The Curious Case of

BENJAMIN BUTTON, Apt. 3W

The Curious Case of

BENJAMIN BUTTON, Apt. 3W

GABRIEL BROWNSTEIN

 W. W. NORTON & COMPANY   NEW YORK   LONDON

The following stories first appeared in the following publications: "Musée des Beaux Arts" in *The Hawai'i Review*, "Wakefield, 7E" in *Zoetrope*, and "The Inventor of Love" in *The Literary Review*. A different version of "The Speedboat" (titled "Party Animal") appeared in *The Northwest Review.*

For information about permission to reproduce selections from this book write to Permissions, W. W. Norton & Company, Inc. 500 Fifth Avenue, New York, NY 10110

This book is composed in Walbaum with the display set in Bell Gothic
Composition by Yor Ffodet
Manufacturing by the Haddon Craftsmen, Inc.
Book design by Chris Welch
Production manager: Julia Druskin

Library of Congress Cataloging-in-Publication Data
Brownstein, Gabriel.
The curious case of Benjamin Button, Apt. 3W / by Gabriel Brownstein.
p. cm

ISBN 0-393-05151-X
1. New York (N.Y.)—Social life and customs—Fiction. 2. Apartment houses—Fiction. 3. Jewish families—Fiction. 4. Male friendship—Fiction. 5. Boys—Fiction. I. Title

PS3602.R75 C87 2002
813'.6—dc21   200223556

W. W. Norton & Company, Inc.
500 Fifth Avenue, New York, N.Y. 10110
www.wwnorton.com

W. W. Norton & Company, Ltd., Castle House,
75/76 Wells Street, London W1T 3QT

1 2 3 4 5 6 7 8 9 0

FOR MARCIA

CONTENTS

ACKNOWLEDGMENTS

Thanks to Richard Brickner, Daniel, Rachel, and Shale Brownstein, Rafael Heller, Roland Kelts, Elizabeth Shah-Hosseini, Ezra Shales, and Matthew Sharpe; to the magazines that published these stories separately; to my agent, Paul Cirone; to my editor, Jill Bialosky; and most of all to my wife, Marcia Lerner.

The Curious Case of

BENJAMIN BUTTON, Apt. 3W

MUSÉE DES BEAUX ARTS

Solly Schlachter lived on the top floor. We never spoke to him, partly because he was older but mostly because of his dad. In those years before we saw our own fathers as nutty, we all understood Dr. Schlachter as cracked. A proctologist barred from public practice, he wore a wire brush mustache and suffered a movie villain's limp. At the least provocation—a Nerf football bouncing across his path in the lobby—Schlachter would wave his cane and threaten to shove it up our general ass.

"For years, kids, I did it professionally."

Strange ravings, strange projects: The elevator door opened and Schlachter lurched forward perilously. "That's right." He'd sneer. "Make 'em think you're a corpse."

October 1975, rain came for twelve days and he rode up to the penthouse bearing two-by-fours. From his apartment Schlachter had access to the roof, and next to the water tower he half built an ark. At the first glint of sunlight, we went out to play in the park and there glimpsed the tips of the curved, bare ribs of the ship. Rumor had it he'd measured in cubits.

Another story worth recounting: '72, when Nixon was running for reelection, Schlachter wanted to fashion a wooden horse, fill it with McGovernites armed with jelly doughnuts, roll it over to East 82nd Street, GOP HQ. He posted maps in the elevator and sign-up sheets, any Upper West Sider who wanted to play Achaeans at Troy. His money came from patents, ass-investigating tools: scopes and wedges, cameras attached to long narrow tubes, a robotic device—FDA approval pending—that would scamper up the small intestine and return back like a Mars probe, bearing precious samples.

After Solly's death, the doctor spent some time in a prison hospital, then returned to the penthouse, drunk, morose, and alone. I was away at school when the Grumbachers caught the smell. Velasquez, the doorman, let the paramedics in and got a glimpse of the naked, bloated corpse.

"A bottle of brandy on the night table, the Bible on his chest, his cock the size of a baseball bat."

"Christ Jesus," I said, and remembered Solly's awful end.

Velasquez, a large, philosophical Dominican whose two children now sing professionally, one with the Met, straightened black glasses on his nose and ran a hand across his bald pate. "Fuckin' madman. Throw a child off a roof. Son of a bitch didn't get half as bad as he deserved."

As a kid, I couldn't fathom Solly's existence, that such a father could have a son. Stark red curls. Hands jammed deep in his pockets. A furtive air of embarrassment and shame. We'd stare at each other in the elevator, that same fascinated quiet that came between me and passing Hasid boys. Understand, ours was a building full of kids. Zev Grubin on six, my compadre; the MacMichaelmans on eleven, Kevin the mad genius and his younger brother Ian. On the sidewalk we played Bob Greise, Fran Tarkenton, tossed balls off the windshields of parked cars. Solly wended his way through the games, slumped and strange and—Kevin said—disgusting.

"Solly the Sissy," we called him. Or "Sally," as if accidentally.

He once babysat for me, and for an evening I admired him. All night we worked on scientific hitting. Solly taught Rod Carew's batting stances—wrists, elbows, squats—and spoke beautifully on the quest to hit .400, Carew seeking to regain one of the lost markers of human achievement. That Carew was a Jew, a convert, this was important, that he wore a *chai* around his neck and drew one across home plate with each at-bat. Solly fetched an atlas and showed off Minnesota: the Twin Cities, the Land of Lakes, names straight out of Tolkein. But the next day, when we were playing in the lobby—Zev and the MacMichaelmans and me—I felt compelled to be vicious.

"Sally the Sissy!" I screamed. "Sally Cecilia!"

We jumped up and down.

"Sally the Sissy Cecilia!"

He kept his fingers in his pockets, glared from under the bill of his Twins cap. Little Ian MacMichaelman—who would later play quarterback for Horace Mann High School—threw a Nerf football right at Solly's face—maybe I encouraged him, maybe, the little brother, he wanted to prove he was one of the guys. And Solly didn't duck, didn't flinch, just let his nose be the ball's target. Then he got in the elevator. The door shut. It couldn't have been more than a few months later that Schlachter saddled him with wings and pushed him off the rooftop toward New Jersey.

As I remember, Solly was a skinny kid—light-boned, long-nosed, a bird. He rose skyward, wings cupping air, then glided down over the treetops and playing fields of Riverside Park. It was mid-Hudson that the project went sour. Apollonian sun melted Icarus's wings; a hard wind wrecked Solly's. A miracle nonetheless: wafting boy, swooping over the West Side Highway. Sewer ducts slimed the river north and south. Seagulls played in the froth of the discharge, and Solly was one of them, airborne. A tugboat captain pressing a bargeful of innocent trash—ragged Levi's, used-up Diehards, Osh-Kosh baby overalls, lead piping, cabbage leaves, bullet casings, Alpo cans, phone books, notebooks, Danskin tights, dead gerbils, cracked Louisville Sluggers— he couldn't stop, not even for a boy falling out of the sky.

As I remember it, we were playing football. I ran a buttonhook. Kevin MacMichaelman covered me. Out as far as the train grate, and then I ducked in quick. Little Ian, at quarterback, lobbed the pass. It flew north to south, downtown, and Solly flew above it, crosswise, toward the water. He wasn't something you mistook for a plane or a bird. I stared skyward, dumbstruck. The ball sailed over my head to Kevin, who ran it in for a touchdown. My father says it's impossible, but I swear I can picture it all, the look on Solly's face, which passed not from ecstasy to terror but from fear to exultation. He flapped his wings, and in one awful heave they popped— blew out from inward like a cheap umbrella. He was too far out. I didn't hear him crash to the water.

It hit the front page of the *Post*, a subheadline: *Doc's Son in Greek Myth Plunge*. I found that recently in the Columbia library, dated August 1979. The larger event, of course, no one is able to forget. Still, I swear I remember particulars: the yellowing, sun-dried park grass, eggplant Parmesan for dinner, the stunned Grubins coming down for dessert, parents conferring in the living room while Zev and I played with the electric football game I'd gotten for my birthday. But I talked to my dad recently, and he said there was no way I could have seen Solly's fall.

I must have confounded things, he said, patched my recollections like a crazy quilt of dream, memory, anecdote, and fear. It was the summertime when Solly fell, he says, July. My mother, my sister, and I were on the Cape. Dad was in the city working at Harlem Hospital. He turned down 89th Street to discover the ambulances and paramedics blocking the street, Solly's smashed body just yards from the sidewalk, insides out like a popped bag of trash, and the broken wings balanced on the roof of a nearby parked car.

No shock that I've got distorted memories, said my father. It was terrifying, also a hard year for me, the cusp of adolescence. Maybe I had once seen a paraglider cross the park, he suggested, maybe it distracted me from a football game. Did I remember Elizabeth Wild, on seven, who had drowned her baby and then leapt from her parents' bedroom window? I was in town for that. But there was no way he was confusing things. He remembered it all, Schlachter being led through the lobby in manacles, bawling. "About suffering they were never wrong, the Old Masters," that's Auden, of course, "Musée des Beaux Arts," Brueghel's painting of Icarus's fall. And me? About suffering? Never right, not once, not ever.

BACHELOR PARTY

Jake's divorce has got me remembering events of a few years ago: that night before his wedding. It's not so uncommon, I guess, for brothers to fight at a time like that. And my brother—well, I've never known him.

Jake is twelve years older than me. In his early thirties—just before he got married—he became Jewish, by which I mean yarmulkes and Shabbas. This seemed odd at the time because when he was in high school, who knew? Take a look at his yearbook picture: the feathered hair, the cocky grin, football helmet under his arm. Then Dartmouth, then UCLA.

When he got hitched at our parents' place in Cold Spring Harbor, the affair was full of ritual. The night before, however, Jake let in some American secularity: boys, booze, cigars. Two A.M., the party had dwindled down and it was my brother and his old college buddy Larry Abrams, who for some reason had put on a skullcap to match Jake's—I think for Larry it was some kind of gag, a freshman beanie—and me and our cousin Tibor. Tibor has always been a strange guy: skin the color of buttermilk, big glasses, thin hair that flies in too many directions. He laughs at inappropriate moments, picks scabs off his face. I feel for Tibor, I'm repulsed by him, and in those days I worried I was too much like him. Just home from my first year of college and the semesters had not gone comfortably.

The porch light was out and Tibor was rocking in his seat. I was a little drunk and a little buzzed on account of some pot Larry had slipped me. A little out of place, too, a little anthropological, peering at the strange macho bonding of the Dartmouth alums. Jake assimilates into any crowd— businessmen, intellectuals, athletes—and that night he shifted out of enthusiastic Judaism and into American guy-hood as easily as if his ego were one of those cars that at a push of a button pops from two- to four-wheel drive.

Larry cracked jokes for him. They weren't even jokes, but something more primitive and private. Larry said, "Milking the cow," and Jake snickered. Larry said, "Butter biscuits, man." My brother shook his head. "Sand in my bed," that was another good one. I must have been staring too intently, because Larry adjusted his skullcap and glanced my way. "You getting all this, Kenny? Taking notes?" Checking out my brother, looking for a reaction. "You working on your novel, Ken?" Larry's jokes, elbows to the ribs. He'd heard I'd taken a class in creative writing.

Larry broke out some more cigars and opened a bottle of brandy and it was clear we would be on the porch for a while. He leaned over and lit the cigar that was in Jake's mouth.

"You must be scared shit," Larry said.

In my family, Jake has always had a reputation for cool. "No. I can't say scared. Maybe you mean anxious? But I'm not anxious."

Somehow this made Tibor laugh.

Larry said, "Tell me something, Tibby. You ever gotten laid?"

White Tibor went whiter.

I said, "Hey, Larry."

"Kenny the college man. Ken." I guess Larry took my point, that it wasn't the time to ride Tibor. "Ken," Larry said, and he leaned back, elbows on the porch. "I hope *you* are getting laid. Every night. Because that, my friend, is the true value of undergraduate education."

He had no idea how much I had to learn.

"My advice to you, Ken, is don't go looking for a girlfriend. Don't fall in love and don't be particular. But you're a Garbus. I don't need to give you advice. Probably prowling the sororities right now. Or do they have sororities where you go to school, what, Green Tofu U.? Shagging the hairy-legged hippy chicks. Let me tell you," he said confidingly, "your brother here, my boy Jake, he might act like quite the religious scholar, but when I knew him, this guy—well."

"Larry," said Jake. "You don't have to—"

"Must I make a list? Reese Crawford? Sabine Bourgeois? The heiress, Winona Van Den Leider? Kappa Sigma Phi? Jake Garbus, man—Long Island Lothario, Kosher Casanova, circumcised scoring machine—"

"I—I have had sex," Tibor interrupted.

"Sure," Larry said. "Sure."

Jake puffed on his cigar. I pictured him trotting up sorority stairs, my brother's athlete's legs and BVDs and some girl in a bra giggling up in front of him. When he was in high school, I once caught Jake posing in front of the bathroom mirror, flexing his pectoral muscles. With me, it wasn't exactly trying on my mother's lipstick or putting a ruler to my schlong, but I have never been a confident guy.

"You and Monica do it, right?" Larry tossed down one

brandy and started work on another. "I mean, being with this whole Jew thing. I don't want to be offensive. But how far do you carry it, Garbus? You? With the little missus?"

"He doesn't want to be offensive," Jake told the lawn.

"Okay." Drunken Larry. "Now he's Mister I'm-not-going-to-dignify-that. But in my day? May I ask something?" He coughed. "Garbus. Okay? Best sex, man, tell me right now. Best sex you ever had."

"Monica." Jake, ever easy.

"Go to hell."

"We don't have that," Jake said. "In our religion."

"Okay." Larry turned to me. "*Okay*." Larry, big and shambling with his tie loose and his suspenders emphasizing the sandbag of his gut. Professionally, he trades Third World debt. "Okay," he said. "Groom's not talking. So you then, Kenny." Brandy sloshed from his glass. "College shenanigans out in that liberal New England outpost. Tell us about freshman year."

"Actually." I looked down. It wasn't my habit to talk. I was the only man in the world with my problem.

A pretty face on a sophomore in sandals brought tears to my eyes, and that Saturday before I had left Vermont for my brother's wedding, Padgett Hastie (who was on the field hockey team and in my Marxist Theory class) had spread her legs for me under a poster of Tracy Chapman, and then all that was solid melted into air. For a second there, in conversation, I felt as I had in her bed: my poor brain flying the white flag of surrender.

"No way?" Larry understood. "You never did it?"

"Um—"

"A virgin? You must be, you *must*—"

"Hey," said Jake. "It's okay. He's eighteen years old. Lots of people haven't done it at his age. Besides, it takes guts—"

"Guts," Larry acknowledged.

I resented my brother for coming to my defense. And Padgett Hastie. A redhead with a raccoon's mask of freckles. "Everything okay?" she asked as I stuttered up above her. "Kenny?" And then did I peel off the condom? Yank up my underwear? Padgett kissed me and her attentions made for an extra heaping helping of shame.

"Guts," Larry said. But he had had too many and was looking for a fight. "Mr. Groom," he said. "Contestant number one," he said. "We need to know the best sex you ever had. I don't think the judges can accept your answer to the question as it was previously posed. *Bachelor Party*." As if it were the name of a game show. "We are here to talk about—"

"Larry," Jake said, "why don't you answer the question?"

"And compromise my role? That would be like Pat Sajak, like, 'Pat, do you want to buy a vowel?' You don't see guests ask dick of Alex Trebek. No." Larry stretched out his arm, reading from an imaginary question card. "You are the leading tang-taker we know," he said. "Our own sultan of salami-stuffing, the great vandalizer of virginity, and so, now, as you go now to retire your roaming steed, we ask you to enlighten us." Larry, steadying himself. "We who have admired and watched your career. Garbus, tell us about your greatest, most satisfying bouts. Your intended—Ms. Monica Schneibaum—we'll call that off limits. But we need information, and tonight. Judges, am I right?"

I stayed quiet, so far out of my depth. Tibor, big glasses on his little face, said, "I could t-tell stories, man."

"At least I didn't bring a stripper."

My brother sucked on his cigar. "You want me to embarrass myself?"

"I've never seen you embarrassed, Garbus."

"You want me to tell you something for old times' sake?" I could see the outline of Jake's face, his curls, the glint of the bobby pin on his white knit skullcap. "Something to freak out the kids?"

"Hey," said Tibor.

"I'll tell you," said Jake. "I'll tell."

My brother left the house when I was six. His room went untouched until I was thirteen. It was like a special exhibition he curated, a diorama, object lesson to my junior high misery: Successful Teenage Life. Shelves heavy with trophies, A+ book reports in the desk, lipsticky letters from old flames. The holy box of Trojans in the drawer of the night table. I'd sneak in there when my parents weren't around and I'd look at the letterman jackets hanging in the closet, the yearbook with hearts drawn on his face, and I'd wonder.

Seventh grade, I got the shit kicked out of me, and then I would haul my ass out of a garbage can and look at my brother in the school trophy case. He held the record for the two-hundred-yard dash and was pictured with a championship football team. Math teachers reminded me all the way up to senior year. Old Mr. Albertson. "You're really Jake Garbus's brother?" He remembered Jake on account of some statewide prize. "You don't look like him. But obviously, you're bright. I think you could take a lesson from Jake. Apply yourself as your brother did—and really, it doesn't have to be in athletics. There's no telling how far you will go. . . ."

Report cards came home, my mother retreated into herself. She saw me as some misted-over genius. My father got mad, threw books, threw telephones. Mysteries of genetics. Jake's got dad's big shoulders and curly hair. He's got a profile, and sitting out on the porch the night before his wedding, I saw it embossed on the night sky.

"It's nobody you know," Jake began. "No one any one of you might remember—"

"You're going to tell me better than Callie Cannel?"

"It was during my postdoc." Jake ignored Larry. "When I had moved from California to New York. I was going to work with the preeminent man in the field, Victor—let's call him—Himmler. But names have been changed to—"

"To Himmler." Larry, deadpan.

"Yeah." My brother, the world's smoothest liar, or embellisher, or (who knows?) maybe it was true. "The work was to be in his labs. I was his chief assistant, a great move for me, career-wise, but socially it was strange. I had been in Los Angeles, UCLA, for years, and even though I was a biologist and a graduate student and by definition a nerd, well, I knew a couple of people in the film business and my social life was easy. You'd be surprised how many aspiring actresses want to sleep with someone just because he's *not* in movies." I pictured Jake in a Venice Beach bar, more confident, predatory, and handsome than any of the young actors or producers' assistants. Jake all the while pretending to be some sweetheart of a guy. "I was working on a cure for cancer. I got a lot of mileage out of that."

"I tell you." Larry. "All the angles. We should be taking notes."

"I don't b-believe . . ." Tibor, petulant.

"What?" I said.

My brother ignored us. "I came to New York and even though I grew up here on the Island and am an East Coast man by nature, well, the city felt cold. I didn't know too many people. I had never really lived in New York. Also, working for Dr. Himmler, I had the feeling that it was time to get serious in my life. I rented an apartment in Queens. I had to change subways to get to Columbia, so I woke up early. I worked out at the university gym before heading to the lab. Then I came home late and reviewed my notes. I would lie alone in bed reading journals and sipping seltzer. I didn't drink, I didn't smoke. Celibacy did me wonders. Dr. Himmler was scrupulously neat, perfectly devoted, absolutely careful. Before him, science had been academic to me, something I knew I could do well. It was a little like football—I didn't choose it, it chose me. But with Dr. Himmler that changed. He presented an elegant world, a world defined by the aesthetics of the laboratory, and I wanted to be a part of it. People think a man like that, with his achievements and Old World dignity, would be unapproachable, but with me he was kind. He accepted me—a twenty-four-year-old Jewish schmuck from Long Island—as a colleague."

"You screwed the Teutonic oncologist?" Larry.

Jake sighed.

I pictured this grandfatherly, severe mentor. Undoubtedly, there had been someone like that. Thin head, rectangular jaw. Deep lines in his face and his gray hair carefully combed. A tie beneath his lab coat, the lab coat replaced at the end of the day with a sports jacket. Really, in my life, I have never had anything against Germans.

"He was kinder to me than I had any right to expect," Jake said. "He invited me to his house for dinner. He introduced me to his wife, Greta, a handsome, neat woman in her sixties—"

"You did the hausfrau?" Larry, mock aghast.

"Please." Jake's hand shot out and I thought he was going to smack Larry, but he just tapped him on the ridiculous yarmulke. "Dr. Himmler introduced me as Jacob Garbus, a young fellow who takes his work too seriously, and since I have never in my life been introduced that way, I was flattered and didn't object." My brother, he'd be diffident in the doctor's home. "Dinner came in courses. There was soup with dumplings, then rabbit served with potatoes and greens. After each course, Greta cleared dishes. She took her apron off each time she came back from the kitchen. I offered to help but was shooed away. How do I explain? I'm no clod. I know which is the salad fork, which spoon is for coffee, but I don't live my life by those rules, and I got self-conscious about the way I handled the cutlery. My knife clanked the plate. I made too much noise."

"Do I remind you at this point"—Larry, the peanut gallery—"we were talking about getting laid?"

"They lived in a three-story town house in the West Eighties. They owned beautiful rugs and gorgeous antiques; there were books everywhere. I have to admit I was surprised. Dr. Himmler was a prominent scientist and Columbia probably paid him well, but this was a house that would have suited a financier. I must have let my surprise show—I wasn't half as smooth as I wanted to be—because as we sat down in the living room for coffee and cigarettes which I refused—he smoked, yes, the great oncologist smoked vicious unfiltered European brands—he told me the story of the house. His wife was washing dishes and that sound made a pleasant background. Apparently the mansion had fallen into their laps. Thirty years earlier, Dr. Himmler and his wife had rented the basement apartment. Their landlords in those days were an elderly couple named Miller and when the old folks became infirm, Greta Himmler tended to them, very decently and out of sheer neighborliness. She cooked their dinners. She tended to old Mr. Miller after his stroke, to Mrs. Miller when her arthritis was so bad she could barely walk. The landlords died childless, but before Mrs. Miller passed on, she gave the Himmlers—and Greta was pregnant then—a deal. They bought the town house for a song. I could hardly believe this. In New York, you know, real estate is the stuff of high drama, of miracle. Dr. Himmler laughed when he told the story and then said he had no right, no right to be so lucky."

"And you two passionately embraced?"

Jake continued. "'Who is living in the downstairs apartment now?' I asked. And Dr. Himmler answered with a twinkle. 'My daughter,' he said, and he showed me the picture."

My brother shut his eyes. A light went out upstairs. In the glow of suburban street lamps, passing cars, and burning cigars, my brother was a silhouette. Tibor picked up a stick and began swinging it.

All that week, I had wanted to call Padgett Hastie out in her parents' Jersey home but was too frightened of what she might think of me. I guessed my brother would have screwed Padgett happily; or maybe, worse, wouldn't have screwed her at all—not cute enough, too stocky. Or maybe in his new orthodoxy he would have disapproved. A shiksa.

"Kristina was dazzling," Jake said. "She was absolutely dazzling. I don't mean like sorority girls or aspiring starlets, I mean the real thing. Here was a simple snapshot of a girl and her parents, a countryside somewhere in Europe; they were all dressed in shorts. Dr. Himmler, of course, had his oxford shirt tucked in, and Greta wore epaulets on her shoulders. The girl had her sunglasses pulled up on top of her blond head and she had raised her arm in the air like she was celebrating something. It was a very ordinary photograph and yet she seemed in a different frame than her parents; she seemed not just more alive than they did, but more vivid, more . . . I'm not expressing it well." Jake leaned back, and though we could hardly see him, we heard his voice, that throaty, confident voice of his. "Have you ever seen one of those Shakespeare films with English actors and American movie stars? Have you ever noticed how the players from the two countries can be in the same shot—Keanu Reeves and Kenneth Branagh are in the same room, standing there, but it feels like a special effect that has been pulled off unsuccessfully? The actors speak the words and mean them, while the movie stars yank themselves out of the picture with each word spoken. It's like there is a hard line drawn between, and it's not just because of the movie stars' failings but because they are juxtaposed with something more real, more artful, more expressive, than they can ever hope to be. This photograph worked something like that. Beside the liveliness of their daughter, the Himmlers barely seemed real—or maybe they seemed too real, too ordinary, too prosaic. I must have gasped."

"The plot thickens," Larry Abrams said.

My brother nodded, sucking on his cigar. Ash glowed red.

"Dr. Himmler called to his wife. He said, 'Greta, darling, invite Kristina upstairs.' And then she came. And then the parents disappeared. They served their daughter to me after dinner, like she was a wedge of lemon meringue pie."

Jake woke me up the morning of his wedding, putting on his phylacteries by the piano and singing. That rich cantor's voice of his. I had given up my bed to Aunt Mimi and was lying on the living room couch. My left eye hurt like hell.

My parents' living room has big glass doors that look out on the porch and the lawn beyond, so morning sunlight shines right in and Jake was praying and bobbing in his blue flannel pajamas, unshaven. So fucking handsome, he could have been a movie star. Prayer shawl over his shoulders, leather wrapping his arm and forehead, looking out at the porch where the night before he had told his crazy sex stories.

Why did he wake me up with those prayers? My face hurt like a bitch and later I took two aspirin and used an ice pack. Why couldn't he just pray in his bedroom? With his yarmulke and tefillin he was draped in the full authority of his religion and I couldn't say to Jake, as any American brother would have, "Hey, will you knock that off?" Also, it was his wedding day. His wife-to-be, Monica, was taking a ritual bath. I pretended to sleep. Sonorous Hebrew ranting all around me. When he was done, Jake snapped his book shut and he looked down at me and smiled.

"Coffee?"

My face with the imprint of his knuckles. What do you do with a brother like that?

On the porch, his voice had been burned and bruised by the cigars and brandy. It got so dark I could only imagine his curly head. Also, I imagined Kristina, the oncologist's daughter. I felt pity for her even before Jake's story began.

"She cannot have been so hot," Tibor snorted. He was a shadow out on the lawn, swinging his stick. "I mean, what— she was like, like Claudia Schiffer?"

"Shut up," Larry said.

But Jake put a restraining hand to Larry's chest. "Claudia Schiffer," he lectured Tibor, "has her hair recut by Hollywood stylists for a single posed shot. She wears hundreds of dollars in makeup and is photographed only under the most flattering light, and then by highly paid cameramen. She wears the best clothing and terribly uncomfortable undergarments that pull and push her body so it's thin in the gut and her tits puff up. She's photographed a hundred times, the best of those shots are selected, the best poses, and then they are airbrushed and recolored and made more perfect.

There are committee meetings about whether Claudia's panties look better in pink or blue. Kristina Himmler—the girl I am calling that name—was flesh.

"Larry." My brother gripped his friend's shoulder. "I don't know how to explain. Ken, you have to trust me. Tibor. Kristina was the easiest conquest of my life. And let's be honest: Girls have never been hard." My brother. "But her attraction was the kind of thing that explodes vanity. I cannot tell you what she saw in me. She was fun, delightful, the kindest, sweetest girl I have ever met. She was not particularly interesting or ironic or artistically gifted. She had beauty and kindness and that was it. But if I may, I'd like to get crude here for a minute."

"Please," said Larry.

"I could have said, 'Blow me,' the moment we met, and she would have gotten down on her knees and sucked."

"Some guys." Larry Abrams shook his head.

"Are you kidding? This girl was crazy. But I couldn't get enough. She wanted me. I was powerless—"

Larry nodded solemnly. "That Nazi bitch."

They fucked right there, on the Oriental, twenty-five minutes after her father left the room. Jake said something like: You live downstairs? The girl said something like: So you're my father's student? Then she was getting rug burns. So the story goes. They went to the kitchen, to tidy the dishes, and did it again on the ceramic floor, mismatched pubic hair all creamy and meshed. Jake on his back, hairy legs up against the dishwasher, trousers in the sink, and pale pink Kristina with the hem of her dress clenched in her teeth—

I couldn't believe what my brother was telling me. It shocked me, by which I don't mean I was offended, but like a jolt of static fuzzed my brain. Those days, I tell you, so uptight: I didn't talk about such things, couldn't.

"We tried to behave like human beings," Jake said. "You know, we'd go out for dinner. We would discuss the weather and the classes she was taking. Kristina studied social work at Hunter College. We would converse, but then in the middle of dinner and as if by some secret pact she would get up from the table and then I would follow her and before you knew it, I was banging her against the men's room door. Thump, thump, thump—then we'd walk out past someone who really had to take a piss, the two of us blushing and tired. We'd bring home moo shu pork and do depraved things with plum sauce, right there, downstairs, in her parents' house. She would giggle, she would shout like a demon, and then the next morning her father would invite me up for coffee and he and I would sit together and read the newspaper like civilized men, except I couldn't stand up when Kristina entered the room on account of my raging hard-on."

"Plum sauce?" asked Larry.

"She had a perfect face, a face at once childlike and womanly. She had wide eyes and a wide mouth and a smile that rose against her cheeks. She had a perfect pan and she liked it if I pulled her hands behind her back and pressed that face into anything: a pillow on a bed, sand on a beach, mud in a parking lot. The girl wanted to be demeaned, and by me. Had she done these things before? I have no idea. She would show up on a date in a white dress with little blue flowers. Her hair would be washed and combed and shining. You know that fine net of stray hairs that sometimes settles above a beautiful head? She never had that fine stray net. A girl so clean and white and fine, and all she wanted me to do was sully her."

"Sully," said Larry. "The words he chooses."

"This is total bullshit," said Tibor. "This is something I

read—I read it in *Penthouse—Penthouse Forum.* Did did you read that, Ken? I mean, I think—"

"Tibor," said my brother. "Give me that stick." And Tibor did and my brother chucked it end over end into the lawn. "Now, please," he said. "Please listen."

Religion and ethnicity, in my family when I was growing up these were facts like the carpeting. Passover, we once celebrated release from Egyptian bondage with take-out falafel, baba gannouj. My parents went to services sometimes on the New Year and sometimes on the Day of Atonement, and when they used to drag the kids along we would all feel uncomfortable together. Both sons had bar mitzvahs, Jake's with pretty girls. But you know how it is in the suburbs. We tiptoe around holiness the way our ancestors did around sex. We have special places for it, we avoid them.

I'm no anti-Semite. And I have the usual apportion of feelings toward my older brother: admiration, envy, worship, hate. I remember seeing Jake play football at Dartmouth, seeing him fly in from the secondary and clock a quarterback cold. I remember the way the underclass girls reacted to his name at college graduation. When I was eleven, he'd come home from L.A. and he enjoyed making fun. I was hitting adolescence. My big nose, my weak chin, my glasses.

"Starting to look like Grampa Abe."

My brother, the Greek god.

"We were competent, scientific men. We injected rats with carcinogens. We monitored progress, examined data and DNA and renegade cells, we counted death rates and measured tumors and kept it all clean and crisp and beautiful. We faced disease in civilized abstraction; we could quantify death. Then at night I would take his daughter to my apartment in Queens and stick jalapeño peppers in her mouth and whip her behind so my belt left streaks on the ivory globes of her ass. She wasn't inventive but she was always game. Kristina flounced around my apartment without pants. She would hand me something hard or cold—a squash racket, a Popsicle—and as if coincidentally bend over or spread her legs."

Who remembers dialogue as it happened? I'm doing reconstruction here. At the time, like half these words must have bounced off my forehead. No way they were getting to my brain. A freshman home from college—I played with my snifter, I fidgeted on the porch.

"The family invited me on picnics as if I were an ordinary boyfriend, as if Kristina and I were to be engaged." My brother in happy tennis whites. "We drove up to the Bronx Botanical Gardens in their BMW. Greta brought an enormous wicker basket full of wine and crystal and china and sausages and breads and home-baked pastries. The next day, then, Kristina came to my apartment with the same basket, this time filled with toys she had bought in Greenwich Village, little metal clamps and leather. She took off her clothes and began to fasten these restraints together, to take them apart, a little demonstration—my naked stewardess showing off the not-so-safety gear."

Larry laughed. I tried—nervous distraction—to count the thumps Tibor's chair's legs made on the wooden porch.

"When her parents left town for two weeks in October, Kristina wanted me to screw her in every room of their house. So we did. With her father away, I was on my own and sex had crushed all my hopes of diligent study. I spent as little time as possible in the lab, left most of the work to graduate students, and went on a methodical sexual rampage. We did it in the foyer, knocking over the coat rack. In the living room, I sat in her father's chair, while she undid my fly, raised up her skirt, and, sitting on my lap, fucked me, all the while feigning conversation with make-believe guests. In the dining room she bent over the table, took a banana from the fruit bowl, and shoved it in her mouth. She wore her mama's apron in the pantry."

"The judges are scoring this high," said Larry.

"Just wait. I'll give you more than you can take."

"That what you gave her?"

Did my hands cover my face?

"Listen: I did her on the stairs and in her father's study and her mother's studio, playing with the paints and brushes. And we did it in the hot tub and in her old single bed surrounded by stuffed animals and pictures of Baryshnikov. In the den, we screwed to MTV. Finally we got to the third floor, her parents' bedroom, actually a suite with French doors and the walls all painted brown. The furniture gave the room the feel of an importer's showroom, everything massive and wood. Curtains on the windows made as if it were a country estate. And Kristina stood girlishly tracing her naked foot across the tassels of the purple rug, waiting for me to undress her.

"This was something of a consummation for her. I understood that implicitly. I undid the little buttons on her back, helped her arms out of their sleeves, and when her little blue dress dropped to the floor around her, I offered gentlemanly assistance as she stepped out of the charmed circle her clothing had made.

"The bed had no canopy but four carved posts. On the walls were black and white photographs, ancestors and weddings. God, was I exhausted from fucking all day. And I suppose with all lovers—even the most beautiful—there are moments when one views their bodies almost clinically. You know you are being objective, seeing them as they are. So I saw Kristina then, the scales of attraction falling from my eyes, and I thought with cool detachment that nothing could be more lovely than her legs. I ran my hands up the arches of her feet, and then her ankles, the calves, the knees—the muscles' curves, a child's soft skin on a grown-up body. I got to the thighs. I began kissing, half wondering where the hell the imperfection might lie." Jake paused. "Bang, bang." He pumped a fist. "Bang, bang, bang, bang. The old bed is creaking. We are damp, our bellies suck and kiss. We rock with the bed. And she is coming and I am totally in the driver's seat, like I believe I could fuck again all night until tomorrow, but her teeth grab my nipple and I am lost, but maybe even then, in the midst of my orgasm, maybe even then—because I was spent, really, I can only do it so many times in a day, my balls were burning—maybe even then bells were ringing. I rolled off onto her parents' mushy mattress and not into blessed postcoital satisfaction but something much more—"

"You were freakin'," said Larry. "Warning siren: Woo woo. Get me the hell out of here. 911."

I wanted to leave the porch.

Tibor coughed. "This is such a load of crap."

"Shut up, Tibby," said Larry.

"I sank exhausted into their old mattress, thinking: Okay, the attic and the roof deck and then what comes after that? And Kristina snuggled under my arm, all that blond hair. Then she said it: 'I love you, Jacob.'"

Larry knew everything. "You fuck 'em, they fall in love."

"And I had no response. I looked up the long, pointing finials of the bedposts, with their intricate squares and carvings, and the peaks like angry flower buds. I looked at the old oak dressers whose mirrors reflected squares of shadows and the frames of photographs. She was waiting for me to speak.

I flicked on the lamp on the bed table. Japanese white porcelain, a seascape. I saw a pack of Gitanes next to a copy of *The Periodic Table*—there were some old brown hardcovers but the Primo Levi was in paperback, all dog-eared, with a playing card for a bookmark. 'I love you,' Kristina said again, as if I hadn't heard her the first time. So I reached for the cigarettes, to give my mouth something to do. I lit up, and pretended to examine a Learn to Drive matchbook. My bare ass against the sheets, I was scared shit, irrationally, and trying to keep my cool, and smoking and studying the room. I patted her head. I didn't want to lie.

"I looked at their wedding pictures, Greta with a streaming white train and Victor young and very thin. I studied her jewelry case and the stacks of correspondence on his dresser. I would stare at anything then so as not to look at Kristina. There was an African mask hanging above a picture of a street scene in a long-ago European town. And then I finally noticed it: the gray face with the high cheekbones, the knobby forehead, the hollow eyes, the heavy lids whose lashes seemed to have been burned off, the lipless, damnable, clever mouth—"

I was so out of it, I thought maybe he was giving us a new way to see the girl.

"Please," said Jake, "don't look in the Columbia University directory for a Professor Dr. Victor Himmler. The names have been changed, as I told you. But Dr. Himmler had been Nazi Youth. There were UJA letters on his dresser—payments for family sins, I guess. I saw those letters when I got up from the bed, buck-naked and smoking, to get a good look at their famous ancestor: a man in a khaki uniform with familiar insignias, and I wouldn't have been able to match the name with the face if the name hadn't been all around me.

"'What the hell?' I said. And this was my response to her 'I love you.' Kristina, flustered in that great four-poster bed, was halfway to tears.

"What came out finally, after fragmented sentences from both sides, me pointing like an ape at the photograph of the Nazi, was her saying, explaining for her parents' sake: 'You would not want us to forget?'"

"Goebbels," said Larry Abrams. "Was the name really Goebbels?"

"We fought there, for the first time, really fought, me naked in the elegant bedroom and Kristina sobbing about how it's all right that I don't really love her, it is enough that she loves me. Then she ran down the stairs, leaving me alone with those glowering photographed Nazi eyes, while I poked around for my socks and underwear.

"I went home that night to my place, rode out to Astoria on the R train, and I felt as if Eichmann and Hess were sitting on either side of me, quiet, gentlemanly commuters, perusing the *Post*, the *Daily News*. And then I got in my little single bed, anxious and exhausted, and I had the most awful dream."

Me? I have never lived in *The Sorrow and the Pity*, much less *Schindler's List*. Padgett Hastie wrote a term paper about the Congo, Belgian mercenaries filling up barrels with the severed hands of black kids—I don't say this to put events of World War II in context. I grew up in Long Island, *that's* my context. And to this day I pray at night in a way that's embarrassingly New Age Protestant American—one on one, extemporizing to The Big Guy as if He were my imaginary best friend. I don't know why Jake's story made me so angry. Was it because I was so damned uptight? About sex, about Jews, about mystery? Did I expect more from him? Less? I didn't quite believe his story and I still don't, or if I do it's as some kind of hyperbole that blends Jake's ambition with his fears and something angry that he wanted to shove in all of our faces: Larry's, mine, Tibor's. Back then I was intimidated by Jake in a different way than I suppose I still am: that he could so easily and publicly talk about fucking, so confidently display his religion, his yarmulke, confident like he was playing football, flying forward in full body armor. I didn't know what to do with his talk.

And then this purported dream about which he told us next—that night in his bed in Queens Jake saw himself in Kristina's place, dressed in a German officer's World War II uniform. Kristina's head was shaved and she was wearing a concentration camp suit and he was barking orders and she was obedient.

"I told her about it," Jake said. "My nightmare. This was a week after the incident in her parents' room. I had been avoiding her, but that day I had come back to the Himmlers' town house to pick up some papers. It was the afternoon—I was hoping not to see her. But Kristina surprised me by being there, fixing lunch in her parents' kitchen. I remember being shocked by the way her jeans and her T-shirt showed off her body—those innocent, those alluring curves. Were things okay, she wanted to know, between us? She was licking mayonnaise off her fingers. Was I avoiding her?

"'I didn't mean to pressure you,' she said.

"We were in the sitting room, standing on the rug on which she and I had first fucked. And I was nervous and a little afraid and couldn't quite face her. So, by way of describing my discomfort, I told her my dream. She stepped closer. She tossed her blond hair. She wasn't tentative—though my guess is she was a little scared of me at that point, waiting for me to dump her—and she, Kristina, said—God—she said, 'Okay. We can do that if you like.' "

Larry said, "Do you still have her number?"

"Oh, please," said Tibor.

Do girls like that even exist?

"I left that day," he said, "like right then, after her offer. It was too much for me. The whole thing seemed so—but she called me, she called me. Friendly, sexy Kristina left messages on my answering machine. I wanted to dump her, I wanted to go back to the way things had once been. Things had gotten out of hand. I knew I should stay away, but you know how it is, you always go back one more time. She phoned and said, 'I'm not making demands.' She said, 'I have a surprise for you, Jacob.'

"So one day—maybe a full year after I had met her—I left the lab a little early and walked downtown through Riverside Park. It was late fall and I had on a pea coat over my lab clothes. My sneakers and jeans were in a bag. I remember the blue sky, the bare trees, my breath making clouds. I walked over on West 89th Street to their brownstone, and Kristina greeted me at the door. She wore lipstick and a pale yellow dress and smiled.

"I was full of misgivings, but I showered as I always had after I got to her place from the lab. That was routine and a psychological necessity after all those tumors, all those rats. In the past, she had sometimes come into the shower with me, but not this day. She was outside, in her bedroom, preparing my surprise. So I scrubbed and the place got steamy and the glass doors of the shower fogged and I remembered the German officer's face, and I thought, Big deal, big fucking deal, so what? Her parents wake with their guilt every morning, and she loves you. Is this a burden you can't bear? I catalogued my worst, most far-fetched fears— that she was her dad's instrument, that she was signing her cunt over to me like it was a UJA check, some form of psycho-sexual reparations—and I thought, What a load of crap. I let the water run over my head. You can't hold family history against someone. We are modern, liberated New Yorkers. That's what I thought. I turned off the tap. I wrapped a blue towel around my waist. I walked through the little kitchen and into her bedroom, and there was Kristina at the foot of her bed.

"Her hair was all over the floor. She had shaved it. And on the down comforter was the actual object, I tell you, khaki with insignias—"

"Ab-," Tibor said, "absurd."

Larry said, "This is clearly some fucked-up kinky bitch."

I said, "A woman would do that for you?"

"For me?" Jake said, indignant. "Of course I couldn't put that on. And she was on the floor, sobbing, bawling, a beautiful bald nude surrounded by her own marmalade hair, naked and soft, her breasts like a teenager's, her ass full. You have never in your life seen anything like that, or if you have, God bless you. I stood there with a towel around my waist. I think I wanted to say something like 'What the hell are you doing?' but what came out, if I remember, was a cross between a stutter and a gasp. I tell you, I ran. I was tying my shoes on West End Avenue. I tucked in my shirt on the subway platform. I left the lab clothes at her house."

Was that it? What my brother wanted, what he feared, what he knew? I leave it to you to dig through the layers of possibility, the desire, the paranoia, the lurid grotesque. But at the time I heard his story, I was frustrated, I was angry, I was a mess.

"I don't know what Dr. Himmler thought afterward: That his daughter was suddenly bald? That I was gone from her social life? I don't know. He said nothing about Kristina to me, and he never invited me to his house again. Still, we worked side by side. These things, I suppose, do happen, affairs between the protégé and the mentor's child. Things do sour. He was very—is the word *understanding*? I'm not sure. I know neither what drove his actions toward me, nor to what degree he was conscious of his motivations. I was good at my job. And at the end of my postdoc, Dr. Himmler wrote me a letter of recommendation, a letter that I am sure secured my subsequent appointment at Hopkins, a letter which in no small part made my career. And he never stopped being good to me. He even gave me coauthorship of our study. He didn't have to do that—nobody does that. Was it all penance? I don't know. Was I his Jew? I never asked. I did good work for him. I'm not saying I didn't deserve the credit I got. Then, before the study came out, Dr. Himmler was diagnosed with lung cancer. I never visited him in the hospital. I didn't go to the funeral. I stayed away. I couldn't face it, you know?"

"And the girl?" Larry asked. "Still looking for Jewboys to fuck?"

"She lives in Israel." My brother sighed. "No shit. She works with deformed Arab kids."

Tibor laughed.

I looked to my brother in the darkness. I wanted him to say something to me, to tell me one more thing, maybe some explanation—was there a point to this story, a lesson? Did he feel guilty? Did he feel wronged? But more than that, I wanted to be one of the guys, or even the special guy, the one who understood. When I spoke I did it mostly to break the silence, or maybe to find a place by Jake's side.

"And this," I offered, "was why you have become so orthodox? Such a Jew?"

"Oh, for Christ's sake." Jake turning nasty. "Take it easy, Ken."

I looked at his yarmulke, its knitted pattern, blue and white, letters in Hebrew I couldn't read. I don't know what overcame me; I had an impulse. I just grabbed it right off his head, chucked the skullcap out onto the lawn, and the thing lofted like a Frisbee.

Jake looked up at me, gape-mouthed. He stood. And that's when he did it, no change of expression. Boom, punched me right in the eye.

At the wedding, I made excuses. Told my mom I had slipped the night before, banged my face against a doorknob. And after the ceremony, I offered a toast full of shit. Like, Jake was the one man I admired most. My dad bit his trembling lip, so proud. "His courage," I said. "And boy is he being courageous now." The kind of thing people say at weddings, ha ha. The bride was charming all dressed in white, and Jake wore his skullcap as if it were a crown. He gave me a hug when I was done rhapsodizing and then I saw his life spreading out before him, justified at all margins: Dr. Jacob Garbus, pillar of the community, father, oncologist, mensch. I could never imagine his divorce just a few years later: that he would leave Monica for this Raina Zweig, a colleague's wife, a few years older than he, a member of his congregation.

The band began to play, a stage in a backyard. Under the tent the family danced in a wide circle, legs stomping to the beat. My mother laughed, my father sweated. I looked at Jake, whom I hated right then irrationally and more than I can express. Still, I smiled and clapped. Just like everyone else, though underneath it all my dark soul imagined him doing different steps in a different costume, a riding crop in hand and a bald girl on the floor in front of him.

THE CURIOUS CASE OF
BENJAMIN BUTTON, 3W

1.

As I understand it, the first large buildings on the Upper
West Side rose up at the end of the nineteenth century on
speculation of the city's growing uptown. The Dakota was
named after a frontier state and plunked down between
farms and shanties where goats wandered near the edges of
Central Park. After the building of the IRT, dreamboat
buildings sprouted on Broadway, for instance the Ansonia,
that Beaux Art wedding cake later home to Babe Ruth. Soon
construction spread to Riverside Drive, solid brick apartments
next door to the mansions of cigar-rolling millionaires. These
had views of the Hudson and the Jersey palisades, but were
within earshot of the trains on the riverbank. Soot caked the
high windows and in summer you could smell the sewage
seeping out to sea. In hot months the fetid water bubbled.
The Old Manse, where I grew up and where my parents still
live, was erected in 1911 between West End Avenue and the
Drive. It combines an Old World sensibility with an early
twentieth century style. Frightening gargoyles peer into the

street, wood beams extrude from the brickwork. A haunted house, the clanking pipes and empty dumbwaiter shafts not nearly so mysterious as our neighbors. Kevin MacMichaelman, Zev Grubin, and I—all of us in PS 75, Ms. Appel's sixth-grade class—watched them and made up stories: Dr. Schlachter, for instance, in the penthouse with his dyed mustache and terrible cane; Wakefield, filthy and furtive in 7E; the voluptuous teenaged Jessica Lenzner; even old Mrs. Button with her Southern accent, enormous hats, cataract eyes, limbs like pale shriveled vegetables, Parkinsonian trembling, wheelchair, and nurse. Halloween we were cowboys, Starsky, Batman, sweating under plastic Woolworth's masks whose rubber bands pinched our ears. We glimpsed foyers with parquet floors or checkerboard tiles, a photograph of a Cape Cod sunset or a reproduction Matisse, on 15 a dog's paws scratching the floor, barking Mandy dragged into the kitchen. Sometime that year a young man moved into 3W to live with old Mrs. Button. His chestnut hair was cut David Cassidy–style and he wore gold chains around his neck. He wandered upper Broadway barefoot, sometimes with a tropical bird on his shoulder and sometimes a black and green snake. To Kevin, Zev, and me, Benjamin Button seemed the ideal of adulthood. We admired his tattered army jacket, his girlfriends, his hand-rolled cigarettes. Those first few times he spoke to us we felt as though he might take us under his wing, and it was like meeting a celebrity. Later we dismissed him, forgot him, and I learned recently that he died an obscure death.

Ask me about New York in the 1970s and I'll remember it as a golden age, the city bankrupt and filthy but full of aspiration. Snowstorms and blackouts and strikes—garbage, transportation, teachers—all of this was ordinary, exciting, and incomprehensible. We marveled at the serial killers—

Son of Sam, whose real name was Berkowitz and who apparently spoke with dogs. Etan Patz was abducted yards from his Soho home and his disappeared face on xeroxed posters became as familiar to us as anyone in Ms. Appel's class. Our local terror, Charlie Chop-off, lured boys to the tops of apartment buildings and with pinking shears took off their dicks. In school we sang "Kumbaya." Ms. Appel swung her guitar and read us Carl Sandburg. She wore keys around her neck and a whistle and flashed on and off the lights when we got noisy. "People! I'm waiting!" The only times we sat in rows were to watch movies. Rosey Grier, the football player who retired long before we became interested in the NFL, liked to knit and he sang "It's All Right to Cry." One cartoon, *William Wants a Doll*, went right over my head. Sex roles, what did I know? Just that girls had cooties, but were also mysterious and fascinating when they patted palms or played Double Dutch or braided each other's hair. Boys who liked girls (e.g., Renny Benitez) were gay. Renny was a skinny, fatherless kid from the projects who wore permanent press shirts and groom in his hair. He had a cleft palate and glasses and all his attempts at good grooming were signs of poverty in our world of T-shirts and jeans. In the open-corridor classroom, we dressed as superheroes, performed plays (*Return of the Pink Pampers*), and drew slaughterhouses. These were Kevin's idea and his were the most intricate. He used a straight edge, drew legends on the bottom of his construction paper, and carefully mapped the entryways and the cutting floors where circular saws took off Renny Benitez's arms, where they sliced away his legs, the gutter where Renny's head fell, the moat where the sharks ate his dick. Kevin included blow-up boxes with close-ups of grisly scenes, vertebrae protruding from the stump of Renny's shoulders. On the way to school, he rewrote the history of West End Avenue. Bars on basement windows were the remains of dungeons. Antenna wires the last vestiges of gallows. And I imagined it all: corpses rotting, screams from the basements, rent-controlled apartment houses doling out medieval justice. He was, without anyone's having to say it, our leader. We did what Kevin told us to, ate cat food, whatever. He had us all line up by his radiator to piss out the window, eleven stories down. "Tor-pee-do!" said Zev, squeezing his dick shut and letting it open again. Our solid strands broke as they fell, intermingled, and showered the roof, the wipers, and the windshields of our landlord's town car. During army training exercises, Kevin decided that we all had to hang out the window, eleven stories aboveground.

"As members of a special unit devoted to the technical surveillance of possible underground attacks by Republican Nazi rebels, you have to develop your technical skills and also demonstrate a high degree of bravery."

He cleared the Matchbox cars and action figures off his radiator cover and under his supervision Zev gripped tight to the window frame, lay on his stomach, and stuck his legs out the window, Zev dangling from his waist and kicking up his heels in the sunshine.

"You guys," I said. What would we tell his mom?

But Kevin was unimpressed. And as if to prove our general pussihood, he went all the way out, hung over the ledge with his chest on the sill, and then eased himself backward until all we could see were his arms and smiling freckled face.

"Bye-bye."

And he became nothing but knuckles and fingertips. I imagined Kevin's arms extended along the grimy brick face, Pro Keds kicking against the windows of apartment 10E. Also, I imagined his fingers losing their grip. I could see Kevin falling, red hair flying, arms and legs swinging, back snapping over the garbage cans in the alleyway, brilliant brain splattered across the concrete.

"Davey," he said when he climbed back in, "you can take your hands off your face now."

I was a spooky kid in my cousin's hand-me-down corduroys, cuffs rolled, knee patches at the shins. My hair was cut in a puffy bell, same as the boys on *Zoom*. I picked my nose, never tied my shoes, wouldn't brush my teeth. One day in gym class, I noticed that Hettie Carmichael had a vaccination scar, a dime-sized scoop, like her maker had puttied over the bolt that held her arm to her torso, and I took that in as we all practiced the Hustle and the Bus Stop, Ms. Appel up front with a boom box, crying, "Step, step, step, turn," and I decided that Hettie was a robot, that everyone around me was a robot, that the world was shaped like a large terrarium and outside lurked watchers in white coats. At night I rubbed my secret penis against my mattress and my first sex dream involved a redhead in Mr. Temple's class across the hall; PS 75 broke out in fire and in the corridor Mary Duncan and I embraced. I resolved in case of nuclear war to go upstairs to Jessica Lenzner's and see if she would fuck me. I was in my own world, that's what Mommy said. A center part on a boy summoned up the word "celery," and blondes were endowed with a seductive haze—invisible to the eye, but there like an aura, I knew it. Certain other things were clear to me, Kevin MacMichaelman's genius, for one. He was Mr. Ace, the smartest man alive, and we were the androids he had built. Zev became Rocket, the fastest cyborg lifeform, and Terry Baldus was Hammer, the strongest. I got to be Arrow, second best at everything. Our primary task as superpowered androids was to keep Renny Benitez away from Kevin, particularly as we made our way from school down the slope of 96th Street to the big yard.

Sixth grade in late September, the sun shone on the big plastic signs for the Mobil and Exxon gas stations that were tucked in the garages across the street, and in four lanes onto and off the highway, cars swept under the arching copper bridge that supported Riverside Drive. Bums trolled the green dumpsters where once I saw a woman draw out a half log of orange cheese. We had left Ms. Appel's class in sized places, but as we approached the yard, order broke down and it was all the student teachers could do to keep us out of traffic. Terry Baldus—a short kid, good at sports, brush-cut blond hair—squatted in his Pittsburgh Steelers promotional T-shirt. Zev said, "Neeee-yowwwwww!" He set his arms in a sprinter's pose and his wild curls blew. Kevin opened my control panel and used special tools to fix me. I argued that Arrow, as second best at everything, could run faster than Rocket and hit harder than Hammer. "Because if my legs move almost as fast as Zev's and are almost as strong as Terry's, then actually, I'd run really, really, really fast, faster than either of them. And if my arms move almost as fast as Zev's and are almost as strong as Terry's, then in real life, I'd punch the hardest."

"No way," said Kevin.

"What do you mean, no way?"

"You're second strongest, but Hammer is stronger than you. Also Rocket. Rocket is really, really fast. Faster than Arrow. But you can punch harder than him."

"Listen," I said. "If I'm going really fast and I'm really strong"—this time demonstrating the actual style of my punching motion and the real power of my legs— "then I'm stronger and faster than someone who is just fast or just strong, right?"

"Davey," said Kevin, surveying the motions of his other

androids, "you don't understand. You're strong and you're fast. But Rocket is faster. Hammer is stronger."

"Be realistic," I said.

"I'm being totally realistic here."

Zev went past, a tangled mass of curls, arms frozen in the comic book sprinter's pose. And Renny Benitez, like he couldn't help it, like even with his glasses he couldn't pick up his head and see the world around, wandered toward us from behind. Terry used the poor kid as a blocking sled, shoved him off the curb and almost into traffic. For the rest of recess, Hammer had to sit on the side.

It was at the end of elementary school that Benjamin Button entered into our lives. He came in around the same time our childhoods ended. Like I said, we noticed him before we ever spoke to Benjamin. He was everything our parents weren't, everything they didn't mention in school, the stuff only hinted at on radio and TV, the grunge and the sex of the city. The first time I remember talking to him was in Riverside Park. Benjamin had his bird with him and Kevin, Zev, and I were inspecting a dead chicken. Early October, late afternoon, a Sunday. The sun was out, puddles evaporating. We could see the tall buildings uptown. The cliffs of New Jersey had fall color.

What Kevin liked to do after a storm was head out to Riverside Park and map the patterns of runoff down the hill behind the Soldiers' and Sailors' Monument. We brought graph paper with us and protractors and tape measures. In our sketches, the puddles and eddies became lakes and rivers, the patches of dry ground islands and sometimes continents. Zev always finished first and then started throwing rocks at trees. His maps were shoddily drawn and places got named things like Suckpussia or Lake Moosey Cocka. I tried to be more careful and mimicked the nomenclature of swords and sorcery books: the Sea of Kalakatan, the Kingdom of Winoola. Kevin climbed over the black iron fence and worked deep in the brambles where the rats lived. He was professional, used a ruler and a compass, striding off yards and trying to get the scale right.

"Davey, will you hold the tape measure?"

The maps he drew captured as much chaos and detail as he could within the ruled lines of his graph paper. He borrowed the names of constellations, calling one rock kingdom Cassiopeia and a string of islands that were the bumps of tree roots Orion's Belt. We were deep in brambles when Zev discovered the headless bird.

"Snap," Zev called. "Oh, snap!"

Kevin gave me his maps for safekeeping, put his pens and tools in his mom's Channel Thirteen shoulder bag, and fixed his canteen behind him. The dead chicken lay feathered, deflated, and scrawny on the concrete frame of the metal grate below which the tracks of commuter trains headed north. Kevin unfolded the long blade of his Swiss army knife and poked the bird, flipped it. The corpse remained rigid. Its muddy feathers caught the breeze.

"Dead for hours," Kevin concluded. "Killed last night before the storm." With his knife blade he probed the gooey pulp where the head should have been. "Apparently, it was torn off, not cut." He pushed at the skin, tapped the bone. "I'm thinking biting, someone tearing the chicken apart with his teeth. I don't think at this point we can rule out the kind of savage rite in which a high priest rips the chicken apart as sacrifice. Devil worshipers."

Zev nodded.

I said, "Bet."

"Imagine the leader there, on top of the hill. He bites off

the chicken's head. Then he drinks the blood and the bird is passed from hand to hand. These are doctors and lawyers and librarians. Our parents' friends, all chanting prayers to Satan. They stand here." Kevin, with his knife, drew a diagram in the mud. "Here and here. Then, when it gets to the back of the crowd, the corpse is discarded. The congregation becomes a raging mob. They rampage through the park, seeking squirrels, pigeons, stray dogs, sleeping drunks, anything to satisfy their bloodlust. My suggestion is we come here at night. The three of us. If we can climb into trees, conceal ourselves, they'll never notice. And I don't know about you guys," Kevin said, "but I am definitely interested in—"

He stopped, distracted by something or somebody, looked away from the chicken and over his shoulder. I turned and saw a pair of bare, long-toed feet, the ragged cuffs of jeans, and a tattered old army jacket. It was Benjamin Button, his hair hanging down to his shoulders, his face slightly acned, his cheeks unshaven.

"How do?" he said. And when he saw the chicken, "You guys do that?" He had a tropical bird on his shoulder, in his left hand a brown paper bag that jumped.

"Is that a parrot?" Kevin asked.

"Cockatiel. Her name is Bessie."

Kevin nodded. "What's in the bag?"

"A rat," said Benjamin coolly. "I'm going to feed it to my boa, Billie. Actually, I'd open it for you, but I can't do that here. It's alive. The rat would just run away. Are you going to cut up the bird with that knife?"

"We're investigating."

I felt stupid to be carrying the notebooks and graph paper. Zev had folded his map and stuck it in his back pocket.

"A dead thing like that gets germs." Benjamin rubbed his nose. "You kids shouldn't be playing with that. Actually, if you guys want, I could show you. You could see Billie eat." The cockatiel on his shoulder fidgeted. "I mean, beats playing with a dead animal."

My mind went to after-school specials. You weren't supposed to follow strangers, you weren't supposed to listen to what they said. But Zev and Kevin were braver than I, and Benjamin was so guileless and so obviously cool that there was no way we could resist. We followed him up the hill, across Riverside Drive, and to the Old Manse. Benjamin's weird, long-toed feet made their way across the checkerboard tile of the lobby, Benjamin moving past the doorman with the smirk of a criminal or a naughty child. He took us up the stairwell because, he said, the elevator frightened Bessie. On the way up he talked to us about the diet and care of a pet boa constrictor.

He didn't feed Billie often, he said, because snakes would just keep eating and would grow and grow and grow. It was important to regulate the boa's size, but also not to let it get too hungry. Hungry snakes escaped from cages. They went hunting. They caught pets, neighbors, ate unsuspecting old ladies. We passed the coiled fire hose at the second-story landing. I touched its dry canvas stitching for what reassurance I could get. Some pet owners, Benjamin said, were afraid to feed their snakes live rats, afraid of diseases the rats might carry and the wounds snakes might receive in the struggle to eat their prey. There were owners who fed boas dead rats; the snakes pounced on these corpses and constricted them. Some even put vitamins in the dead rats, a little injection to keep a healthy snake.

"But that's so uptight," said Benjamin. "I mean, boas don't get vitamin shots in the wild."

Kevin followed him, then Zev, then me, and where the stairway elbowed between the second and third floors, Benjamin's feet were at eye level and I saw the chipping yellow calluses at his heels. He opened the door to 3W, the cockatiel clawing his jacket's shoulder. The apartment smelled of medicines and disinfectants and as we crossed the dusty threshold, Benjamin put a white finger to his lips. The ancient carpet was worn. The wallpaper bubbled. Confronting us in an ornate wood frame was a portrait of what had to be an ancestor—a striking resemblance to Benjamin Button—a mustached middle-aged man in the gray uniform of a Confederate officer. I saw the back of a wheelchair behind the half-open door of the master bedroom, a withered arm hanging by its side. Mrs. Button, I guessed. Was she Benjamin's grandmother, his great-aunt? In the kitchen dishes clattered; that had to be the sound of her nurse. Benjamin gave Zev the paper bag to hold, instructing him to grip the top. Zev might get bitten if he put his fingers on the sides or bottom. Then Benjamin cajoled the cockatiel onto his right forefinger and dropped his army jacket on an old maple wood dresser which behind lead-ruled diamonds of glass displayed an astonishing collection of crystal and dust.

We walked down a narrow hall past a bathroom to his bedroom, which was the same shape as mine but seemed as much a storage closet as a place where someone lived. It had the furnishings of an attic in a long-kept family home, and the feel of a museum exhibit fallen into disrepair. Peeling from the walls was paper in an ancient nursery room pattern—smiling locomotives pulling carloads of happy cows. Antique trains lay on the floor beside miniature pistols in hard leather holsters. In one corner was an old-fashioned crib with a high headboard, delicately carved. Above the crib hung a mobile, wooden angels with trumpets. I saw a coronet and a synthesizer, a xylophone, an old Victrola phonograph with a trumpet for a speaker and a needle like a serpent's tooth, a hamster cage with cedar chips and a little rodent running on a wheel. There was a sleeping roll on the floor on top of an old quilt and carpet, folding chairs against wooden chests, a clarinet, a nudie poster by the dartboard. By the far window was an enormous birdcage, climbing from the radiator top all the way to the ceiling. Benjamin slipped the cockatiel through the wire door and Bessie flew to the top, past the mirrors and feeding bottles and perches and swings. Then he turned to the other window, whose shade was drawn. In a gigantic tank with a sunlamp sat Billie the boa constrictor, green and black and lethargic, resting on some withered lettuce leaves by a ceramic water dish.

"Hey," Benjamin said. The snake did not respond.

We three gathered around as he lifted the sunlamp off the top of the tank. The movement of the paper bag's top as he unrolled it must have excited the rat within because it bumped and bulged against the brown paper sides. When it was opened, Benjamin neatly upended the sack and the rat poured out like white spotted jelly. It bounced on the pebbled floor of the cage, little paws pressing madly against the glass. Then Billie the boa moved like a gunshot, like a piston, like a whip. The coiling and crushing were all one action and most of the sound came from the rush of pebbles at the bottom of the tank. Then the rat was dead, a tail protruding from the smiling mouth, along with a bulge of fur and a foot. The snake's expression remained stupid and resentful.

"Do it again," said Zev.

"Does it swallow the rat whole?" Kevin asked. "Do its jaws unhinge?"

"Let's feed it something bigger," said Zev.

"How about Davey?" Benjamin's hands rested on my shoulders. "Want to feed her him?"

I won't pretend we ever became intimate. Sometimes in the lobby he said hi, sometimes he seemed to avoid us. Benjamin was always outside our understanding, mysterious and disturbing. Halloween that year, we stumbled on a party he threw. He had invited a bunch of Columbia students or maybe high school seniors over to his place to get stoned.

The next year we would be too old to go begging for candy, but in 1978 we dressed as the World Champion New York Yankees, no need for costumes beyond plastic batting helmets and polyester pinstriped shirts. Pudgy freckled Kevin of course was Thurman Munson, the catcher, number 15 and our captain. He wore his helmet backward with a face guard on top of his head, and a navy blue chest protector with ridges like a turtle's belly. His red hair was cut in a bowl; think *Rubber Soul* Beatles. Olive-skinned Zev wore a jockstrap and dressed as Sweet Lou Piniella. ("They're not booing," he said, with his fist to his mouth, trying to include crowd noise in his soprano imitation of announcer Frank Messer, "they're Lou-ing.") I had to be Willie Randolph, slick-fielding second baseman, and with my black autographed glove, inhabited the role. We all felt mustached and macho, ready to swat homers, chew tobacco, spit, scratch our crotches on national television. According to tradition, we started at the penthouse apartment, Schlachter, and worked our way down, so we hit three with plastic bags and hollow pumpkins filled with Goobers, Kisses, and SweeTarts. In the elevator, we had the usual trades and arguments, Mellow Yellow vs. Starburst, the relative value of Charleston Chew. Ms. Appel had prepared us for Halloween. Never accept home-baked goods, she warned, not even a cookie, not even from someone you know. There could be drugs, there could be poison. Avoid fruit. Razor blades got hidden in apples, so everything had to come in its original packaging. And never go into anyone's home, that was the main rule. We were jittery and jumpy at the door to the Button apartment, wondering if Benjamin would be there, wondering what he would give us, hoping he would invite us in.

"Davey's excited," Zev said. "Davey has the hots for Mrs. Button."

"Quit it, Mr. Raging Boner."

"She's your girlfriend, right?"

"*Excusez moi?*"

"Did you just say Mrs. Button was your girlfriend?"

Kevin rang the bell. Music crept from under the door to 3W, bass notes, drums, and chanting. A smell of something smoky, too. Kevin knelt to get closer to it, but at the sound of approaching feet scrambled back upright. We shushed each other, rearranged our helmets with our mitts, ungloved hands clutching candy. The lock turned. Out peered Benjamin Button.

"Wo."

He wasn't wearing an army jacket, wasn't even wearing a shirt. There was no cockatiel on his shoulder, no snake around his neck, just gold chains against his freckled skin and wispy chest hair. "Hey," he said, and rubbed his eyes. His pants were unbuckled. Maybe we had woken him from a nap. "Come on in." Then he turned around, showed us the pimples on his back, and disappeared into the dark foyer. The door swung back ajar. We stared after him stupidly.

"We should just go down to two," I said. "We should skip this guy."

"Don't be a chicken," said Kevin. "Chicken."

He pushed the door open and edged across the threshold,

looking left and right from the old wood dresser to the picture of the Confederate ancestor.

"You guys," I told them, but I also entered that place which was shaped like my family's apartment but furnished like someone's crazy grandmother's. And it had been violated. Strange articles of clothing lay on the floor, draped over chairs, hung on glass doorknobs. A feather boa lay on an old hooked rug. Kevin moved toward the music and the light. I put a fist in the cool leather of my mitt. It was like we were entering a scary movie, complete with soundtrack. The shadowy furniture seemed to me to be apart from the party, dignified and quiet. In the living room candles burned and unusual pillows were strewn across the floor. By the piano, a group of four sat cross-legged and passed from mouth to mouth a pipe shaped like an experimental plastic woodwind. Two men, two women, long-limbed and squint-eyed, their hair blossoming in all-natural puffs and folds. They had made a nest of rugs and sweaters; they reminded me of campers by a fire. Goodies spread around them, a box of cookies tipped on its side, a yellow cake which had been pulled to pieces. One of the girls wore no pants. Her blue jeans were in front of her, near a scattering of playing cards. There were a few other pieces of clothing there—a leather vest, sandals, socks, a bracelet. The pantsless girl giggled. "Baseball team!" she said. Benjamin Button sat apart in a green wing-backed sofa, shirtless, his legs folded under him, and he whistled a tune that had nothing to do with whatever came from the stereo. Above him hung two old-fashioned paintings, black kids in rags playing with fiddles, dogs, and drums.

"Oh, right," he said, when he finally looked up. "The Yankees."

"Trick or treat," said Kevin.

The smokers laughed. One offered up the pipe. Kevin might have taken it, if Benjamin Button hadn't gotten off the couch and led us into his kitchen. He seemed to have no idea what to do when he got there, flicked on the overhead light and took a paper bag from a closet, grabbed a jar of peanuts from a shelf.

His refrigerator was old-style with levers on the doors and an oversized icebox. We could see the bumps of his vertebrae when Benjamin bent to fetch us plums. From the shelves he pulled a jar half filled with olives and then a sticky one with maraschino cherries. He wandered over to the countertop— there was no table in this kitchen, nowhere to eat, just an ancient black stove with a kettle. From dusty glass jars Benjamin grabbed handfuls of prunes. He tossed these into the bag that lay open and standing in the center of the narrow kitchen. He found a box of graham crackers and sprinkled these lavishly over the other prizes. Outside, from the living room, more laughter. I thought of the legs of the dark-haired girl without pants. She was tall and not very pretty, but in the glow of the candles I had seen the way her pubic hair curled out from her panties.

"That enough?" Benjamin's eyes could barely open. "You guys set?"

We were all quiet for a moment, considering the horrible buffet. The paper bag stood on its own, an absurd monument. Kevin finally spoke up. "I don't want prunes," he said. "Or really the peanuts, actually, on second thought. Davey, do you like prunes?"

Zev said, "Prunes kind of suck." But he said it softly, with a hint of apology.

"Not the cherries, either," I managed to say.

Benjamin sighed, leaned on the countertop. The bag sagged on its own. It seemed miraculous to me that Benjamin's pants, unbuttoned and without a belt, stayed up, supported only by his narrow hips. "Got it wrong, as usual," he said. "Anyway, you can see that I wasn't quite prepared for visitors. You guys, I mean." He rushed a hand through his chestnut hair. "We've got to get you guys something good. Don't want to waste your time here." He scratched his chest, his naked nipples. "Why don't the four of us share some of the maternal stash of dessert wine?"

Before I could even think of what to say, Kevin assented and Benjamin disappeared, leaving us alone with his bag.

"Sucks the big moose cock," Zev offered.

"Quiet," Kevin said.

I took off my helmet, which contained a warning, not for actual use in games.

Our host returned. Four yellow goblets dangled from the fingers of his left hand, silver stems and rims around cut glass. The wine had an ancient brown label. Red wax wrapped the bottle's neck. Benjamin's hand trembled as he poured, and when he passed me a glass I touched his cold damp fingers.

"We gotta make a toast, guys," said Benjamin. And we all felt very old, drinking that grown-up drink in his weird kitchen which had tiles and not linoleum on the floor. It was the end of trick-or-treating of course. After that visit to Benjamin there was no point going down to the second floor for miniature Mr. Goodbars or Nestlé Crunch. We went right up to the MacMichaelman apartment, where Zev explained it was marijuana they were smoking and I fantasized about girls without pants. We ate too much candy and spun around in circles. Kevin put on a 45, Wild Cherry. And as I lay on the floor in the MacMichaelman living room, watching their ceiling turn, I remembered Benjamin Button looking out his door after us, and had a sudden worry—one of those wild paranoid rushes kids get. It had something to do with Benjamin's teeth; they were yellow like my grandmother's with black cracks in the canines. It had also to do with the fact that he had referred to ninety-year-old Mrs. Button's wine as maternal—I thought suddenly that he wasn't a young man at all, that he was ancient, and that he should have had a long beard, a cane, and eyeglasses.

2.

In 1912, no Jews lived in the Old Manse—no blacks, no Catholics, no Chinese, no Mexicans, no Irish, no Italians, no Finns—and the first Benjamin Button moved into 3W with his pregnant wife Lilly. They decorated the big rooms with furniture from her grandmother's North Carolina plantation: four gilt mirrors, one oak table, two oil paintings of black children at play, the green wing-backed sofa, the maplewood dresser with its crystal display, and of course the portrait of Lilly's great uncle, Colonel Fitzgerald Key, in his bushy mustache and Confederate grays. The only new purchases were the marriage bed and the piano on which Lilly played sometimes Chopin and sometimes a Scotch air. Button was a merchant banker, an army veteran, small, dark, and energetic, had grown up among Essex Street pushcarts, the grandson of a rabbi, but had buried his heritage along with his family name. The birth of his first child promised to incarnate his dreams of an American future. He imagined a son, Benjamin, Jr., attending Yale, and there acquiring a nickname, maybe "Cuff."

So on the morning consecrated to the birth of this child Button rose at six, dressed himself fussily, and hurried out to a Broadway thick with brick and wooden houses under which the subway had recently begun to run. He caught a trolley uptown, nervously stroking his mustache, worrying his cheeks for spots he had missed shaving. The car was empty except for a young black man whose feet beat a complicated rhythm and an old Jew who ate fish straight from its wrapping. Button had skipped breakfast and the odor of herring tempted him. He shot greedy glances at the old man's bites. The Jew's lips made a clucking sound. The handsome young black passenger carried with him a coronet in a black case. His hair was short and soft and shined with oils, his face chocolate and friendly and satchel-mouthed. The tempo he tapped with his foot ran contrapuntal to the old man's puckers, and the crisscross rhythms must have pleased him because he began to moan, long, soft, harmonic gasps bridging the two times. Perhaps unconscious of the music in the back, perhaps in response to it, the driver burst in with a bit of Verdi. His tenor was not grand but insinuating, and as the trolley crossed 96th Street, the old Jew began to clap. His lips stopped smacking and he sang out, "Yeedle-deedle-dee," in a chord complementary to both the coronet player's groans and the driver's aria. Button, frightened, leapt off the car and walked the rest of the way, brushing his clothes as he went. He turned a corner and there saw his wife's doctor, a civilized figure in black, rubbing his hands together in a washing motion as he descended the hospital steps.

"Dr. Keene!" Button shouted. "Doctor!"

The physician faced around.

"What?" Button read something awful in Keene's expression. "The child! Where—my wife—how? Why—"

"Come!" said the doctor. "A sentence! In English, please!"

"The child—is he born?"

Keene frowned. "After a fashion." He straightened his tie. "Yours, I suppose."

"Boy?" Button asked. "Girl?"

"Hear, now!" An ice truck rumbled past, horse hooves clomping. "If you had only been honest with me! Told me the truth! But this? Do you want me to spend my last years tending to sick colored children? Climbing tenement steps? What about my reputation? I cannot enter into your world of—"

"What?"

"See for yourself! Though I suppose you know the worst already." Cane in hand and silk hat readjusted, Keene climbed into a waiting cab and was driven serenely away.

Button was frightened. He wondered if Lilly had let the truth slip—somehow mentioned circumcision or refused the attentions of a minister. He doubted such a thing possible. She had always done what was Christian and proper and had never placed any significance on his origins. Like Button, she ignored them, assumed that his damp European heritage would evaporate in the warmth of American life. He entered the front hall of the hospital and snatched his hat off his head. It was a fashionable boater but on his shadow looked like a peddler's derby.

"Good morning," the nurse on duty remarked.

"Good morning," he said. "I am." And he seemed momentarily to forget his name. "I am Button."

A look of terror spread itself over the girl's pretty face.

"My child. I want—" His teeth caught on his usually labile *w*. "I want to see my—"

"Upstairs!" cried the nurse. "That's where we put it!" And she ran from her desk in terror.

Button saw his mother's face projected on the ceiling of the great hall. A wig, a frown, wet, knowing eyes. He lowered his head and climbed to the second floor. There, he addressed a dark-skinned nurse who approached him, basin in hand.

"I am—" Again he faltered. "I am Button—"

"Sweet Jesus!" the nurse exclaimed. Clank! Her basin

clattered to the floor. Klink! Bank! Bong! It rolled down the stairs, a melancholy tolling.

"I tell you!" Button shrieked. "I want to see!" Was his child not as human as any other?

The nurse regained her composure. "All right," she agreed. "But if you knew what state it's put us in all morning. It's unfair to your—our—I don't know what to call it. And your wife! This hospital will never have a ghost of a——"

"Ach," cried Button in his meticulous fashionable dress.

At the end of the long hall they reached a room from which proceeded a variety of howls. Six newborns were on display, color-coded pink and blue, pinched faces and tiny hands. The third bassinet from the left was stuck with the name Button and in it lay no child but a tall thin gray-bearded old man—older than eighty and naked but for the small cotton blanket that covered his groin. Sad-eyed, wet, liver-spotted, and bony, jammed into a tiny crib, he kept his arms crossed, and his withered chest shuddered. His breasts sagged, his nipples were purple, veins crisscrossed skin as white as cake icing. His knobby knees dangled over the crib sides, his ears were messy with vernix.

"Oy," the vague old newborn muttered. "*Veys meir.*"

"Is this some kind of joke?" Button yelped.

"To us it doesn't seem at all funny," replied the nurse. "This"—she pointed—"was removed from your wife's womb, and just this morning."

Horror-struck, Button smoothed down the front of his suit, imagined his son's miraculous birth—the screams and the surgeons fainting and the old man's body unfurling from Lilly's gut. His fingers twitched at the thought of the wrinkled newborn skin. A picture formed itself: He would be wandering the streets with this apparition by his side, a living illustration of his embarrassing origins, long-nosed, simpering, and bearded—his son. He would lose his wife, his apartment, and his good name.

"Get this thing out of here!" cried the nurse. A heavyset orderly loomed behind her.

Days later and home from the hospital, he sat the old boy on the toilet in the back of 3W, the bathroom closest to the nursery, and worked with sewing scissors, one hand on Benjamin's head. Snip! Snip! White tufts of beard fell onto the lap of an ill-fitting dressing gown. Button forced Benjamin's head back, saw the turkey neck and throbbing veins, and had to fight the urge to stab there. Hot water ran, the bathroom mirror steamed. Button rattled a brush in a cup of soap, foamed the newborn's sagging cheeks, and stropped his razor. Benjamin sat working his gums, a lost hillbilly on the crapper.

"Hey! I might be in the wrong here, but it's only—" Button gestured. "Whatever got into your head to come out this way, I don't know, but it's terrible, and you are going to be much happier—your mother will be when I—Now sit! This craziness! If you had only come out a normal child!"

He nicked the loose skin beneath Benjamin's ear and gasped to see blood mingle with creamy soap bubbles. Button's nervous fingers trembled, tore out a piece of chin, and drew a red line under the nose. And when he had cleared Benjamin's face of suds, he rubbed it violently with a hand towel. Two fingers slipped into a pat of Shinola, then ran in dabs across Benjamin's eyebrows. Button took a step back, bit his lower lip. Pleased with his work thus far, he massaged the black wax into his son's head, applying it to the scalp where no hair was available. So Benjamin was welcomed home. His father's robe hung slack from his shoulders, displaying his withered chest. Long strands of yellow hair extended from the front of his imperfectly shaved neck. Blood had retreated from his cheeks and lips only to gather and flow from the nicks around his mouth. His blue eyes focused nowhere, taking in nothing, and his hair was clumped in a mockery of fashion. Shoe polish fingerprints marked his brow.

"Better, though," said Button. "Much better. You don't look good, but you look a lot less . . ."

He got out a set of dentures and clamped these into the old boy's gums, Button working up a sweat. Benjamin, meek and obliging, squealed only when pain became unbearable. The father dressed the boy in a sailor's suit that had been made to order by a flabbergasted tailor and pushed him into the living room, where Lilly, taking laudanum for her pain, smiled genteelly, mistaking Benjamin first for a neighbor's boy and then for a peculiar-looking salesman.

She had been in her youth the single white rose that flowered at the top of Chapel Hill, but now looked tired and wilting, cut and kept too long in dingy water. In her palest blue dress, with her face powdered and her blond hair set in ringlets, she watched little bent Benjamin make his way across the plantation rugs, the newborn nodding like an idiot. Behind Lilly stood Nandie, her childhood nurse, with a pitcher of ice water and a querulous smile.

"Where is the baby?" Lilly asked.

"Baby?" said Button.

"I—is this—" Lilly could not rise from her chair. "Do you—where—the baby!"

"I tried . . ." Button wanted to tell her more—that this wasn't exactly what the boy would look like; it was only a suggestion. With better dye, better dentures, a more professional barber—

"What have you done?"

"I don't see—"

And Lilly broke into sobs.

It's difficult to guess how Benjamin understood this. He was getting used to the feel of his feet, the way sound traveled in air, the shadows and shapes of his parents and Nandie and the furniture and the window frames—all this after the dark waters of the womb. Button insisted they be a family. On the first Saturday that Lilly could walk, he marched her out for a stroll. He wore his mustache waxed, his best high collar, and a new straw hat, pushed the carriage into which Benjamin would never fit—though his son did not object to holding a bright red ball. Button's bravery in the face of calamity was lost on Lilly. Dizzy and terrified, unsure what to make of the ruse childbirth had played on her, she rode a whirligig of confusion. In the promenade of the park, she stared over the river toward New Jersey, trying to hide her limp and to pretend the two eccentrics with her were not relations. Then came the inevitable chill in the spring air, the face of social disapproval. Mr. and Mrs. Parkinson Childs, philanthropists who lived on the drive and whose family, on the husband's side, was distantly related to her father's, were sauntering toward them, over a rise in the wide path, under the shade of the maple and sweet gum trees. Lilly began to fidget. Button felt her tension and steeled himself. Benjamin, who waddled painfully—he needed support, a cane and not a rubber ball—looked up to see what lay ahead. The Parkinson Childses came close, they were near. The impulse rose up within the boy. He touched a hand to his blue sailor's cap.

"Good *yontif*."

Lilly bolted, darted through traffic, and was almost run down by a honking Ford. Within days, the news spread. All of transplanted Southern society knew disaster had befallen the Buttons.

So Benjamin learned to keep quiet. At home, Lilly sobbed

as she knitted colored socks for him and then cringed at the sight of her son. The heirloom crib, carved by slaves on the ancestral plantation, was pushed to a corner of the nursery. Maybe, Button said to himself—since that day in the park, he and Lilly rarely spoke—the boy would need it later, Button thinking as if Benjamin's premature dotage were a passing phase like colic or an illness like the croup. In the meantime, he bought the boy a cowboy hat, a six-shooter that used caps, and a set of model trains which some days little Benjamin tripped over and others he ignored. As a provisional measure—until the crib became useful—Nandie laid out a cotton bedroll for the boy and a quilt over a thick rug. Lying down at night under the shadow of a mobile of angels with horns, Benjamin felt the wood floor against his delicate bones. Nevertheless, he was an easy baby. Only when morning light broke through his windows did he pull himself from bed. Something working within him that he did not understand, he put on a sailor's cap, took the leather strap from a quiver of arrows, and wrapped it in ritual patterns around his forearm. Button woke to hear the faint singing at sunrise. In his nightshirt and tasseled cap he padded down the hall to the nursery, where he discovered his son—there beneath the choo-choo-train wallpaper, dressed in footed pajamas with a teddy bear pattern, knitted blanket draped around his shoulders—bobbing instinctively toward Jerusalem.

"Not—no! Here—never!"

The boy learned to apply his own hair dye and makeup, to shave, to dress himself as what he was not. After days of snapping argument, his parents sent him off to kindergarten. Lilly insisted that it was pointless, his presence in school would only publicize their disaster, but Button countered that it was essential the boy be Americanized. Useless.

Benjamin dozed while the other children pasted together scraps of colored paper. Presented with juice and cookies, he asked, "A cup seltzer, maybe?" And, "What Benjie Button?" He scratched his head. "I used to be, if I remember correct, Mr. Solomon Uschitz sounds right." He joined in the singing of songs, but always too enthusiastically, clapping his hands in wild rhythms and singing bass-line harmonies to tunes that properly had none. At the request of his classmates' parents, he was removed from school. The Parkinson Childses in particular advocated against Benjamin, insisted that despite their own distant relation with the boy he was an improper influence on the other children. I've found their letter, browned and crumbling, signed by an attorney and expressing a combined sense of urgency and regret. Lilly kept it folded in a volume of German legends.

She locked herself up at home, could not face the pointing and whispers on the street. To her medicinal laudanum—which she persisted in taking long after her physical pain was gone—she added a dose of gin, spent her mornings dressing and her afternoons slipping into an untidy stupor, left off her piano playing, dreamed at night of North Carolina, one day even began packing suitcases to head down there, but when she considered the humiliation she might face—old friends who would know that she had given birth to a freak and that her marriage was a failure out of folk tale—she collapsed sobbing, an awful sight which Benjamin could only observe from a distance. As for Button, a man so finicky and self-conscious, so jealous of his position in the world—it was unbearable. He felt the grocers and butchers snicker at him, whether he was purchasing apples or pork. Laughter in an odd corner of a restaurant, and he would assume he was the subject, the object of a stranger's joke. His anxiety erupted in spasms; he screamed at secretaries and doormen. At his furious insistence, the family attempted dinners. He dragged foggy Lilly to the dining table, crammed brittle-boned Benjamin in a chair, but just as old Nandie was laying down bowls of pea soup before them, Button turned on his son.

"Damn it!" he shrieked. "It's just bacon!"

Meals ended in chaos, the roast uncarved, the front door slamming, Lilly in her bedroom. Benjamin slunk off to the nursery, where on his xylophone he plunked out sad tunes, old folk songs from tiny European towns, but with his left hand syncopated harmonies, slinky, insinuating rhythms. The sounds entertained only the toys he ignored and the crib in which he could not fit. Then in 1915 *Lusitania* sank and neighbors were finally distracted from the family's disaster. President Wilson declared war—or announced that war was already in progress—and Button reenlisted as an officer, motivated less by patriotism than by a desire to flee his home. It wasn't until he was gone that Lilly and Benjamin realized how thickly his rage had filled 3W. After his departure, there were no more dinners, no more walks in the park or hopes that Benjamin's condition could be relieved. She distracted herself with hours at the piano, kept Button's photo on the mantel, and hoped for the best for him, but while she played, her mind was elsewhere. Head turned to the right, she bit her lower lip intently. From the edge of the room, Benjamin watched the smart rise of her wrists, the way her fingers spread and contracted, the brown flashes among the white keys. Once, Lilly caught him there, standing almost hypnotized.

"Do you like it?" she asked.

Blushing, he could not answer.

Benjamin snuck out from the apartment, investigated the city all around. At first, traffic and noise startled him—

Broadway with its backfiring trucks and bell-ringing street-cars, the fresh piles of manure, grocers selling fruit, and above it all, painted ads for hats and soda pop, cigarettes and soap. Benjamin lingered by the empty lots, peered through holes in wooden walls, watched steam shovels at work, I-beams swinging on wires. He brought home gifts for his mother—wind-up toy birds sold on the sidewalk, a box of lemons individually wrapped in pink paper, magazines with pretty pink women drawn on their covers—and left piles of offerings by her bedroom door. He snuck down to the river-bank, through the mud and brambles, risking his old bones to get close to the trains, the clanking couplings, the whistle's hoot. He followed the tracks downtown where they crossed into the avenues and once saw a flag-waving cowboy lead a locomotive through San Juan Hill. At night, he went to Paddy's market where pushcart vendors sold fish by the light of oil lamps and he brought home sardines folded in news-paper. Over the years he had become stronger, his legs better adapted to his weight. He walked sometimes without his cane, and his neck jutted less precipitously from his shoul-ders. The old boy spent hours riding on the Sixth Avenue El, knees against the wicker-seat bottoms and his dyed trimmed eyebrows on the window's dusty glass. The lives of the city passed by: women in blue muumuus airing heavy arms on fire escape stairs, families fighting, policemen strolling. After sundown, these scenes flickered past in a montage more com-pelling than any Benjamin witnessed in the movie theaters with their rattletrap pianos, more surreal than any cartoon he had seen in a hand-crank arcade. The train's percussion provided the right score for his peep show and if once he saw a girl in a window twirl so her skirts rose, the shades before and after were discreetly drawn. He would hoot, he would whistle, he would groan.

A policeman tapped his shoulder. "Old fella, you okay?"

The cop looked over Benjamin: the short pants, the parchment skin, the inky eyebrows—a pervert? a lunatic? a suffering, sickly boy? And when Benjamin in his immigrant's accent offered up his mother's name and Upper West Side address—a drop of mucus dangling from the tip of his nose—the patrolman didn't know what to think. He brought Benjamin home, big red hands clasping the fishy knuckles.

Lilly answered the bell. "Yes?"

Hat in hand, the horrified officer mumbled apologies. Aghast, he felt he could in one glimpse see the whole history of the Button disaster (did he remember an item in a scandal sheet?): the child with the awful disease, the fall of Southern gentility. Lilly spent the next week in bed and Benjamin grew lonely for her piano playing. On a Monday when she was either unwilling or unable to leave her room, he tiptoed over to the instrument, caressed its keyboard, and sat down on its bench. Benjamin jumped at the sounds it made—so loud in the quiet apartment—but persisted. He fiddled as he played, exploring the scales, weighing each note tentatively and then with assurance. Old thin Nandie was startled by the noise and came out of the kitchen, her apron white with cake flour.

"Benjamin! You'll wake Miss Lilly!"

"Oh."

He let his hands drop, then lifted them again, tried a flat key, then a natural, then a chord, inhaled, exhaled, and reached his fingers across the scale. Out came Beethoven, *Für Elise*, exactly as Lilly played it, all her stops, repetitions, and missed keys. The failures in her music captivated him, and they were the source of his initial improvisations. He would take a hitch in her *Auprès de Ma Blonde* and then drive it through the tune, forward and back, until he had broken up the music so that it worked like a piece of faulty machinery. He did the same with the spirituals and lullabies that Nandie hummed: learned them by ear and then ruined them. Benjamin experimented with keys and tempos to capture the heave of Broadway's traffic, and in his walks around the city lingered in front of taverns where accordions played. English was not the only language he understood. Yiddish, Hebrew, German, and Polish, these came to him as naturally as eating. Benjamin eavesdropped on the Germans in the East Twenties, the Chinese downtown, the Jews below Delancey Street, but even though he watched and studied the big city, he was isolated in the polyglot crowds, a funny little wide-eyed man in shorts. His desire to know beat out his inborn prohibitions and he sampled schnitzel, chitlins, and chow fun. The flavors played on his tongue and when he came home the piano would roar. His music drew Lilly out from her bedroom. She sat in the green wing-backed couch and watched his bent back as he played. The two might have become intimate if Button, Sr., had not returned home, a twisted, angry version of his former self.

His mustache was gone and his right leg shaped like a question mark. He wore an officer's cap and a green army overcoat, but the left sleeve was empty and pinned. Up he limped from the subway station, duffel bag dragging. Broadway boasted fewer wood buildings than when he had left, more automobiles and coughing trucks. Large brick apartment houses towered above, terra-cotta facings in the sun. One of those March days whose coolness seems only to intensify light, and lipstick was coming into fashion. Button turned down 89th Street, crossed West End Avenue. When he came to the Old Manse, his eyes teared, whether from nostalgia or wind off the river, I can't say.

Benjamin answered the doorbell when it rang. The boy

had changed. He stood straighter. His face was less wrinkled. There were perhaps fewer liver spots on his hands. Still, he wore a floppy collar and his hair dyed black.

"You," Button began. And if there was more to that sentence, he never finished it.

Benjamin inched to the left, under the portrait of the Confederate colonel. There was an odd resemblance now between the two: the wide forehead, the sensitive eyes. Benjamin offered to take his father's coat or bag, but Button would give up neither. He smelled Nandie's ham hocks stewing, Lilly's perfume, eyed the furniture, the familiar wallpaper, and limped across the threshold dragging his bag.

"Is someone?" Lilly called from the winged-back sofa. "Oh, Nandie, will you check if the——"

In the living room, sunlight streamed in from the south-facing windows and the air hung with dust. The shadows of the window frames cast a net of parallelograms across the furniture, and Lilly sat with a novel and a blunt knife to cut its pages. She hadn't heard her husband enter. She thought the doorbell might have been a plumber. And in those suspended moments before she looked up, Button glared at her critically. She had put on weight. Her face was puffy, her eyes bleary, her hair no longer honey-gold but the color of wood left out in the rain.

"Mama," said Benjamin softly. "Daddy's home."

Book and knife flew from Lilly's hands. She swung her feet to the floor, reaching out for her husband, who stood there stiffly, challenging her to accept his new shape. Lilly patted her hair, her shoulders, her hips. And it wasn't until she had caught her balance that she noticed the extent of Button's deformity. She knew he had been injured—the army had notified her—but she had not understood. There was nothing on his left side, not even a shoulder, just a curve belling gradually from his neck, the folds of his overcoat loose as curtains until they reached his belt.

"Oh!" Her hands covered her mouth.

Button stepped away, stumbled against the rocking chair. "This place is a little more cramped than I remembered—"

"But it's home." Lilly pushed stray hairs from her forehead, struggled against her tears. "You're home. I didn't expect—why didn't you tell—we're— Nandie, fix sandwiches. Take off your coat, dear. Champagne!—a—Benjamin—play something for your—"

"Play?" Button asked.

Pots clattered in the kitchen, Nandie fixing food.

"Champagne!" Lilly called again. "He's dressed just the same, just as you wanted him to. We've been trying to continue—we both have—as you would have—but things have changed. Well. However to explain? Benjamin, help him with his duffel—or just—"

"What exactly does the boy play?"

"The piano," said Lilly. "He is the most marvelous." As she looked across the room to her son, there was a sweetness to her smile that hit Button like a punch to the stomach.

"Well, kiddo," he snapped. "Let's hear."

So Benjamin stepped to the bench. He settled his long, thin fingers across the keys, began by testing a scale, then fell into a rhythm. His left hand worked chord changes with confidence, then the right came in, tapping out high notes like a chickadee's call, music as anarchic and hopeful as a summer afternoon in Central Park. Benjamin's fingers fell in loopy circles like sycamore seeds to the ground, and then, to give the tune an improvised bridge, he clanked out hectic downtown rhythms, musical analogies for the coffee roasting and the docks clanking below the Brooklyn Bridge. It was the city he was giving his father, a welcome-home gift wrapped in klezmer blues. Button chewed his lower lip, might have been counting the flowers on the wallpaper. An evil scar climbed his neck. Lilly prayed for a smile from him, a sign of approval of the music and by extension the family, but when Benjamin finished with a flourish, crossing his right hand below his left, Button frowned.

"Boy plays coon music."

The clatter of Nandie's tray on the coffee table had to stand in for applause.

Button and Lilly slept together that night. She tried to kiss him, to massage his good arm, but he pulled away, haunted by visions of combat, then of the delivery room. When he finally slept, Button dreamed of carnage seeping from between Lilly's thighs. So in the years after the war while the rest of the nation was exuberant, 3W seemed older than ever, the paintings more somber, the furniture more dilapidated. The colonel in his confederate grays had never looked more disapproving, the black kids more sorrowful in their play. Nandie's dusting got careless, as if even her old hands were weighed down by the apartment's misery. Benjamin did what he could to please. He played the piano for his mother and then skedaddled every time his father came home, wore the clothes of a child and lurked at the edges of rooms. Button railed at Lilly. Doors slammed. Unabating tension. The scene repeated itself more than once: Benjamin hoping to entertain his godforsaken mom (who lay in bed, disconsolate), his bony hips planted on the piano bench, his back bent so his nose almost touched the keys, his body transported by a rhythm that almost captured an East River sunrise, when—whack! He never heard it coming, didn't smell the rummy clothes, didn't hear the footsteps, only felt his father's hand crack his delicate jaw. Seeking peace, Benjamin rode the subway up to the fish markets in the Bronx, and there amid the general screaming, the slapping of eels on cobblestones, he stood on tiptoe and cocked his ears. Of course, he got threats from the rough kids, a little man in a cowboy suit, his hair dyed and his eyebrows stray and reedy, trembling wattle beneath his chin, a look of apology in his eyes as if he understood every stranger's desire to smack him, but he wanted it all: the screaming Italians, the Polish children's games, the city like a smorgasbord laid out for him. Benjamin stayed out late, lingering at the doors of clubs and speakeasies. His very eccentricity allowed him entry, so he traveled to fashionable 133rd Street, Jungle Alley, the Nest, Mexico's, Dickie Wells's, saw the Jim Crow crowds, the debutantes in sleeveless dresses, and the floor-show women with feathered asses, heard the stomping bass drum, the orchestra's roar, and at Pod's and Jerry's barrel-chested Willie "The Lion" Smith, there with his cigar chomped in his mouth and his bowler hat tipped low, playing the keyboard with razzle-dazzle more beautiful than Benjamin could imagine. He sat at the bar, ordered a top and bottom, and ignored every sight in the room except the piano player's fingers. As for Button, in those days he took on a raucous life of crime. He was seen less often in 3W—wiping shaving foam from his chin, dropping a suit in a valise—then began to appear in the newspapers delivered to their door. The one-armed lieutenant strode the Boardwalks of Atlantic City with Legs Diamond, got photographed in the company of Texas Guinan. I've read the printed rumor that he killed a man. He moved to a mansion in Long Island and there threw wild parties. There's mention of these in Winchell: Gilda Gray from the *Follies* spotted at his place, a famous young writer tossing his wife into a pool. If you want to extrapolate affairs with jazz singers and bootleggers' wives, go ahead, but my bet is the man was a mess, doubly trauma-tized. He never got over his own war injuries or the twisted birth of his child. I imagine a man who knows he is hideous and is frightened to boot by the historical load in his gonads. In a train car once, he broke a show girl's nose.

And Benjamin may have made his way into the papers, too. I've unearthed something odd, and I'd like to share it with you. In a club in the West Forties there was a pianist known variously as the Hey-Hey Hebrew, the Jitterbug Jew, and the Kokomotion Kike. We're talking 1927–1928, the heyday of Miller Huggins's Yankees. This showman tottered out onstage nightly in shtetl drag, dusty black clothes, a long white beard glued to his cheeks, an exaggerated stoop. He'd wave a fishy hand at the crowd and then sit at his instrument and let loose wild rhythms. Owney Madden, Pola Negri, Commissioner Mulrooney dropped by to see the shambling humorous entrance, to hear the occasional "Oy-yeh-yoy" between sets, and to witness the surreal riffings that quoted here Schubert and there the Hebrew *Shemah*. Gossip of the time suggests the performer was in fact a prominent young Southerner, but you know what I think? I'd like to draw you a scene. The tough guys shuffle in, four of them in wide lapels, the boys accompanied by six dyed-blond molls, the girls' sequins glittering in the light of the tabletop candles. It's two A.M., the last set, and the gangsters are grouped at the balustrade by the back. The maître d' is terrified. There's no place to seat the tough guys and, forced to stand, they grow outrageous, hoot, pinch the waitresses' behinds. The fattest points and bellows and his elbow digs into the ribs of his one-armed confrere.

"Will you look at that, Zipper—the genuine article!"

Button squints through the cigar smoke to the spotlit stage. The piano player is messing around with "Yes, We

Have No Bananas," making it go faster and faster until the piece is an all-but-unrecognizable set of repetitions and trills and stuttering rhythms. Father knows right away that the beard is phony, the forelocks from a wig maker's, the black coat a sham. He can see the pianist naked as the day he was born and if he can't understand the music, he knows the musician is making fun. The boy doesn't know anything about what he's doing, can't know a thing about the Lower East Side, the shtetl, this pampered Americaner grew up with his pretty Southern mother in the goddamn lap of luxury. Button wants to reach for his gat. Also, he wants to cry. He rushes into the street, retinue in tow.

And in his dressing room that night, Benjamin turns thoughtful. He's read stories of what's happening in Germany, and it makes him uncomfortable. Jewishness is, after all, not a part of his upbringing but something weirdly entwined with his memory and birth. He takes off his makeup, lingering in front of the mirror as if answers to his questions lie there. With warm water, he washes layers of translucent glue from his cheeks and when the cotton-ball beard begins to hang, he peels it off gently. With a quick tug, he snaps the right forelock from his sideburn. Then he touches the talcum powder on his head and, leaning close to the mirror, discovers a shift in his hairline. It's thicker and lower than it's ever been. Bending over the paint pots and newspapers, he touches his fingers to his scalp. There at the roots, where neither black dye nor white powder have penetrated, the natural color has turned from white to gray. He has always suspected that his body is slowly adapting itself to the world, but for the first time he begins to hope that he might be growing young, or at the least middle-aged. He palpates his cheeks and decides, yes, the network of wrinkles there is growing shallow. Some winter color has come into his skin. He takes off his suit. The jacket is thin, powdered at the shoulders. He pauses in unbuttoning his shirt—the sweat stains at the pits. Equally revolted by his Jew outfit and his short pants suit, he stands helplessly in his drawers, pinching his skin, inspecting his belly button. Born with denuded thighs, hairless in patches as though through a life of pants chafing, yes, he is sure of it, there has been some stubbly regrowth. Certain only of things he is not—neither of his costumes suit him—Benjamin leaves the club, his dyed hair under a wool cap, his clothes concealed under a rain jacket. The sky is clear. A waning moon. He walks all the way to 89th Street and arrives at the Old Manse before dawn, newspaper trucks clanking, deliveries of ice and milk and laundry.

The 1930s: He continued to wander the city. Hale and fit, a trim gray beard, blue eyes, worsted suits. He spent too much time in 3W, entertained his mother's friends at the piano and the middle-aged women pressed smiles and sweet-cakes his way, but night found Benjamin trembling and sweaty in Bowery dives and Chinatown bordellos. A line of hovels stretched across the great lawn of Central Park; Benjamin trudged through snow, bringing potatoes and whiskey. By stewpots and campfires, he tapped his toes to blues tunes and on his harmonica cried like a hobo in the rain. On the Lower East Side, he tried synagogues on Saturday, prayed in the back row beside men who resembled his newborn self, but the words didn't come to him as naturally as they had in his youth. At home in his room afterward, Benjamin tinkled the old toy xylophone trying for childhood tunes but was unable to reproduce the melodies. So when Pearl Harbor came, he listened to Roosevelt on the radio, then made his way to the recruiters' office in Times Square.

A proselytizing band thumped as he climbed the subway

stairs at 44th Street. Light-bulb skeletons loomed overhead. A couple from Illinois murmured when he passed. Was that Aloysious Tompkins, whom they had seen last night as the judge in *Chippawah?* He was handsome like his father, with narrow shoulders, an uncertain glance, and a tentative worry in his grin. His mother's characteristics had also come clear in him: a softness to his features, a sympathy in his eyes. The army recruiters, of course, saw none of this, only his neatly trimmed gray beard, the crow's feet that ringed his eyes.

"I am twenty-nine years old," remarked Benjamin coolly.

"Why," said the corporal at the desk, Adam's apple bobbing, "I'm sure we could use a fellow with your experience, but Uncle Sam does say right here—"

"Twenty-nine," Benjamin repeated.

"Will you get a load of—" The line behind got antsy. "Move along, old-timer!"

And a sergeant burst into the room, voice spiky as his thin gray hair. "Corporal, what's all the ruckus here?"

"I am in the right," Benjamin protested, even as he dropped his birth certificate on the floor. "I really am twenty—"

"And I'm the Queen of England! Get out of my building or get out of town. You mean well, sure, but we ain't got the time!"

"He thought this was the old men's home!" cracked a voice from the back of the room. "Must have been the Wandering Jew."

Under the accusing gaze and pointed fingers of recruiting posters, Benjamin made his way out into the street. He had told the truth about his age, worn no disguises, demanded something he actually wanted, but even with dignity and truth on his side had been found as ludicrous and out of place as he had been in preschool. He thought of his mother at home, her musty, transplanted Southern gentility. He thought of his father, ever since the Crash balled up like a crippled fist in his mansion on Long Island. Clouds shot by overhead. Papers swirled off the pavement. Benjamin wandered dizzily up Seventh Avenue, from the Roxy to the old Yiddish Art. He had twenty dollars in his pocket, his grandfather's watch, a ring on the second finger of his right hand. At a hock shop he traded the jewelry for a blue wool sweater, a traveling bag, and a cheap set of clothes. He ate a chicken sandwich at a Tenth Avenue lunch counter. Then he disappeared. I imagine him in a black knit cap, working as a merchant seaman. A dose of gonorrhea in Belize, odd jobs, entertainer, saboteur, piano player in a Casablanca dive. Then in 1943, thirty-one and mature beyond his years, Benjamin emerged from this underworld and signed on with the Allied army as a civilian translator. He rode with tank troops into the heart of Germany. I have a picture of him, newsprint golden with age. Benjamin stands with a group of officers who have gathered around Omar Bradley. He is on the far left, bearded, carrying an attaché case.

And it was during his last year in Europe that he wrote a series of letters to his father. I've collected these, stored the pages in a set of vellum envelopes. Benjamin's style is colloquial but succinct: descriptions of listing walls, German soldiers begging behind barbed wire, civilians emerging from the rubble of Hitler as if from a period of hallucinogenic delusion. Some tell of the stockpiled starved bodies, the tall black chimneys.

I have been appointed to converse with the survivors and this sometimes upsets me but I don't mind telling you that my upset makes me ashamed. These people don't seem to have anything, no hair no sex no nothing but eyes and bones and

they press their hands on you talking crazy, like they were
starving for talk and not bread. In Italian in Hungarian in
Greek. They all think I'm the translator so I can understand
them which is not true, believe me! You want to keep a level
head and sometimes you just want to vomit and other times
you want to kill every German you see and other times you
want to kiss the DPs (that's when the DPs aren't around).
They are nothing but skulls on sticks. Suffering suffering
everywhere. I try to do the best I can and talk to them as I
would anyone on the IRT in good old New York. An old
man—but who can tell—he told me he was a musician so I
gave him my harmonica. After he had played the instrument
for a minute it came out of his mouth covered in blood, his
lips and gums I guess they weren't up to it.

I have the papers. I can show you. The son came home
healthy and horrified and delighted with the ordinariness of
life, but the father died alone. Button must have been one of
those phantom suburban corpses discovered by a stranger
who has come by to check the gas. Lilly was brought to the
morgue sixteen days too late.

1948. Skinny, clean-shaven, chestnut hair speckled gray,
Benjamin formed a jazz combo, the Button Down Three. In
the fall, they drove up to the Hudson Valley, Benjamin and
his drummer and a bass player, for the reception of a wedding in which the famous King Moncrief Orchestra was to
play the dance. His bandmates were younger than he and
took the front seat, gossiping. Benjamin lounged behind,
smoking cigarettes, eyes shut behind dark glasses. The back
door of the station wagon was tied shut and it clanked as
they went, an uneven rhythm out of sync with the engine
and the wheels.

"I would say Italian women," said Buddy the drummer,
brushing the square of beard that grew beneath his lip.

"Particularly out of Sicily."

"I would say you don't know shit."

They crossed the bridge over Spuyten Duyvil, the wide Hudson on their left.

"How about you, Ben?"

Whose fingers played keyboard in air. "Depends who's cooking."

"Cooking." The rhythm section laughed.

Out of the Bronx, houses began to thin. An hour north, forest gathered around. They pulled off the highway and into a territory of open fields. Benjamin rolled down his window, let a yellow cloud of smoke escape. Early afternoon, the meadows were filled with late-blooming harvest flowers. The station wagon turned into the driveway of a mansion and rolled toward the delivery entrance at its back. A sighing crept toward them—it could have been the plaint of violins through the open windows, a string quartet warming up for the two jazz bands, or maybe just the rustle of birch leaves from the woods nearby. They parked behind a large bus from which the big band was disembarking.

"There's the King," said Buddy. And Benjamin's eyes opened to take in a Cadillac, the trademark captain's hat, Moncrief's long hands dangling from the sleeves of his overcoat. The girl who followed him was small but voluptuous. "Hildie," said Buddy. "His daughter. Sings with the band." Her skin was honey-colored in the sun and ashen under the shade of the porch, beautiful as sin.

Benjamin nibbled the earpiece of his sunglasses and nodded, affecting indifference. "Pretty." He climbed out of the station wagon—middle-aged, slightly drunk, stretching his legs—then added, "You might introduce her to me, Bud."

Inside, the house was abuzz with caterers and florists, maids with dustbins and brooms. Benjamin watched as the more famous musician tested out the piano, feeling the action of its keys. Hildie bent over Moncrief, whispering. Her evening gown showed off her back, the curve of her neck, the shape of her sweet behind. When Benjamin's trio began, it was with Irving Berlin, "Always," as the wedding party entered. Buddy tickled the high hat. Joe laid down bass notes like satin sheets on a bed. Benjamin's right hand slinked along the keys, his left stroked lush chords. The open rooms filled with passed hors d'oeuvres. The piano warmed with innuendo.

"Slow down, Pops," Buddy said.

When their set ended and the cake got cut—a pause in the music while the big band arranged itself—Benjamin found Hildie on the back porch, warming up her vocal chords by her father's Cadillac. She was staring at the stars, so much thicker here than in the city.

"Hey," he said. "It's Cassiopeia."

"What?"

Benjamin introduced her to the constellations.

"Some playing," said she.

"You know Orion's Belt?"

"Who are you, man? That's what my daddy kept asking. Why hadn't we heard of you before?"

"Will you look at that sweep of stars above the mountains."

She sighed and accepted a Chesterfield.

"I ought to quit this singing. You don't know what I have to put up with. All these eager sidemen, pestering me. Young boys are so idiotic. Do you know what they talk to me about? Card games. I drank such and such with so and so. My car is so—"

"You should hear my drummer."

"I'd rather hear you."

"Ah." He swallowed to keep his heart from thumping. "An old man like—"

"Old?" asked Hildegarde. "You don't seem old at all. Let me guess. Fifty? Why, that's just the romantic age. Established in the world, free from overwork and worry." She smiled. "Fifty."

He expected fireworks from the Big Dipper.

The day they were married, Benjamin lifted her out of a white Chevy. The skirt of Hildie's gown billowed, her heels kicked. He stumbled up the shallow lawn and the stairs of their new house. Benjamin carried laughing Hildie over the threshold, laughing, too, at the fetching kitten he had managed to scoop up in his arms. Upstairs, he dropped her on the bed. Then, tipsy from champagne at lunch, bride and groom giggled as he flung up her skirt, its billows of white chiffon. She grabbed his bow tie and he fell. It was like plunging into a cloud or a special airy pastry, and she was somewhere within, the creamy center of all that tulle.

3.

I rode the 7 train out to Queens some years ago, to visit Hildegarde Button. She was in her seventies, a thin handsome woman whose gray hair had been straightened and cut in a style out of the Kennedy administration. She still lived in that same semidetached house, not too far from the Louis Armstrong Museum. A wagon wheel marked the rise of her lawn, and she had grown the hedges high; otherwise her house was identical to the ones to the left and right of it: brick steps, an ornamental front porch. Pakistani children biked in the narrow streets. Teenage Sikhs in turbans played football between the rows of parked cars. All of Asia pours into Queens. You can walk a block where no two neighboring shops are decorated in the same alphabet. The day I stopped by, no car was parked in Hildie's driveway, so I was able to walk right up to the fence of her garden, where she knelt among the raised beds. Her back was to me. She wore canvas gardening gloves and a smock. Still, I could make out something of the figure that had so astonished Benjamin: the lines of her hips, neck, and shoulders. Everything around her, including her collection of trowels and watering pots, even the mud she was turning over, seemed perfectly in place. Pansies edged the brick patio. Basil and tomato plants grew high. Crabapples hung above.

"Hello," I called. "Hello?" And she turned, pushing a strand of hair from her forehead with the back of her gloved hand.

"My name is Birnbaum."

She squinted, wondered what I was trying to sell.

"We had Jehovah's Witnesses yesterday."

I smoothed down my tie, told her what I was trying to write. Hildie hesitated. I worried she might chase me away, might take offense at my project, but, revealing some of the impulsiveness that had led her to marry Benjamin Button, she smiled.

"I'll be." Stuck the point of her hand spade in the ground. Removed her gloves, plucking fingers free one at a time. "Let me—I'll meet you at the front door, please."

And when she did, Hildie wore the smock no longer. A bright scarf around her neck matched the color of her pleated skirt. She had changed from sandals to pumps, all in just a few minutes, and she led me through a sparely furnished living room. The piano showed off her wedding picture, also a photograph of her father in a top hat and tails. The furniture was 1950s modern: one Scandinavian couch alongside a coffee table with a hole in the middle, abstract curves, and three legs. She placed me in a high-backed wicker chair in the cool of her screened-in porch, headed back to the kitchen, and returned with a tray bearing a pitcher of lemonade and two tumblers full of ice. We watched the birds and butterflies flutter around her garden. Her tools had all been put away, the patches of mud smoothed. "You really ought to have called before coming."

"I didn't——" I began.

"You thought that if I saw your pretty face, I'd trust you. Quite a plan." And her smile was more than a little flirtatious. "Mr. Birnbaum."

"Call me Davey." I coughed.

The record of her marriage was divided into twelve maroon photo albums whose vinyl covers were molded on the surface like leather's grain and padded beneath around cardboard centers. Each volume contained five years' worth of pictures. Green dividers separated the seasons, yellow the years. Photos were placed four to a page, spaced regularly under clear plastic sheeting, and I cannot remember one out of place, a corner of a plastic sheet bent, a crease or an air bubble or a stain on a snapshot. Hildie edged close to me and turned the stiff black pages one at a time, and I knew enough to keep my hands, damp from the condensation of the lemonade glass, off the carefully curated memories. She wore no jewelry except for a silver watch and a golden wedding band. Her nails were manicured in clear polish and they played lightly off my shoulder, off my forearm, off the images of her husband's face. She chattered as we sat. Her voice was light and thin and musical—you can hear her on a few recordings by the King Moncrief band. There wasn't ever much range or texture to her singing, just a swinging brightness that did well with light, uptempo tunes. Her laugh was like that, high notes pinging.

I kept notes as I looked over the books. My scribbles are in ballpoint pen—I remember being embarrassed by the tooth marks in the cheap Bic I'd bought just days before outside a subway station. The pages of my green spiral-bound pad now ripple. I got caught in a rainstorm on my way home. Just as well. All that writing is useless: *pg 2 B & H by bbq*, or *H in Fla, fishing, 1953*. May 1961, I noted three photos: the couple on a boat, a beach, a porch with drinks and friends. I wrote down names as she gave them to me—*Larry Moses, Pauline Paulson*—but she was lying, misremembering, or my research techniques have failed. Not one of those leads has proved identifiable. Her refrigerator seemed to contain nothing but lemonade, which she pressed on me glass after glass. I must have gone to the bathroom half a dozen times. I scooted through her living room, noting the expensive rugs, the lack of books, the massive record collection. In her medicine cabinet I found antidepressants and blood pressure drugs. And the photographs? A shot of Benjamin in 1951 in the backyard in a chef's hat and apron, his young wife looking up in laughter, the colors all gone pale.

"I had quit my singing," she told me, "but wanted everyone to know we were show biz."

Another cute one, black and white, Hildie playing with a baritone saxophone almost as big as she is. Singly, the pictures were bland, but collectively horrifying. If the shifting of a man's carriage from forty to fifty is gradual, how much harder to gauge the changes in reverse. Between 1947 and 1955, his hair becomes thicker and he puts on a little weight. In 1956 they are sailing in Key West. She is girlish at twenty-eight, Benjamin has a middle-aged paunch to go with his Hemingway beard. 1962, they are in Vegas. His face is wide, getting florid. A cigar juts from his full-lipped mouth. He wears a Hawaiian shirt. Hildegarde in her mid-thirties attempts a cosmetic dewiness, shiny moisturizer and thick

mascara. As his face becomes smoother, hers develops lines
and cracks. In the final shot, an older woman kisses her post-
pubescent husband full on the lips.

"Even then," she said, "we were happy."

She closed the album. I finished the last of the lemonade.
The remaining ice, former squares melted together in a
cubist hunk, fell *plish* into the syrup at the bottom of my
glass.

"It wasn't"—I struggled, ashamed to raise the obvious—
"difficult?"

"Child." She laughed, laid a hand on my knee. "No marriage is ever easy. The secret to a happy one, I think," she
said, "is staying young. Why, if you look at these pictures, he
never seems a day over sixty—"

"That must have been—"

"Love," she said. "Love keeps you young, you know."

I have a recurring nightmare in which I enter the elevator
at the Old Manse—the wood paneling, lights recessed
behind shiny brass ledges into which Kevin and Zev and I
threw chewing gum and candy wrappers and cigarette butts,
the linoleum floor with the brass plaque set on a diagonal at
its center. I am boarding from the seventh floor, my parents'
floor. The brown door opens and a fat man is waiting for me.
Something about him makes me hesitate. I get on the elevator anyway. He wears a checkered sports coat. His short tie
ends at his gut. My vision is at the level of a child's—I am a
child. I stare at the fat man, his spongy crotch, the belt that
wraps his tummy, the wet folds of his neck. He smiles. His
teeth are wide-spaced. His hair is matted. He leans down
toward me and heat fills my gut, pure terror. I'm up before I
know what happens next. The scene feels like obscure memory, half forgotten, like I recognize this stranger but can't

place the face, can't figure out what he'll do to me. So I get out of bed, walk around my apartment. Pick up dirty socks and underwear and drop them in a sack at the bottom of my closet. Take a piss. Go to the little three-quarters fridge and get a sip of milk. If it's not yet three A.M., whiskey. Sometimes in bed again I'll search my memory for the fat man, for the fear, for its source. Did something awful happen, something I have forgotten? Was that Charlie Chop-off, pinking shears behind his back?

My friend Kevin lost his mind when we were seventeen. That's how I put it when I tell the story, if I tell the story at all: breakdown, Kevin, once sane, turned erratic, as if at a discernible point the friend I had ended and was remade along less compelling lines. It's a disingenuous locution, and covers up a mess, forgives me for having failed Kevin in the years following his hospitalization, because if he was *broken*—well, then, the Kevin I loved disappeared. Don't get me wrong. I'll be the last to romanticize mental illness, to claim it's difference and not disease. I won't rail against the compulsory normalizing of psychopharmacology. But there is a continuum. All the stuff of Kevin—his enthusiasm, brilliance, humor—lay encoded in his brain like and unlike mine, ineffable but real, and with a hitch built in its workings: Step on the gas and you wouldn't know *when* it would hit 250 miles per hour—or let me reject that metaphor and try another: I see his character composed of not individual traits but aspects of a single form—intelligence, wit, insomnia, paranoia, competitive anger, love of pizza—hovering in a darkness beyond my reach, its edges indistinct, but how the curves shine. . . . I was awful to him. After his breakdown, terrified—after he was put away and drugged and named *crazy*. I was interested in girls, in poetry, in being someone my parents were not. Zev was much better, still is. Visited

Kevin in college, hangs with him now and then. Not me. Oh, it's easy to rationalize: old friends, you lose touch. But I wasn't rational. I was scared.

I'd tell the story straight, but senior year of high school? Like a blur to me. I remember no chronology, just incidents, my brain a jumble of odd snapshots. Here is Robert Claxon in the back of French class trying to see if Cheese Doodles are flammable. There's Vicky Takahashi, some guy's muddy handprint on the butt of her Sassoon jeans. Or me, walking down the steps of school, thinking: Better get some now because girls are never again going to be this beautiful. My grandmother, when she was in her seventies, visited my uncle's house in Boston and, exhausted from a plane ride, picked up a novel in German, a language she had not spoken since she was twelve. For several pages my grandmother did not realize what language she was reading until my uncle came in and interrupted. With the German, a flood of memories came back: World War I, when she was a refugee in Czechoslovakia: dogs, apple trees, walks, songs. Maybe someday I'll put the right CD in the player (or download it from a computer or mainline it through an IV or however music will flow in my old age), pick up the right piece of pornography, or read a particular swords-and-sorcery novel, and then—whammo!—my last year of high school will return to me and I will remember how shy I was and what an asshole to my friend Kevin.

There are facts. Like, one day, Kevin went over to Zev's apartment and the two of them smoked a joint and then Kevin took everything in Zev's bedroom and threw it out the window, starting with a bicycle, then a desk chair, then some lamps, then the jujitsu trophies, then the books, then the records, then the record player, then a bookshelf, all six stories down, smashing cars and scaring the hell out of passersby. (Zev locked himself in the bathroom, sat on the toilet shaking and crying, his face bruised where Kevin had hit him with a baseball bat.) Kevin hurled Zev's pillow and blanket and sheets onto the street, shoved the mattress out the wide-open window, broke the window frame when he was trying to heave out the bed, but that's when the cops came and smashed down the door and put Kevin in cuffs and leg irons.

I missed all that. Still, I do have certain memories of the days leading up to Kevin's big freak-out. There was the time I was at his house watching television and Kevin emptied a deck of playing cards in a hat and then emptied the hat on his head. When he was spinning out of control, he became obsessed with the Alger Hiss case: Whittaker Chambers, the pumpkin patch papers, 1950s skullduggery. It began with a paper for AP history but snowballed. Kevin was up every night and on the phone with me the next morning while I slurped Rice Krispies and looked over the Yankees' box score.

"Yo?"

"Davey? Good. Find the chart I slipped under your door."

I went to the foyer and picked up a manila envelope. Inside was a sheet of paper with boxes and arrows and unfamiliar names and Venn diagrams and a complex curlicue border as if that lovely touch were essential to comprehending conspiracy.

"Just follow along," said Kevin. "I'll explain. What I want you to see is that it all comes down to him, some ninety percent of postwar U.S. history. The bizarre cancer incarnate, the one that survives bouts of chemotherapy and reemerges, here in McCarthyism, there in Vietnam. Watergate, that's the least of it. The whole Reagan White House—Haig, Bush—they all came out of him. William Safire, Diane Sawyer—don't tell me there's a liberal bias in the press. The

American left, contemporary liberalism, it's a twisted set of capillaries, an organ grown constricted and bent in the harsh conditions of blastula R.M.N. Literature? Imagine Mailer without that man. Pynchon, those paranoid fantasies? No, these are footnotes, annotations to the sick fantasy life he foisted on us. A pumpkin patch—who keeps tapes in a pumpkin? The bad guy in a comic book, that's who. And the good guy would dress just like Our Boy Dick, maybe in more saturated colors, the yellow trench coat and fedora; he'd have a more chiseled nose and chin, maybe a two-way radio wristwatch."

"Dude," I said.

And other things come back to me. For instance, a blessed last conversation in Riverside Park. A chilly fall day after baseball season, we came down the path behind the Soldiers' and Sailors' Monument, down the steep hill where once we had drawn maps, and we sat on a park bench not too far from the train grate where we had discovered that headless chicken. Joggers passed, their breath steaming. Bare trees, so we could see traffic whistling up and down the West Side Highway, and to our left the playground where overzealous parents pushed swings in the cold. Kevin sat, hands in his pockets. Zev and I stood. All of us in long coats bought at secondhand stores and wearing more or less the same shaggy hairstyles we had in elementary school.

"You're only using ten percent of your brains," Kevin told us, smiling. "That's ninety percent unused. Just think if those capabilities were harnessed. I think I've learned a way, through meditation, to access that power. I want to teach you my techniques. Once you've learned them, we can work together to spread the word. And there's no end to what we'll accomplish."

He spoke of an end to disease and famine. The triumph of

peace. And I think he pictured himself like Buddha reigning over a golden age.

"Not really possible, Kev." Like it was rational, like the time we had argued about the relative strengths of Arrow and Hammer and Rocket. "Like a lot of your brain, the hypothalamus, it's just there to do standing up straight and stuff."

"Actually, body temperature and a range of metabolic processes. But what you're saying is beside the point, Davey. I'm not talking about the diencephalon, here. Think memory, for a second, okay? Think Plato, think Jung, major philosophers throughout the centuries who argued that there is so much more in our heads and knowledge than we habitually call upon. At fifteen percent, man, do you know what kind of problems we could solve?"

He talked about ratios of excess food produced to amount needed by starving people, numbers at his fingertips like he was a spokesman for Oxfam. I was routed at every turn.

"Okay, but how are we, you know, a bunch of seventeen-year-olds, going to get people to listen to us anyway? I mean, if you are right, how would we get anyone to listen? Like, if you can access all this brainpower and you become Mr. Super-Einstein, do you really think people are going to pay attention in any significant way?"

"Davey," Kevin asked, "are you willing to try my meditation techniques?"

"Kevin, I'm your friend. I'm talking about other people who—"

"Just try the techniques, Davey. You're a perfect test case. If I can convince you, I am sure I can convince anyone."

I looked at Zev, who knew better than to argue with Kevin. I looked at Kevin and his clear eyes were unblinking. Maybe I would have tried, just then, given his meditation techniques a whirl, if we had not been interrupted. It was some weird kid, a little younger than us, though his clothes seemed ancient, a green outsized army jacket, blue jeans frayed where the cuffs were rolled, and he wore no shoes. Between his lips was a bent and broken cigarette. He shivered in the cold.

"Any of you guys got a light?"

"Um," said Zev.

"Would you like to join us in a meditation session?"

"Oh, man." The stranger giggled. Chestnut hair, horrible acne.

Zev extended a Zippo. The guy stuck his face out to meet it.

Those were the Reagan years. Tortellini and arugula at our parents' tables; moms and dads talked stocks. Meanwhile, the hospitals for the poor and crazy emptied, the real estate boom shoved the half mad into the street, and a new drug-dealing business began, crack cocaine, with shoot-outs on Amsterdam Avenue. The addicts congregated in Riverside Park, gothic parades of washouts. Nights, I'm sure, he crept out there, to all appearances a messed-up white teenager, but really someone with as little future as the oldest, poorest addict.

He puffed twice on his cigarette, then smiled and showed us his cracked and ancient teeth.

"That was," I said as he padded away, bare feet on the chilly asphalt, "Benjamin Button, 3W."

"Davey," asked Zev, "what the fuck are you talking about?"

"You remember, Kevin, don't you? The guy with the cockatiel, the boa constrictor, that party, that Halloween?"

And Kevin didn't answer. He just sat on the bench, his hands balled into his pockets, the smile of enlightenment on his face.

I come in from Brooklyn now occasionally to visit the Upper West Side. From Lincoln Center past 72nd Street where Broadway swells and intersects with Amsterdam Avenue all the way up to 89th Street, new buildings reconfigure the landscape of my childhood. These are huge and glossy— glass, steel, and stucco—but they feel portable and weightless, like architectural models grown large. The terraces all stacked and identical, there's no brickwork variation. You know the marble in the lobby and bathrooms is laid on in strips like veneer, that the Sheetrock walls bruise easily. And in the glass bottoms, you find the same coffee shops, bookstores, houseware retailers, and clothiers that you would in Peoria or Dubuque, the same countertops and signs, identical merchandise. What are you going to do? I still like Riverside Drive, the sculpted curves. But they've opened a new deli on Broadway. The place gleams. It's gigantic. Chrome and floodlights, underneath which they have imported guys who seem typecast to slice pastrami. "Pistol, whiskey-down," they shout the ancient code of countermen. Corned beef complexions, jowls like bloodhounds, and the dispositions of beat cops nearing retirement, perhaps they are actors, or maybe the real thing, flown up from Miami. The sandwiches are decent, but cost. You pay for the surly treatment, the steam clouds, and the smell of garlic. Guys in leather jackets and baseball caps yack on cell phones over matzoh ball soup. What Benjamin Button, Senior or Junior, would have made of it one cannot possibly guess. Bafflement, tinged with disgust in the case of the father, and for the son—I think it would have been a music he could not understand. The last year I saw him was 1988. Home from Ohio, stooped under a backpack of paperbacks and dirty laundry, in the lobby of the Old Manse I caught the glint of Lilly Button's wheelchair, saw the white-socked calves of her nurse, then a kid's legs, his feet in green Velcro-strapped sneakers. He emerged slowly from behind the nurse, a skittish little moonfaced boy, chestnut hair faded almost to blond. His mother's trembling hand reached out for him, those skeleton fingers making their way through his bowl cut. We three waited together for the elevator. No one said a word. Benjamin held on with two hands to his stoic nurse's pleats. She was wide-faced and solemn, her hair in a bun, one of the army of Caribbean women who come daily to Manhattan, to tend to old people, to tend to kids. The elevator finally landed. I didn't want to get in. The nurse pushed Lilly's wheelchair through the open door. The boy's head came up to my hip. I knew he was staring at me, waiting for something—what, I'm not sure. Greetings? Acknowledgment? I imagined his big eyes on my face, his T-shirt with a picture of a dinosaur.

"Benjie," said the nurse. I looked at her—maybe because I couldn't face either Benjamin or Lilly; I studied her wide, high Asian cheekbones, the small moles that grew in a cluster by her left eye. "Benjie, come on, now, get in the elevator."

Which he did with a burst of speed, childish hands in fists. "And you, sir," the nurse said to me, who wore his hair shaggy and his T-shirt with holes, who had been looking too closely at her thick lashes, the flesh rings that circled her neck, her white shirt open at the collar. I entered, then turned my eyes to the floor. The nurse pressed the brass button for three and asked me what I wanted. I stammered, then pressed seven myself. We passed two, approached their floor. The cables clanked, then caught themselves with a jerk. I had to peek, just to see, maybe to assure myself of the impossibility of my suspicions—but it was him, the shock when you see an old friend's baby picture and recognize the adult present in the child, but here the child was come to life.

"Come, silly boy," said the nurse. And he scampered away, never to be seen again.

Benjamin died in that plantation-carved crib, I'm sure, his mother expiring in a room down the hall, a nurse shuttling between them. I imagine that through the months, weeks, and days, he mewed and wriggled in wet diapers. There was a little brown bear and a little brown ball, and light filtered through the bars of the empty birdcage, the empty snake tank. The shadow of the angels on his mobile fell across the dusty Victorola on the floor. And as time passed it all grew less distinct, language and consciousness ebbing. The sounds he made became indistinguishable from the sounds around him. Soon, he could not tell day from night, pain from want, and finally presence from absence. Long after he ceased to feel the movement of time, he faded completely from its progress.

SAFETY

I drove without a safety belt. Feeling freer, I drove better. This made us all safer. Alice in the backseat gave me hell, same way she did about cigarettes. "Do it when I'm not in the car, Dad." One hand on her mom's seat, one on mine. "We don't have to see you die, Dad." She and Reiko made a big stink. I'd weather it and after the first few minutes they'd shift their focus, give me shit about the way I changed lanes. I said they should quiet, that if they'd just quiet I'd be more relaxed. I'd drive better and that would make us all safer.

"Safety first." Reiko pushed back her thin dark hair.

Husbands got in the way of doing things reasonably—this is what my wife taught my daughter, with me as exhibit A—but husbands could be charming. She and Alice started singing to the tune of "Guys and Dolls": "When a man named Dad has ideas that are bad . . ."

We were heading up to my parents' country house in Vermont, the Oedipal ranch. I didn't like to go, but Reiko—always against imprisonment in childhood resentments—cajoled me. "Four acres!" Her comedienne's exaggeration.

"A house by a lake! Get the kid out of the city!" Fourth of July, traffic thick as it gets on I-89. Everyone doing about sixty-five. I rolled down my window, lit another Lucky Strike. Reiko said, "Just because you're seeing your parents doesn't mean you have to go through the whole pack." Alice said, "I thought you were trying to quit, Dad." Some Connecticut hothead in an Isuzu Trooper snaked up from behind. "Look at that asshole," said I.

"Pete," Reiko told me.

Isuzu rode the ass of the cars in the passing lane, weaved right and left. At a hill, the old VW in front of him started to drag. I checked out my daughter in the backseat, dark hair, pale skin, her mother's teddy bear eyes. Hothead Isuzu honked his horn, slipped into the right lane, and clipped the hood of a Mercedes coupe. "Shit!" The Mercedes with its wonderful brakes avoided a worse accident. Isuzu sped off into the great beyond. My brakes needed repair.

Alice screamed as we flew into the Mercedes' rear end. Reiko extended her arm in front of me the way she did at stop signs, my wife's thin limb as if she might protect me from calamity. Metal struck metal, the Honda crumpled. My head went through the windshield. The steering wheel snapped my ribs. Reiko and Alice saw everything: my final twitches, the extruding ribs, the body impaled, demolished, dead.

The phone rang in their country house and my dad answered and he didn't wait to tell my mother. He forgot his wallet and glasses. Hunched up, big head over the top of the wheel, hands squeezing it, gray hair flying, my dad drove to White River Junction. My mother heard the news later, a second phone call, and it struck her as the steering wheel had struck my chest. My mother bawling on the floor of her country house, a gray-haired full professor of English crumpled like a baby.

In the emergency room, Alice talked to no one. Sat in a molded plastic chair. Hair hung down, dark and wet. Her sneakers, her socks, her blue jeans, her tie-dyed T-shirt, all were splattered with her father's remains. A social worker offered her a soda. Alice wouldn't drink. A nurse offered her a bed. Alice wouldn't move. Her lips swollen as if they had been punched. Her eyes glassy as an old woman's.

After an hour and a half, she said: "I need to go to the bathroom."

My wife came out from sedation and screamed my name but with syllables exploded and unrecognizable. Reiko, all layers of personality stripped down, no control, infantile terror, her face tomato-red and screaming.

My father showed up. The social worker said Alice shouldn't go back into a car. My father said: "Fuck you, fuck you, fuck you." No one there knew how to deal with a panicked, aged New York Jew from West 89th Street. He buckled Alice carefully into the seat beside him. He kissed Alice's head. My father said: "Do you want to change your clothes? We could buy you new clothes." Alice stared at the dashboard. He said: "Do you want ice cream? We could buy you ice cream."

She said: "Grampa."

He, too, drove without his safety belt. Alice cried. No tears, no sound, just a spasm in her throat. She vomited. My father pulled over. With pickup trucks whipping by, he struggled to clean her clothes. My father, past seventy, bending on aching knees, one folded napkin in his hand. "Mommy," Alice said.

"Mommy will be all right," my father told her.

There was a funeral. Reiko was incapacitated, a neck injury, a leg injury. We had written a will. In situations like this, our daughter was to fall into the custody of my sister-in-law Sue. But for the days Reiko was hospitalized, Alice stayed with my parents in Vermont.

My parents' lives were settled. Retirement had been laid out like a dinner service: the house in Vermont, the co-op off West End Avenue. Then the car crash, and the white linen had been pulled out from under, and all the china and crystal was suspended in air and might fall down in place as in a magician's trick but more likely would crash and shatter. And my mother would offer my father no consolation, would accept none from him. When my father ran out the door without telling her the news, without staying to console her, he had betrayed her. At the essential moment—the realization of the fear against which they'd organized forty years of sex and dinner and conversation and checkbook balancing and furniture purchasing and financial planning—he had gone AWOL. My mother did not talk to my father at the funeral. From her wheelchair, Reiko gripped Alice as if the two were surrounded by snakes.

For a time, the house was crowded with guests and relatives. My father wanted only Alice. She is small for a twelve-year-old, thin and dreamy, with my wide mouth and her mother's cheeks and eyes. For weeks after the crash she had trouble sleeping. Five in the afternoon, the Wednesday my brother Isaac finally split, the place was empty and Alice was bawling. My dad brought her from the sitting room to the kitchen, and she cried there while my mother sat at the table, eyes on a saltshaker. Dad walked her through the rambling house, past the workbench and firewood pile and rusty tools. My exhausted father finally lay down with her on the bed in the barn that had once been mine, under a picture of Saturn that had been taken by the satellite *Voyager*. There like an infant Alice quieted, licked her lips, and slept.

My mother in the kitchen was awakened from her trance by the teakettle's whistle. She shut off the burner and went to the barn.

"What are you doing?"

My father, standing up, put his fingers to his lips.

"She can't stay here. She can't stay alone. She'll stay where she's been. In the room under the stairs."

My father said, "Shush. She's sleeping."

"She can't stay here," said my mother. "I'll get sheets and blankets."

My father grabbed her arm. My mother had to pull three times before he let go. She came back with blankets and my father said, "Leave her alone," and my mother laid a sheet over Alice, then a blanket that smelled of mothballs, and Alice slept on the bare mattress. The sun sank and the room went dark. My father came back with a cup of tea.

"I made spaghetti," he announced two hours later. My mother stared at Alice. Another hour elapsed and she heard a screen door slam.

My father parked by a Presbyterian church in Randolph, a lot where farmers' markets are held on Saturdays. He cut the headlights, turned off the windshield wipers, let the drizzle beat down. In the house in Brookfield the phone rang, my brother Isaac calling from the road.

Spaghetti jelled in its colander. Tomato sauce cooled on the stove.

When my parents visited the house to buy it, the old women who were selling the place posed on the front porch, one with an accordion, the other with a tambourine, a little tableau vivante: Country-time fun. My little brother Isaac and I wandered across the front lawn. At the edge of the barn, a large maple tree grows, and beyond the maple we saw a rolling meadow, a sliver of lake visible beyond the meadow's edge. High grass grew across a bumpy scoop in the land. The old ladies kept only one strip mowed, a path that ran down to the lake. Isaac and I took off simultaneously. Down around a fir tree, past some raspberry brambles, we found a gravel beach. I pointed at the beaver dam across the way. A gray heron took off. Little Comanche scouts, we turned tail and ran back to tell our parents.

The old ladies called it Lake Oakee Fanoakee, "shimmering water" in Indian, they said. Some call it Colt's Pond after the one man known to have drowned in it. On the state map, it's labeled Sunset Pond. Isaac and I would float in inner tubes there and try to upend each other. We would sing songs: "I am a monarch of the sea!" Neighbors from the Upper West Side, Dave Ballarini and his sister Laura, would visit and we would splash each other and scream: "Time out!"

One summer when I was thirteen, their twelve-year-old cousin Lucy Darwin came, and she was taller than me, with chestnut hair and a wide face and a tendency to hesitate when talking. Her father was dying of throat cancer, she was staying with her cousins. Her black bathing suit was wet against her breasts, white edging by her shoulders and below her neck. Her hair was wet with bright streaks where the sun played. She flipped a lock while floating in an inner tube. I took this as an invitation.

Underwater, gravel played against my chest. I could see her bottom clasped by the ring of the tire. Beneath her shadow, I shot upward and flipped her and she yelped and when she came up, smoothing hair from her face, she smiled. Then her cousin Dave splashed her too violently. Lucy started to cry.

She was sensitive, my mother explained later. Her father was sick.

Next time, I promised myself, I would protect her.

The house in Vermont is decorated with gentle, ironic, literary jokes. There is a picture of a meeting of American men of letters: James Fenimore Cooper, John Greenleaf Whittier, Henry Wadsworth Longfellow, Oliver Wendell Holmes, all their heads cut out and pasted onto dignified bodies. There is a clock with William Shakespeare at noon, John Donne at three, Milton at six, and Shelley at nine. A poster that says BYRON in large letters and has pictures of women's undergarments beneath. Dried cut flowers. Hooked rugs. A sewing table with a pouch for needles and bobbins and thimbles.

My father has torn up and replanted the grounds every weekend of every summer since he bought the place. In a bathing suit and unbuttoned Brooks Brothers shirt, he hauls wheelbarrows of dirt; he jogs with buckets of water. He picks a sapling by the vegetable garden and moves it a hundred yards to the lake. He uproots the thyme by the back porch and fixes it by the old stone wall near the lilac tree, then the next year puts it all under the back of the barn, where it gets afternoon light but is blocked by morning shade.

These are my memories of summer: My mother cross-legged on an aluminum folding chair, reading the *New York Times,* and my father goes tearing past, face strained and splotched with mud and dripping sweat, a spade in his left hand, a garden hose in his right. 1984, asparagus, 1987, fruit trees, 1994, delphiniums and pansies.

On the way down to the pond are nine tiny spruce trees, eighteen inches tall at the highest, which my father sees as the elegant walk that Alice's children will travel after he is dead. My mother pays a local boy, Dennis Carton, to mow the meadow. Dennis is thirteen years old and string-bean thin, sometimes mows five lawns a day in summer. His dark hair takes on hints of blond and the muscles in his legs are visible under his skin. He calls my mother "ma'am," he has a small, nervous mouth, he lays traps for crayfish, his father is the local real estate man.

Just past seventy, too youthful to be called spry, my mother bent over her granddaughter like a shortstop waiting behind a ground-ball pitcher, like a scientist ready for an experiment to go awry. She fell into familiar patterns of vigil, marching around her brain like a drill sergeant, instilling discipline, ridding herself of desire. She needed to urinate, she held herself. She heard the spring of the screen door, my father back from Randolph, scraping his feet on the doormat. She didn't move. The phone in the kitchen rang, my brother Isaac.

"Things are," my father answered. "She's sleeping. Your mother's watching her." He unscrewed a whiskey bottle and filled a juice glass. "Your mother's upset. Alice was crying. She's sleeping now. Have you heard more about Reiko?" My father's quiet analyst's voice breaking. "She won't leave her. She just sits there. I bring her tea, she waves me off. I cook, she won't eat. I cook and that's a slight. She won't look at me, for God's sake she won't face me. I just wish she'd be nice." My father drained his glass. "No. I'm all right. No. You go to work. No. No. My love to Carla. Please."

At midnight, my mother held tight to the wooden desk chair so it wouldn't squeak. She got up, held her breath, and tiptoed slowly. She found the couch that had been there when the house belonged to the old ladies, when the old ladies had rented the barn out to tenants.

The old ladies had found that couch when they were young enough to haul it into the back of a station wagon, had bought it secondhand from some young people moving to Massachusetts. The springs and pillows were shot then, and now hold not even memories of firmness. The original fabric is a muddy yellow that might once have been green, and that ancient upholstery is covered by a red and black slip. Above the slip lies an afghan crocheted by my grandmother.

In my mother's sleep she saw her, my grandmother, young as she had been when my mother was twelve. They were in the country, the Catskills bungalow they had rented with hordes of cousins—my mother's cousin Saul, now Saul the Dentist, her two cousins Alvin, Big Alvin, who is now dead, and Red Alvin, who has gone white. In the dream, Alice had died, and my grandmother—same age as my Reiko—heard the news and focused her eyes on the horizon and said, "Oh my Godt, oh my Godt, oh my Godt."

In the kitchen, my father dumped the balled pasta into the trash, and it fell in a lump, bearing the pebbled marks of the colander. With a damp sponge, he wiped down the countertops.

The next morning, Alice woke early. Across from her sat the card table, the mug of cold tea, and a window. Twelve panes all blurred because the hundred-year-old glass had run. Alice watched the swing of a maple branch. She heard birdcalls and recognized the chickadee's.

I could name the Big and Little Dipper, but not Orion's Belt. I knew poplar, but could not distinguish pine from spruce. I liked weeping willows and Alice did, too.

She made her way slowly through the barn and was surprised to see her grandmother asleep on the old couch. She used the toilet and headed into the back lawn. Dennis Carton didn't know how to approach my family in its grief, so the grass grew high. The dew was icy. Alice pulled off her wet socks, hopped twice, and found herself in the sunshine and blinking. She headed out from the yard behind the house and wandered, getting used to her legs, down the path to the lake, surprised by the number of buzzing flies and snooping birds, the bustling country life of the morning.

It wasn't sunlight that woke my mother or the sound of a closing door, it was a sense of Alice's absence.

"Alice!" She sat up startled. "Alice!" She shuffled through the barn kitchen, saw the empty bed. "Alice!"

She walked through a small room filled with science fiction paperbacks and old rock and roll albums and wrecked sports equipment—badminton nets coiled around branches, and croquet mallets with loose heads. My mother went into the bedroom which had once been Isaac's. She fumbled with a swollen door.

"Alice!" Barefoot, she sloshed through the dewy grass out into the sunlight, and looked to her right, the length of the house. "Alice!"

She was embarrassed to find her granddaughter down by the pond with Dennis Carton. Dennis was pointing at a crayfish and was explaining that the pincers were not so dangerous and that the thing darted backward when it was scared. Alice had the legs of her trousers rolled.

"Oh. Hello, Mrs. Weiss." Dennis was the first to see her. Alice turned around, took my mother in.

"So you've met my granddaughter," my mother said.

Dennis shaded his eyes. Then he turned to Alice, who was no longer staring at the crayfish, but at a school of minnows by her feet. Dennis hadn't assumed that this girl was my daughter. He'd never met anyone whose father had died.

"I ought to go," he said.

"Dennis." My mother searched for normalcy. "Will you be coming by to do the lawn?"

"The lawn?" he said. "Oh. Sure."

"Saturday?"

"Well. Fine."

My father had been awake since five in the morning. His shoulders ached and he was hungover and he wanted to take a bath. He had made himself tea and picked up a magazine from the pile of papers generally used for kindling, and had read it for half an hour before he realized it was a year out of date. He sat in the Morris chair in his damp bathing suit and dirty gardening shirt and drank cold bitter tea and listened to the barn doors opening and closing and the calls of birds and the calls of my mother.

The phone began ringing, people who had returned to New York after the funeral, people who wanted to give him comfort.

There's a picture that hangs in the kitchen, taken the summer of Lucy Darwin.

Yves Clos, who was a friend of a friend of my father's and who worked at the time for *Paris Match*, posed us all carefully in the front of the house, arranged and rearranged us. We were exhausted by the last time his shutter snapped, all intelligence drained from our faces. In the picture we are reduced to objects of the lens, my family as a French comment on the American bourgeoisie. My mother—Yves had hectored her about her posture for half an hour—peers off nervously into the distance, as though in her anxious American way she is worried that her Volvo will roll into a lake. My little brother Isaac is posed behind her. In preparation for his portrait Isaac took an Afro pick to his usually matted hair, and worked and worked until his curls were loosened and his hair stood comically above his head.

Pictures of Isaac at this age are almost universally amusing: Isaac with his two fingers clutching his tongue as though it were a half-swallowed goldfish, Isaac as Junior Birdman, Isaac the trickster with googly eyes. But Yves Clos took the picture seventeen times, pulled Isaac through his entire repertoire of faces: mouth wide and one eye shut, lips puckered and eyebrows raised, fingers in nostrils and ears, tricks with the neck of his shirt. Isaac was too proud to repeat a single pose and in the end too weary to keep watch of the photographer. In the photograph Yves left us, his hairstyle is a joke played on him.

Dave Ballarini parted his hair carefully. He and my father kept to their poses: my father staring into the distance like Herzl gazing out over Zion, Dave on one knee like Cleon Jones on a baseball card. I am slouched and tired and skinny and long-haired, my Adam's apple prominent in my throat. Lucy Darwin and Laura Ballarini sit on the porch rail. Laura looks as though she is about to sneeze. Lucy in her boredom and meditation is watching God knows what and the result is accidentally picturesque—a beauty which violates the tenor of the photograph and is our only triumph over the Frenchman's tricks.

Denise and Harry Ballarini were forced by Yves to stand waist-deep in ferns which ring the front of the house. This emphasizes their shortness and makes them, handsome people in life, seem uncomfortable, absurd, even homely. Denise, whose brother was sick, seems in retrospect to have been very brave that summer, working hard to keep up Lucy's spirits; in the picture, she appears anxious and cowardly. Harry Ballarini has a much-photographed face on account of the successful novels he's written about the lives of working-class Italians in Philadelphia. Generally, he appears as a clever tough guy with a mustache, a plumber with a comic soul, but in this one he comes off as his own father does in Ballarini's stories: sheepish, diffident, concerned. He is worried that his daughter, once she sneezes, will lose her balance on the porch rail and fall and sprain her wrist, which is exactly what happened.

"You stupid son of a bitch," Harry yelled at Yves Clos even as he picked up his screaming daughter. "You goddamned moronic photographic French moron."

As Harry helped Laura into their Saab, my mother apologized to Denise Ballarini. My father the psychiatrist put together a sack of ice from the kitchen, wanted to give Laura a shot of whiskey and aspirin for the pain, had an idea that he could fashion a splint from some cloth and gardening stakes. Harry waved him off, started the engine. Denise Ballarini leapt into the backseat behind her daughter and they were gone.

My father said everyone could go out for pizza.

"Terrific." My mother was furious. "Let's all go out for pizza." And she went to make potato salad.

In the kitchen, my daughter Alice looked at Yves Clos's picture and put a finger on Lucy Darwin's face. "Who's that?" she asked. The sink ran. My mother washing mushrooms, making an omelet. Alice moved her finger from Lucy's face to mine, and it was strange for her to see me at her age, to guess what kind of boy I might have been. My mother shut off the water, moved the handful of mushrooms to an old wooden chopping board that had come with the house. She and Alice had picked chives together on their way back from the pond.

"Was Daddy in love with that girl?"

"What's that?"

"Nothing," said Alice, again putting her finger to Lucy's face. "Who is that pretty girl?"

My mother came up from behind Alice, wiping her hands on a dish towel, looking over her granddaughter's shoulder to the picture on the wall. "That's Lucy Darwin. You see that?" She pointed at the photograph below. "That's my mother." In black and white, young and beautiful, an immigrant girl dressed for 1920s nightlife. "Your Great-Grandmother Rose." My mother paused. "Or I've told you that before?" She had a feeling she was repeating her stories. "She called herself a 'flepper.'"

I seduced Lucy with a fantasy of revenge. While Denise and Harry Ballarini took Laura to the hospital, while my little brother and Dave played in inner tubes by the lake, Lucy and I searched for a toad to drop in Yves Clos's luggage. We slipped into the house while my mother was boiling potatoes, got into his bedroom, and among the Frenchman's socks found rolling papers, a lighter, and a clear plastic sandwich bag. Lucy crammed the drugs and paraphernalia into her pockets. I was awed.

Then, in gestures and whispers, we argued. All of a sudden, Lucy was gripped with pity, not for Yves Clos but for the toad. She didn't want it to die alone among a Frenchman's briefs. So the original purpose of our trip was abandoned. We made a dash from the house to the woods, smuggling drugs, dropping the shitting toad on the lawn.

"Isaac?" My mother called, when the screen door slammed. "Peter? Lucy?"

Two days moved indolently. Alice felt as if she had misplaced a set of keys or a special pen, but as though she had forgotten exactly what she had misplaced, whether it was a set of keys or a special pen or something else altogether. She had to keep reminding herself I was dead. When she didn't, tear storms took over her whole body so that her feet curled and her knees bent and her stomach ached and her lungs went flat and her throat tensed and her lips spread and her nose ran and her eyes grew red and poured tears until there were no more to pour—as if she spent her tear glands the way she had once lost everything in her stomach when she had the flu and had puked and puked and puked. Late one afternoon, she heard voices of boys down by the water.

Alice crept slowly down past the ferns and blackberry brambles. In a canoe were Dennis Carton and a stranger, the two of them casting for pickerel. My daughter peered over the brambles. Dennis reached a thin arm back and cast his rod and the sinker licked the sky and flew out over the water.

A fly buzzed her, Alice dodged it. Dennis looked over his shoulder and saw the dark hair of the girl he had been thinking about for days.

"Hey!"

He had to shout to her again before Alice wandered diffidently down to the beach. Caught spying, she expected some kind of rebuke or laughter and was surprised when Dennis had his friend direct the canoe toward the shore.

"Hey," Dennis said again.

"Yo," said Dennis's friend. He was wearing a Bud Light cap and his lower lip curled.

"This is Bradley," Dennis said. "We were—well, I guess it's obvious." Dennis reeled in his line. "We were fishing."

Alice squinted. "Hi."

"I guess it was obvious that we were fishing," Dennis said again, looking now at the lake.

"*Obvious.*" Bradley giggled.

"Hi." Alice dipped one foot in the water. "I guess, did you have luck? Did you?" Words swimming in her brain, elusive as minnows. "Did you?" My poor Alice. "Do you catch things and then throw them back?"

"Catch dinner if we can," said Bradley.

Ripples from the canoe splashed Alice's ankles.

"You up here for long?" Dennis talked while he paddled. He worried it was the wrong question. "Beautiful day," he said. "Did you ever go fishing?"

Alice shook her head no. She put the back of her hand to her forehead.

They were in the shallow water, the canoe bobbing and Alice waiting. Then Bradley's line went taut and his rod bowed. Everyone watched his wrists during the little struggle. The fish shone in the sun, writhed on the line. Bradley held it up. He laughed. A trout. Then he swung his gleaming prize—a game, frighten the girl—toward Alice.

Who gasped. "Wo," she said, smiling.

But then she recognized the twitching, the look on the fish's face.

"Bradley, you asshole," Dennis said.

Alice froze in the water. She tried to swallow her tears, to suck in her breath. Bradley laughed and Dennis whacked him and this made Alice cry more.

Bradley said, "What's she crying for, man?"

Dennis half whispered, "I *told* you."

"Her?" Bradley said. "Holy shit."

Dennis clambered out of the canoe, and Bradley had to hold tight to the gunwales to stay aboard. His rod, line, and fish tumbled into the pond. Dennis stood shirt-deep in the splashing water. He put his hands in his pockets.

"I'm really sorry, I am." He paused. She had never told him her name, but he'd figured it out. He said, "I'm really sorry, Alice."

Then my father came treading heavily down the path, two

pails swinging. He needed water for two young spruce trees he'd planted a month earlier. My father was bleary-eyed and worn down, the gardening impulse working in him like the mechanism of a battered music box. On seeing the kids by the water, he tried his best to affect heartiness. "Halloo," he said, as if this were the summer vacation he had once hoped for. Alice had her back to him. Neither she nor Dennis knew how to answer.

My father looked old and bent in his muddy bathing suit and open shirt and with his white hair on end. He seemed to have no conception that he was in mourning. Dennis looked at him and had the feeling he had intruded on the doctor's privacy. Alice's throat spasmed, her shoulders high and clenched.

"Beautiful day," my dad said, and he waded into the water, loading buckets. "You want to help me carry these up? I have these beautiful young spruces and I think I put them in just the spot."

"Um," said Dennis.

Bradley had clambered out of the canoe and was searching for his rod. Alice collected herself, wondered what she had ruined.

"Soon as I get this rod back, I'm gonna paddle out," Bradley called to Dennis. "Pick you back up later."

Dennis didn't hear. He was lugging a bucket across the meadow.

Much of the marijuana scattered across the pine needles and mud of the clearing. Lucy looked at the wet rolling paper where I'd licked it and said, "Gross!" On my third try I had managed to put together something that looked like a tiny abstract ceramic turd.

"Is anything happening?" she asked.

"I don't know."

"I mean, do you feel different?"

"I don't know."

"You're stoned." Lucy whooped and covered her mouth.

I touched my lips to her shoulder, then to her ear. We kissed closed-mouthed. I put an experimental hand to her breast. Sex was like jelly, she was filled with it. We lay on our backs and looked up at the trees and the oval of sky where the evergreens parted. We had no idea where the joint had gone, but Lucy found the lighter ground into the dirt near the empty plastic pouch. She ran her fingers through her hair, combing out needles and leaves.

"Did you ever kiss before?"

"Did you?"

"Why?"

"'Cause."

"Yeah," she said.

"I kissed," I lied, but I thought if I didn't make it specific it wouldn't be a lie because I had kissed, for instance, my grandmother.

Surgery, chemotherapy, but the throat cancer went into remission. Lucy's father survived.

My wife would be arriving via taxi, accompanied by her sister Sue.

My mother said: "We'll take them to the train station in Rutland. Everyone will wear their seat belts and Reiko and Sue will sit in back with Alice. I'll drive, and slowly. We'll stay off the highway. We'll accompany them to Rutland and put them on the train to New York. I offered to ride down to New York with them, but Sue said no. Sue said she would go with them. I offered. Sue said no."

My mother finished this speech and looked at my father.

It was the first time she had spoken to him at any such length since the crash. My father was by the kitchen sink, sectioning peppers into slices. He washed his hands and shook them out twice, raising his elbows in the air as he had been trained to do in medical school.

"What's the hurry?" he said. "Why doesn't Reiko stay here with us?" It was Saturday, Dennis Carton's motor whirred across the lawn. "It seems silly to go back—to the apartment, to New York." He blinked, his eyes were wet. "It seems silly," he said. "But if that's what they want. I think Alice should stay here."

My mother opened her mouth, her lower lip trembled.

"Oh," said my father. He took a couple steps across the room, and she took one step toward him. In each other's arms, they began to cry.

Reiko showed up about an hour later. My wife came across the lawn on crutches, my mother beside her, Sue and my father in the rear. My parents, walking one in front of the other, held hands. The sound of the lawn mower had died, and they searched for Alice.

Along the clothesline past the back porch, yellow flowers bloomed, bumblebees were buzzing. Reiko shook her dark hair. Her eyes and mouth were swollen and bruised. My mother was talking about weather, traffic, train schedules, trying for social contact. Reiko pressed on. My father's fingers squeezed my mother's palm. They walked around the fir tree, the blackberries, the brambles. Down they went, to the lake. Then, "Alice!" Reiko said, and the name could have been, "Eureka!"

They were standing by the water, my daughter and Dennis Carton, a boy and girl.

WAKEFIELD, 7E

Under the pretense that he was taking a short trip, Zauberman cut out from his family one day and rented an apartment on the other side of 89th Street, directly across the hall from us. In disguise and under an assumed name, Wakefield, he lived in our building for more than twenty years, looking out his window, watching his wife and daughter age.

He stared through a telescope while they cried, skipped meals, lost weight and friends. He examined little Shoshana as she read Nancy Drew or practiced her violin or undressed before a shower. While Ada sliced chicken, Wakefield focused binoculars on her knuckly hands. When she took lovers to bed, he gazed at the shade of the window to what had been his bedroom.

What was he like before he disappeared?

Clean-shaven and nervous, I imagine, a lawyer specializing in estate taxes. Neat, but not stylish. A le Carré novel on his jittery lap, he falls into dreaming, but vaguely—he isn't imaginative; his thoughts aren't energetic enough to seize on concrete ideas. If you had asked the guys in his office,

"Who's the man in New York most likely to do nothing this weekend?" they'd point to him: a cautious family man, easily startled. The only person who might have guessed otherwise should have been Ada. She knew about her husband's quiet selfishness. She understood his rusted vanity, his obsessive tending to secrets. He refused to talk to her about his work, for instance, always acted as if she suspected him of carrying on an affair.

So let's picture his leaving. A cold October evening, his daughter is ten, a pretty, even-tempered girl, but her father pays her very little attention; he's aloof, and sometimes she reacts to this with ferocity. Tonight she runs circles around him. "Daddy, Daddy, Daddy, Dads, Dads, Dads." She tugs on his coat, steps on his boots, pulls on his suitcase. "Where are you going, Daddy? When will you be back, Dad? What's the hurry, man?" Careful Wakefield carries an umbrella, though it's not raining. He talks to his wife, lecturing in his fussy, hectoring way. He tells her not to expect him positively on Tuesday, not to be alarmed if he doesn't return Thursday, but to look for him certainly by suppertime Friday.

"Tuesday! Thursday! Sunday!" Shoshana flings her arms around his leg.

Wakefield extricates himself, almost stepping on her toes. He adjusts his cap. When the door closes, Shoshana goes still—she's got a mass of auburn curls. Ada, spying casually on her husband, sneaks a look out the peephole while he waits for the elevator. He surprises her, brings his face right up to the lens. He grins. It's an ironic smile, too big, too aggressive, and it's exaggerated by the glass. Ada jumps.

Shoshana says, "Mommy?"

"Nothing, nothing," Ada says.

She dismisses her husband's little joke, but months later the grin recurs, becomes strange and awful. Ada sautés onions in her kitchen and mistakes the crescent moon for Wakefield's mouth. She opens her bedroom window in the morning, a glint of sunlight flashes on a window pane across the way, and in the flash Ada sees her husband's spread lips and teeth.

That day he leaves, little Shoshana is furious. Daddy didn't kiss her good-bye, didn't say a thing. She goes to her bedroom and puts her hands in fists and tells her mirror, "I hate him, I hate him. I wish he never, ever comes back." And her wish comes true. She sits up late at night on her radiator, surrounded by stuffed animals. Under her covers, she listens for the gears of the elevator. It's her fault, she knows.

The first evening on our side of the street, his fake mustache and sunglasses lie on the floor. Binoculars are in his hands. Across the way, he sees his wife fry meat—he's guessing it's pork; there was pork in the refrigerator when he left. He has his notebook open in front of him and he's scribbling in German, the language he studied in high school. He wants to keep everything in code.

Ada has her hair pulled back. She wears a man-tailored shirt, open at the neck, no jewelry. Shoshana's in bib overalls. The girl sits at the kitchen table and talks and her mother nods. Wakefield peers into the empty master bedroom—his dresser, his wife's mirror, the lower left-hand corner of a queen-sized bed. In Shoshana's room, he can see baby animal posters on the walls, stuffed giraffes and bears on the radiator cover. So this is what life is like without him!

Ada cleans the dishes, then she and Shoshana disappear into the living room—out of sight. Ten o'clock, lights go out in the bedrooms. It's midnight when Wakefield stretches out on his army cot, wearing only underwear. He props himself up on one elbow, and thinks of his wife's warm body.

"No." He adjusts himself. "I didn't know what to expect. But I'll go home soon. I'll just sleep here for one night."

He could make an excuse for an early return: a canceled meeting, a canceled flight; maybe he would make no excuse at all, just—but then a light flashes on across the way. A shade opens.

It's his daughter, wearing a giant T-shirt. She stares across the street, but doesn't see her father. His lights are out, hers are shining. He sees her face, her auburn hair, the strange birthmark on her cheek—she's got a pinkish brown spot there, shaped like a sea lion. Wakefield flattens himself on his bed, takes quick peeks through his binoculars.

Clever nincompoop, he can't understand his own glee.

Friday rolls around and he's too excited to quit. In the morning, he watches his daughter leave for school. Shoshana wears blue jeans and a jeans jacket and a shirt with a daisy on it. On her army surplus book bag is an iron-on patch: Tweety Bird. Wakefield wants to follow her, but he's too timid. Fifty-seven minutes later—he keeps count—he sees Ada drawing a shopping cart toward Broadway. Thirty-one minutes after that, she returns, cart stocked with groceries. Ada carries dry cleaning over her shoulder, two dresses wrapped in plastic, the hangers hooked through her fingers. Wakefield scribbles in his journal, consults his English-German dictionary: "shopping cart," "dry cleaning."

Three-thirty-six, Shoshana skips home. Soon after, Wakefield expects to see his old self returning, fingering his keys as he strides home with his umbrella and suitcase. He imagines seeing himself vanish into the building's front entrance then reappear in his old bedroom, tossing his suit jacket on the bed and peering into his wife's dressing mirror while loosening his blue and red tie.

But he doesn't come home.

Five o'clock, six o'clock. Out the window, he can see Ada put her hands on Shoshana's shoulders. Seven o'clock, she's fixing dinner. Eight—she's expected him an hour ago and makes phone calls. The cord curled around her fingers, Ada's not anxious, just wants to know if she should serve her daughter food now or wait another half an hour. But the temporary secretary has no idea where her husband has gone. There's been no Chicago meeting; he's been calling in sick. Wakefield sees a strained, unconscious smile on Ada's face. She hangs up, but does not let her hand off the receiver.

It's only eight-thirty, but the worst thoughts have crossed her mind. Wakefield consults his Cassel's dictionary: "adultery," "mistress." At nine o'clock, his wife and daughter eat. Then Ada goes to the bedroom, back to the telephone. Shoshana washes dishes.

At ten-thirty, the girl is in bed. Ada inspects the plates drying in the rack and gives them a second scrubbing. Twelve-twenty-seven, she lies in bed, waiting. Wakefield uses his telescope's highest magnification to read the title of her book: *The Way We Live Now*. Ada looks away from the Trollope, flips backward, reads the same passage twice. Her light goes out nervously, on again, then off, tense fingers flicking the switch.

One-thirty in the morning: Wakefield steps out in a fisherman's cap, a pair of nonprescription glasses, and a gray overcoat. He tiptoes down the stairway, seven flights, doesn't want to be stuck in the elevator with any neighbor. He leaves our building at a trot, then saunters down West End Avenue, thrilling at the cloak-and-dagger fun.

It's all morbid vanity, there's no going back; the thing evolves in a natural train.

Shoshana, when she is twelve years old, sits in the front row of a memorial service for her father organized by his old firm, Brown, Fane, Molineux, and Phips. She can't believe he's dead, and this belief is to her consciousness what the birthmark on her cheek is to her face: the blot around which the rest organizes itself, something that forces her not into despair or ugliness, but composure. Habitually, she imagines his spirit looking at her, examining her, and maybe it's this sense of super-self-consciousness that provokes her to acts of wild generosity. She takes off her sweater and gives it to a beggar on the street. She practices the violin constantly, more out of devotion than love. Wakefield, across the way, is astounded by the tenderness of his daughter's skin.

He is sure she does not miss him.

And what did we think—my family—when he moved in across the hall?

In our building, apartments were marked East and West, two to a floor, with each pair caught in a complex, incestuous embrace. We had been friendly with the previous occupant of 7E, Mrs. Bullivant, a widowed beauty queen whose husband had had something to do with the making of the atomic bomb. I kept watch in the weeks after her death, wanting to see who would take her place. I hoped for another kid or at least a team of movers, but Wakefield came in like a cold front, invisibly and without warning. You'd be waiting for the elevator and you'd hear his peephole open and shut. You'd come downstairs from a neighbor's and find him in the hallway, sweating and nervous like a Peeping Tom.

I looked out my window at night and watched him stealing down 89th Street. I told my mother that he liked to put on disguises and she ran fingers through my hair. I told Zev Grubin, and he said, "Come on, Davey, I'm serious here: Cheryl Tiegs or Farrah Fawcett Majors?"

"He doesn't clip his fingernails," I whispered. "They're longer than my mom's."

"Everyone says Farrah," Zev opined. "But I prefer Jaclyn Smith."

Zev had drilled a hole in his floor so that he could stare down into Jessica Lenzner's bedroom; he'd seen interesting things there, he said. I decided to drill a hole in the back of my closet so I could spy on Wakefield.

Zev said, "Davey, you're crazy. Davey, this is, like, a disgusting old man." But then he watched me do it—lounging in the dimness and the smell of dirty laundry.

I lay on the floor with the first baseman's mitt and hiking boots and tennis balls. I worried about plaster flakes blinding me and also about hitting a water main. It was hard work, noisier than I guessed. Zev sat behind me, perusing a copy of *Oui*.

Concrete spat. I was going to break my father's drill. But I shut my eyes and pressed until I heard a sound that made me think I had snapped the bit. The tool bucked forward into Wakefield's. I drew back and, with Zev crouching behind me, peeped through the hole I had made. There was a funny shape at the other end. A mouse? A piece of jewelry?

Wakefield's eye.

"Holy shit!" I dropped the drill, struggled through my winter clothes and bar mitzvah suit. "Shit! Holy shit!" We braced ourselves. We expected to hear a madman pounding on my parents' door. But he didn't. Instead, the next day, a letter came:

> *Pleased if you would water my plants while I am away. No remuneration but you are free to look around.*

He lurks in the African halls of the Museum of Natural History. Concealed in a burka, he watches Shoshana on a first date. He lowers himself in the driver's seat of a rented Chevy; with binoculars, sees Ada jog through Riverside Park.

The years pass. Helplessly, he scrawls notes.

The first time I went to his apartment, I was terrified. I made Zev come with me. We knew the layout of the place—the Grubins lived on the E line, three floors up—but neither of us had ever seen a home so barren.

"Leave it alone, man," Zev objected when I opened Wakefield's closet.

There were stained scraps of paper in the pockets of Wakefield's clothes, receipts from liquor stores and supermarkets, marked in a foreign language.

"Dutch," I guessed, holding one slip up to the light, "or more likely German."

"Davey, you're nuts. You know that?" Sometime in tenth grade, Zev had taken to wearing a bowler hat. "Water the plants, man, then let's tip."

A case of wine blocked the door to the refrigerator. The only room in the apartment Wakefield seemed to use was the one that in the Grubins' served as the dining room. But he had no dining room table, just a cot, a shelf heavy with notebooks, a pair of binoculars, a telescope, dozens of gorgeous plants, and an open garbage bag filled with empty beer cans and containers of Chinese food.

"How long is he gone for?"

I didn't know. "A week?" Wakefield had called from an Italian airport, blips and bubbles running the line.

I sat on his cot.

"Wouldn't sit there if I were you," Zev warned. "Don't want to imagine what he does there. Guy's a pervert, a wanker, a fag."

I got up, dusting my ass, and took one of Wakefield's note-books off his shelf.

"Davey, leave that alone!"

"This is also in Dutch," I said. "Either Dutch or in German or something."

"Come on, you got to put those away, you——"

The notebooks were coffee-stained and blotted sometimes with blood and sometimes a stiff yellow residue Zev was quick to name. The pages were off-green and rippled, the penmanship sloppy, but always blue ballpoint and without a single scratch-out. I noticed recurring figures, A—— and S————, the straight lines repeating themselves page after page, dashes always preceded by the same two capital letters. "I think this is German," I said. Wakefield was tracking people, A—— and S————, but I couldn't guess whom.

"Maybe he's Stasi," I whispered.

"I got an idea for you." Zev adjusted his hat. "Maybe he's German."

A train is running from Rome to Paris, Shoshana and Ada in a private sleeper, Wakefield two cars behind. For his European journey he has dyed his hair a happy shade of blond. He wears a jaunty cap and a pair of sunglasses that fade from dark on the top to clear at the bottom. He has cut and cleaned his nails and wears a baggy suit. Over the years, trying to emphasize his disguise, he's broken his own nose thrice. He reads the *Berliner Zeitung*, and might be mistaken for a survivor of a kidnaping or a man with a heart condition. The train sways and buckles toward southern France.

Late in the day, Wakefield gets up to go to the bathroom. He's tired, he's barely slept, he doesn't really take in the girl—Italian, maybe—walking the aisle toward him. Then he picks his head up and glimpses (among other things) the birthmark.

The lights go dark. The train sways. Shoshana stumbles. Her hands brush Wakefield. Then the lights flash again and the train pitches and Shoshana's shoulder bounces against her father's chest.

"Excuse me," she says.

She's just walking to stretch her legs, that's all, an elegant girl who has cultivated her shyness almost into glamour. She turns back after a minute or two to get a peek at the man she bumped into—something about him makes her turn—but he's gone. She goes back to her mother, doesn't mention a thing, picks up her copy of *Frankenstein*.

And Wakefield? He's on fire. He hurries back to his seat, throws his hands in his face, and his mind bursts. He cries out, "You are mad!" But what can he do?

He doesn't see Paris, only his wife and daughter pointing at a Brueghel in the Louvre.

He left home often. I had his key. I bought an English-German dictionary, examined the journals for hours, and determined that their three most common words were bedroom, bathroom, and kitchen.

"What he's doing," I told Zev, "is he's following two people around an apartment." Dictionary, German grammar, and notebook cluttered my lap. "You see that, don't you? The notations are almost identical, same routine, every morning of the week, and most nights."

Zev shrugged. He sat cross-legged on the floor, drinking Wakefield's pinot grigio.

"I think I should go in for charitable work," he said. "Volunteer work is an excellent way of meeting chicks, don't you think? I mean, if you could volunteer for, like, Greenpeace or No Nukes, you could come off with a really good impression of yourself. You'd be doing the right thing, and the chicks would dig it. The chicks would think you were automatically the good guy, the all-right guy, the nice guy. And the liberal girls, the radical girls"—his voice choked up a bit— "they put out, right?"

I paid no attention. "I have to learn better German. To really crack the case. But A and S. They live across the street. All I have to do is find out who across the street has these initials. Given this view, it's, what, twelve to sixteen apartments? In any of two or three buildings? Can't be too hard. . . ."

Kneeling on the radiator, craning my neck, and pressing my face to the panes of my window, I got almost the same view of 89th Street that Wakefield had. So at night I sat on the heater which had long ago been decorated with decals of Bugs Bunny and Elmer Fudd and I stared across the way, trying to see my neighbors with Wakefield's eyes. Involuntarily, my gaze stuck on Shoshana practicing her violin. I took notes on her in the margins of my American history textbook, drew her picture on the inside cover of a paperback of Hawthorne tales. I named her the Girl with the Shoulders, and it never occurred to me that she was the one Wakefield watched.

We did meet once, sort of, in Shakespeare and Company Bookstore. I was sitting on a rolling ladder, flipping through the pages of *Dharma Bums*. Shoshana picked up a volume by Kawabata, *Thousand Cranes*, and I tried to say hello to her but my voice caught in my throat.

"Excuse me?" she said.

I grew flustered. "Nothing, nothing," I told her, and, red-faced, ducked out of the store.

Was Wakefield watching surreptitiously from the calendar rack? Was he excited that I'd spoken to his daughter? Disappointed that I'd run away? As though carelessly, he left his old driver's license on his cot, let me see his old face, his real name. He was intimating it—the whole story—but I couldn't guess.

The wind blows and his pants ripple. He's forty-eight but looks older. He dyes his hair and beard a shocking orange—the hair like a flag, daring people to notice. But on Upper Broadway, Wakefield passes former neighbors, people with whom he has had dinner, men whose wills he has organized, and no one sees him. Something about the weight of his madness, the shocking extent of his change. He wants to jump in front of old acquaintances and shout, "Boo!"

He glances into restaurants, watches Ada alone. What would she do if he pulled up a chair? He would live a life in her debt. It's Shoshana who really scares him, her straight back, her gorgeous hair.

I'll go back tomorrow, he thinks, maybe next week.

The summer after junior year, I got a job in a restaurant on Amsterdam Avenue, and with the money I made bought myself marijuana and used clothes. I spent a lot of time in the park with Zev, the two of us getting high. He'd been busy canvassing for Greenpeace.

"Oh, it's a good strategy," he told me. "Volunteer work." We were sitting on a bench above the highway and the boat basin. "My problem is I fall for the wrong girls. Proof of self-hatred? What would my shrink say? Listen: There are plenty of chicks canvassing, most of them cute, but what do I do? I pick the snob."

A tug pushed garbage toward the mouth of the river.

"You have any luck?" Zev wondered. "Busgirls? Waitresses?"

I didn't have any luck, just the Girl with the Shoulders. "I can't fucking wait," I said, "to get to college. I will move as far away from the city as I can."

Zev passed the joint. The wind pushed his curls to one side.

"So, Greenpeace," he said. "So do I know how to pick them? Beautiful. This girl won't talk to anybody—least of all me. Oh, yeah, she gets real enthusiastic in those houses in Westchester, making pitches about, like, narwhals and baby seals, but in the van, on the trip out? Just sits by herself, head up straight, and, while we're sitting around bullshitting, reads, like, actual poetry in French. And I am just mooning over her, right? It's my fault if I don't get my dick sucked this summer."

I laughed and he pushed my shoulder with his forearm.

"No," he said. "This is what happens when you fall for Joan of Arc."

"What happens, Zev?" I had to shelter the burning roach with my palm.

"The truth? I turn into some kind of stalker. I find out where she lives, who her mother is, and it turns out she lives right across the street. So, without my parents knowing—trying, I mean, to keep everything from my mom—I set up shop in the living room, with a pair of opera glasses. I'm like your weirdo neighbor, what's his name, I stare down at this girl, Shoshana Zauberman, this fucking tight-assed violinist—"

"Violin?" I saw her playing Mozart, and three pairs of eyes staring from across the way. "Tell me, does the girl—Shoshana?—like, live with one Zauberman parent or two?"

Zev looked away.

"Come on, you've been spying on her." I was stoned, but my focus was narrow. "She lives with her mother, whose first initial is A—A. Zauberman."

"Yeah," Zev admitted. "Ada. I looked it up."

And I felt it—Wakefield—as if he had stepped soundlessly from behind us and laid a long, dirty hand on my shoulder, congratulating me. The next time—the last time—he asked me to tend to his apartment, there would be directions and a map.

We stared at the big gray river. "Maybe," I said, "I should write her a letter." And I saw myself not as a run-of-the-mill nerd, but as her savior, her protector. "I could introduce—"

"Well, you can't do that now."

"What?"

"Oh, right." He coughed. "Didn't I tell you? She left. No more Shoshana Zauberman. Went away." With his hands he made a flying bird. "I looked out the window this morning and saw her packing the car. Got in a year early. Some special program, like, biology and the violin. Ohio. Oh, God," he groaned. "I know too much."

Wakefield's long, dirty hand lifts off my shoulder. His feet scurry away. He's beckoning me, and I follow. Seventeen years old, and with a picture of Shoshana Zauberman in my head, I travel to a midwestern college. The bus I take is full of New York City private school kids, all looking for a place to go. The driver is an old man; he wears sunglasses and a brilliant set of orange curls, a gray mustache under his thrice-broken nose.

Once in Ohio, I don't go through the course catalogue or the weekend activities for prospective students. I don't say hello to my hosts. I study the student directory. I touch my fingers to the cinder-block walls of Shoshana's dorm.

We do not introduce ourselves until a year later. Then I lie in her bed, running my fingers across her shoulders, kissing the birthmark on the side of her face. She is telling me that her father left when she was ten, confessing her misery. She cries and I leave the window shade open out of sympathy for Wakefield, who stares in as if from the land of the dead.

THE INVENTOR OF LOVE

This is the saddest story, one my wife told in pieces. Two men, a boy, a park in another city, the men in close communion, the three of them not quite a family.

My wife and I lie awake in bed after we've put away the magazines, turned off the lights. The warmth of her body. The safety of the dark. I say anything to hear Julie talk. "Most embarrassing blemish you've ignored on a friend?" Or, "*Rodomontade.* English word? Really?"

"To brag, I think. Also a parking manuever. Something you do with fish."

And then this story. The men are dressed fussily, the boy a ragamuffin. He leaps in mud puddles. He screeches and hoots. And I've gotten a little flat, a little desperate in conversation. "What do you figure are the major issues facing us today?" And Julie won't say a thing.

This sad story, it's punched a hole in our bedtime conversation. We stare at the ceiling. Fat furry failure squats on our chests. My wife heard the story and told it to me in pieces. She'd come to bed after phone calls to New York, then let me have it chapter by chapter, a sick real-life serial told long-distance by her friend Klara.

"What do you think, Jules," I'll keep at her. "The major issues facing us today?"

"Oh, Charlie. Not tonight."

I get up. I wander the house. The story concerns her friend Klara, Klara's partner Claire, a crazy child called Napoleon, and a couple I don't know, Michael and Brad. All in Brooklyn, a couple hundred miles away.

I like Klara. She's my wife's oldest friend. Scandinavian washerwoman build, big arms and big shoulders, rough and ready, a mothering type with the face of a baby or a nun. Klara's features are tiny in her pan-flat face, a bump of a nose, squinty eyes, nearly lipless mouth, but the mouth is liable to gape and beam. If my wife the skirt-wearing financial analyst seems to have nothing in common with Klara the lesbian social worker, well, they've known each other since they were kids. Daughters of prep school teachers in Long Island, they grew up in faculty housing and watched their fathers swap wives. On field trips Klara and Julie packed tuna sandwiches; the other girls carried credit cards and twenties. They lost their virginities almost simultaneously, Memorial Day weekend, eleventh grade, and confessed to each other while drinking beers by the Montauk lighthouse. Klara leaned down and kissed my wife's mouth.

Think of her as my almost sister-in-law, also as the world's most idealistic practical woman: big legs rooting her to the earth, but sometimes she gets a faraway look like some Valkyrie explorer staring out at the horizon for newfound land.

Claire is Robin to Klara's Batman. Tiny girl, and her blond hair is a mess of curls the color of masking tape. The two of them together suggest a comedy team—Klara the giant, slow-moving straight man, and Claire always getting them into some kind of fix. The stories they tell in car rides: The time they went into a Kmart photo booth in Ames, Iowa, spent time smooching in front of the automatic camera, and Claire stripped and did some nude shots. Neither of them realized that the shots were being broadcast to the whole store via a monitor beside the makeup counter. The guard rushed over, ready to have Claire arrested. Klara talked him down. She explained that the shots were for Claire's boyfriend, overseas in Kuwait. They'd never do it again and never, ever would return to the Ames, Iowa, Kmart.

Claire weighs about 98 pounds wet, but at the dinner table I can't keep pace with her drinking. Wine and liquor, when she gets rocked she turns raconteur: The time Prince's "1999" came on the jukebox and she couldn't help herself, started dancing on the table of a biker bar. Or when she wanted to take Klara out for dinner, ordered all the most expensive things on the menu, then realized she had forgotten her wallet. These are like butch episodes of *I Love Lucy*, Klara in the Desi Arnaz role. Claire tells stories of her childhood, too, sniffing shoe polish, sniffing glue, the kid she knew in her teenage years who used to shoot up deodorant. Punks in Lincoln, Nebraska, they drove all night to see X play Des Moines.

The women keep a menagerie of strays in their one-and-a-half-bedroom Brooklyn apartment, three dogs, two cats, no room. Klara's favorite is Quasimodo, the ugliest and most useless pooch you can imagine. Half corgi, half sheepdog, stomach hair that's always filthy on account of its being longer than the legs. Klara works in a children's shelter in Brooklyn. In late-night phone conversation for years, she calls us in Philadelphia and fills my wife's head with the worst stuff imaginable: an infant girl who had been severely scalded—she'd either fallen or been forced into a pot of boiling water. The macaroni-cooking mother claimed it was some kind of cockamamie accident. Cops came and so did medical examiners, put the lie to her story. The circumference of the burns was too even around the ass. There were no splash marks. It was obvious: The baby had been plunged into bubbling steam.

My wife burrows her head into her pillow as she tells these tales. She gets off the phone with Klara, she climbs into bed, she puts her hands over her ears—like she's expelling the bad news and wants to block the routes back in. Once she gets the story out, she can sleep. Then it's up to me to play insomniac. Klara tells one story that pops right out of nightmare: A little girl was explaining to a doctor that her mommy pressed a searing hot iron against her palm, when a nurse contradicted the stuttering kid: "That's not what you told *me*." I don't want to pretend all these stories have led my wife and me into some permanent depression. We talk. We giggle. I'll get her imagining our roles in a family future.

"You'll be superdad." She laughs. "Waking up the kids early, clapping, hearty breakfasts." Or, "Rules," she'll say. "Because kids like that. To understand there's rationality to a house." Or, "In good cop, bad cop, don't make me play the bad cop ever. Okay?"

"Alfred."

"Kakushka."

My wife and I list names.

"Oswaldo."

"Cherise."

We've said Alice or Elaine if it's a girl and Jacob if it's a boy, after my brother.

Klara wants a baby, too. When she and my wife are on the

phone and they're not talking about the suffering of Klara's charges or the wacky antics of Claire, they bond over this shared longing. Klara doesn't talk about names so much as methods: sperm banks, possible donors, adoption. You can imagine how Klara is around all those kids at the shelter. She must daydream about adopting all the time. The pudgy child of a deported Ecuadorian drug smuggler frolicking in the park with Quasimodo. Claire and some crack-addicted seven-year-old building castles on a Maine beach. Klara has worked in the same place for six years, but she never actually spoke of taking in any child before Napoleon showed up.

"There was something," my wife tried to explain, "I don't know, about this one. Ratio of cuteness to suffering. Or a multiple, take the cuteness to the suffering's power. This Napoleon."

He was five years old, of mixed racial parentage, and desperately affectionate. I never met the kid, but imagine him with gold-toffee skin and a loose Afro. His eyes are wide. His hands are cool. He runs around the room like a banshee, can't for a minute be one of a group. Put him in naptime with the rest of the kids and he will shout, hoot, whip his blue mat in the air, knock blocks together—a *crack* that registers deep in your skull. You single him out from the group, punish him or dote on him, and Napoleon will charm you, love you with all his love from the moment he first gets you to smile.

But facts: He spent the first two years of his life locked in a windowless room, astew in his own shit and juices. His mother is dead. His aunt is a crack addict, his uncle in and out of jail. A miracle beyond miracles Napoleon survived. Most of the time when I heard about the kid, it came after my wife's phone calls with Klara. After they hung up, my wife gave me the news in bed, hands over her ears so she could sleep. But once when Claire and Klara were visiting us in Philadelphia and we were all sitting in the garden behind our little house, Klara produced her theory of the kid's survival. This was two months after she met him. Late summer, brown leaves.

"He survived because of who he is," Klara said. With her infant face and massive body, she looks like some Norse goddess of decent charity. "Call me crazy, but I'll tell you this child has a self-saving power. He learned—and you've got to believe it was his own invention because no one around him could have shown him much of it at all—he learned how to love people. There he is, tiny, neglected, malnourished Napoleon, in a room in some hovel in Brownsville. Brownsville 1992, which for God's sake to this day refers to Mike Tyson as its pride. Undeclared war zone, and if you're a low-level, unaddicted drug dealer, you're doing well. And useless, fractured people stumble into this cave with a crying babe. They stumble in, they stumble out. And the child somehow gets fed, gets people to teach him language. How?"

Cats crawled fence tops. Squirrels leapt between the branches of trees. We all stared at Klara—my wife, who's a financial analyst, and me, I work at a bank, and Claire, who thinks she's an actress but as far as I know only takes movement classes and has never in her life been in a play. We stared at Klara—it was dusk, our nice, tidy garden, arugula growing in pots next to rows of snapdragons, basil, and tomato plants—and Klara had that faraway, ocean explorer's look. She'd seen something on the horizon that none of us could name.

"I'll tell you how. He learns to love people. Invents it on his own. The bumbling addict in this nowhere room comes in and stumbles upon a child, and the child stares up at the useless, broken man, and *loves* him. I'm not talking about passion but some miraculous, Darwinian, self-preservation response. Affection like magic spills out from the infant arms and eyes. The addict knows he is loved and in response musters some return affection, manages some cousin of sobriety, and calls out to the baby's keeper, 'Damn, Marian, you best get this kid some food.' That's the way the baby survives. Love."

I don't know if Klara was talking with her own love-blindness then, but she's no sentimentalist. You can't be with a job like hers. We sat in the half-light. Klara doesn't make speeches. I stared at my wife. She had on a pair of shorts and a T-shirt with the name of her alma mater. I pictured her with a bulge in her taut belly, tried to guess what she'd look like pregnant.

Claire said, "My God. Wow." Then she broke out some marijuana, which we were all grateful for. I thought then what a good couple Claire and Klara were.

So in bed, I'll ask it again, prod my wife unimaginatively. "What"—I don't even know what I'm saying here— "are the major problems in our nation today?"

"Oh, Charlie. Oh." She grumbles. "Problems? One: Are we going to get enough sleep tonight? Two, I guess: Why can't people just be a bit more decent with one another?"

My wife's got things pretty well planned. She looks at our world like it's a runaway train which she's been deputized to guide to its station. She says she wants to make assistant director, the next rung up, before she takes time off for a kid, wants our money-market account at a certain value, a certain distribution of stocks, bonds, property, and guaranteed trusts. "I don't want to be thirty-two, have a gaping hole on my résumé, Charlie, a kid in preschool and me trying to find a job." This all sounds rational but papers over fears. Any child will just bring chaos.

She thinks of herself as the practical one. Before I worked in the bank, I had a band, Happy Hippy Hugo. My wife found this at first attractive, but in the long term a drag. When she was a college girl, she thought of me as earthy and dangerous, which is funny now that I'm a chunky bank manager with a bald spot. I split up the band and took the job at the bank mostly because of an accident that happened last year. Contraception failure and my wife got pregnant, and this thing led to the other and she decided that we had to end it. Two weeks there sent my head swimming. My wife, Julie, knew from the start that she couldn't have it, couldn't carry it to term, and there was nothing I could do but plead. I had this vision, this zygote tadpole in her gut.

Julie said, "Look. You're thirty-three and basically unemployed and living, like, some teenager's dream of rock and roll. I don't think, right now, you're ready. And God knows I'm not ready, either, to be a mother, not now." She was sorry, of course. She didn't mean to snap. "I'm under a lot of pressure on this one, Charlie," she said. "Don't pressure me more. Stick by my side." My wife knew what she wanted, we took care of it.

She doesn't have parents to talk to. Her mother is dead. Her father's a jerk. She is all the family I have. I don't talk to my parents, either. They are Christian Scientists, very devout, in a town a hundred miles west of Philly. My little brother was born with a heart condition, a cluster of defects, the cardiac muscles and valves. A heart full of holes and it worked like a sieve. He was born in the early seventies, a blue baby, and there were ways of curing Jacob, surgery not exactly routine but certainly not experimental. We didn't see doctors. Jacob was never officially diagnosed, not until it was too late. What I remember most was the praying, the sense of the unity of illness and sin. Jacob changed over eight years from a joyful, playful child to a doughy, blue-cheeked, bloated body. His feet, little kid's feet, got to be fat like a drunk old woman's. Toward the end his legs leaked water from their pores. He was eight then, I was sixteen, and a couple of years later, I left my parents' house for good. They're lawyers, had the money to save him. It's a thing that can't be forgiven on the grounds of faith or ignorance or stupid, crazy bliss.

I remember them mostly as they were after Jacob's death. My mom, tensed as her frizzled hair. My dad the soldier, plodding heavy-legged around the house. The morning they put Jacob in a coffin, Dad kept running his hands over his bald scalp, reminding himself how little was left up there.

"Jedediah."

"Portia."

"Constantine."

Of course Napoleon fell in love with Klara and Klara fell in love right back. He had never witnessed something so large and so tender. And Klara had never felt so tugged at by the strings of love. She fed him cookies and apple juice while he drew crayon pictures of bats with purple fangs, or of daddies murdering rabbits. He played with toy airplanes and trucks and always made them crash.

This is how I imagine it: Klara comes home in a blue dress, but with her round face grim as an admiral bracing for war. At their kitchen table, she makes the case for adoption. Picture Claire in their crazy apartment, Quasimodo easily mistaken for an unwashed rug or a mop head that's sprouted legs, the two other dogs, Hero, an aging, gimpy toy poodle, and Muttley, a lame Doberman that drools. The cats are hiding under the sofa, claws bared. The place is a haze of unvacuumed fur mixed with steam from Claire's cooking. She's making something healthy and indigestible. The things those people eat, not just soy hot dogs, but soy corned beef, soy orange cheese. The main dish is always stir-fry.

So this is what I imagine Claire cooking, sloppy chopped carrots, her hair in a rubber band, and the tiny kitchen filled with the smell of nutritional yeast. October, Klara's dress emphasizes her shoulders, her big legs. And while they eat, Klara lays down her plan. Claire is at first dumbfounded, then excited. But she's no fool. She stops and thinks and finally says, "I'm not ready."

"But you do want to have a kid with me—you do want—I mean, we're together—"

"Yes—of course—honey. Yes." Claire tells Klara she loves her. Then she bites her little thumb—I've noticed this about Claire, her thumb is as thin as the other digits on her hand and she's got a mouth with big healthy teeth and when she bites her thumb, which she does nervously, there's a strange effect—you could see how someone in love with her would be dizzied. She's heard all about Napoleon, and while she is proud and awed that Klara works with such children, she knows that she doesn't have the patience, the ability. "I couldn't keep up." Claire, after all, has plans. She's been taking classes in speech and movement—walking and talking classes, she calls them—and she figures the next step is to find an acting coach, one really good coach, and then maybe to start going for auditions. She's also been working on the Alexander Technique. She wants to become an Alexander Technique instructor. It will be a way for her to make money while she acts. She has all these plans and doesn't see how she could manage a child at the moment, especially not a troubled one. And she thinks about it—Claire quite sober and not so wacky—and lays her decision down.

"I don't think I could do it," she tells Klara, and she holds her lover's big hand. "I do want us to have a child. And I think it's wonderful that you are ready to give so much. Maybe I'm being totally selfish here. I'm sure he's great. And I'm sure if I went in and met him I'd fall in love—and I don't want to fall in love with a wounded, crazy boy. I'd love to think I could shelter someone who had suffered so much, but, I mean, he's got to be haunted, right? Full of visions of all the people who abused him. And it'd be like bringing all those people into our house. I couldn't do it, Klara. No."

I know they had that kind of conversation, because later that night, Klara called my wife. She told Julie the whole thing, and then, in bed, Julie told the story to me.

"It's that kid, that kid she talked about, that inventor of love. They're not going to take him in. Thank God, Claire reminded her that they can't. You don't know people like Klara, people who give it all to the suffering of others. There's something wrong with them—if they took the kid in, I mean, it would be crazy, crazy. Right? And I know Klara, she's going on the warpath. The great defender. The great avenger. The savior of suffering children everywhere."

I picture Klara girding for battle: her Norse social worker's armor, in her right hand a two-headed battle-ax, in her left a sack of Huggies. My wife lay on her back and squeezed her eyes shut as tightly as she could. The skin on her nose curled and wrinkled. She fell asleep. I went downstairs and fixed a whiskey and sat on a couch in my bathrobe and stared at the blank TV.

We have a nice little two-story place. A woman comes and cleans once a week. The furniture is new and the carpets come from my wife's family, inherited from a grandmother. It's an old Federalist house—not too hard to come by in Philadelphia—two stone steps leading right out to the sidewalk and a narrow garden in the back. After I learned that Klara would not adopt Napoleon, I headed out there into the cold and did what people do when they can't sleep. I was wearing furry bear-claw slippers that my wife had bought me as a joke. I drew my bathrobe around me but it did no good. There was a freak meteorological incident that night, I swear, though no one else seems to have recorded it—a sudden October flurry. Snowflakes dusted my head and robe.

I've had trouble sleeping ever since I was a kid. When I was younger, I'd worry about God or death. I'd lurk around my parents' house tiptoeing. I'd hide in closets so no one could shoo me back to bed. As I've grown older, what worries me is not the end of my life or the infinite horizons of the universe but things like money and the future, having children, growing old. My job is a job for an idiot. I lied on my résumé, was encouraged to do so. I'm a glorified teller, a big white guy in a tie who's memorized the rules. When people give trouble to the tellers—black women, Hispanic women, all of them—they feel good giving their gripes to me. I nod solemnly, restate policy, and tell them who to write if they want to complain. I sell home equity loans. A moron's job, ground-level enforcement that allows the money to flow smoothly to the glass buildings downtown. Julie talks about it in terms of its stability, its practicality.

"You're lucky to have it," she says.

"I'm lucky to have you."

I've thought about going back to school but I figure it would only give her an opening. Four more years till we have a kid. I used to work as a bartender, but then I'd work nights and she'd work days and I'd never see my wife. I think about what Klara does and it just about breaks my heart, but to take care of frightened children and get paid, you need a master's degree or a doctorate.

I can't remember when the guys entered the story, when my wife began to talk about them at night. They were dog-walking friends, Michael and Brad. They had purebred pooch, a Jack Russell terrier, and perversely it liked Quasimodo best of all dogs in Prospect Park. That's how Claire and Klara knew them: The dogs ran circles, sniffed each other's butts, slobbered over tennis balls while their masters talked.

Somehow, Claire and Klara knew Michael and Brad were thinking about having a child. I don't think Klara would have even approached those guys with the possibility of adopting such a desperate kid, but Claire is impulsive. She takes things as they come. When you talk to her, it's like that. You mention yogurt for breakfast; she says her mother ate a tub of cottage cheese each morning and then puked before sending the kids to school. And so one chilly day in the park, after Michael said something about health insurance, Claire brought up Napoleon.

I never met the guys but I can imagine. In the wintertime, Brad goes running in the park. With his thick muscles, pink cheeks, and auburn hair, you could mistake him for a stocky dancer or cute frat boy. Seventh grade, he was the fat kid in Columbus, Indiana; one third period he burned his own hand against a steam pipe so he wouldn't have to take his shirt off in gym, show his tits. These days, he's got a lightning smile, gracious, easily fashionable, you have to look close to see the underbite. Michael is taller and thin-faced and anxious, the child of divorced Manhattan art dealers, the Upper West Side, 89th Street. It's Brad who's the catch, Michael who's the catcher—a miracle that sensitive Michael has managed to keep Brad down home. And yet Brad has come to love the life. He argues over decorating, washes Michael's socks. He'll talk about it like he's the victim of a prank.

"I am *so* the wife," he'll say.

Michael is a lawyer who works for Lincoln Center. He calls his mom on weekends; she kept the rent-controlled apartment with the view of the park. He has occasional lunches with his dad. Afterward, bitches with Brad. "No, I don't *mind* the German wifette." Their apartment is a chilly place, a view down across Brooklyn to Wall Street's towers. They're as serious about having a kid as Julie and I are—which is to say parenthood is an enormous lake around which they wander daily, thinking maybe soon it'll be warm enough for a dip.

With Claire in the park that December day, conversation slides around a *New York Times* article about gay marriage in Hawaii. Dogs yap. Brad chucks sticks and then hops on one foot to avoid puddles and half-frozen mud. Claire is beaming up at skinny Michael, who nods and keeps his arms crossed. Talk moves on to the difficulties of their lives. From a distance it looks like Claire is flirting, but they're just discussing insurance and domestic partnership laws. Brad is covered by Michael's job, Claire by Klara's. She runs her hand over her messy hair and then asks, point-blank, if they've gotten any closer to having a kid.

Michael laughs. He can't believe the question or, what's more, that he's going to answer it.

"Yeah," he muses. "Oh, yeah. We're getting close to ready." Then he chuckles, embarrassed.

"Adoption, right?"

"What else is there? Inseminate Brad?"

Claire's open face is impossible to mistrust.

She dodges bounding Muttley and gives Michael the news: "I know a sweet kid in and out of foster care, but really sweet and he needs a home." Talking about the kid like he's an apartment for rent.

And then, with a strange hesitation—or maybe I'm not imagining this right, maybe I'm making it go too fast, but soon enough careful Michael says it. "I think," he says, "I think—well, we've talked about this. Brad and I. A kid. A kid in need, yeah. We. Yeah." Reality drops like a wedding cake smack into the middle of their conversation. "We're—I think—interested in, maybe, talking or meeting—uh, Brad?"

Who flips. "Oh, my God!" Brad's hopping around, and all the dogs start barking. "Oh, my fucking God!"

"Oh, my God," Michael agrees.

Claire claps and hops and hugs Brad and Michael, who seem dazed. The dogs leap up, muddy feet against clean clothes.

It was impulsive. They must have seemed decent—they *are* decent guys, no doubt. They didn't do anything *bad*. They acted with the best intentions and from their friends I bet they get sympathy all the way. It helps, for me, to think of my parents. These guys were just following the rules they knew best.

My brother Jacob lay bedridden for months before his death. He'd flicker in and out of consciousness twenty-four seven. Sometimes if I got up at four in the morning, I'd find him rolling and wheezing. I'd help him to the bathroom. I'd get him a drink. Toward the end he was incapable of much of anything, even talking, but he liked it, I think, if I'd creep in there and for lullabies play Bruce Springsteen tunes. "Say good-bye, it's Independence Day." My father would peer in, catch us. He knew he was losing both sons.

"Athol," I say to my wife. "You know—O. Henry's daughter or the South African playwright. It can be a name for a boy or a girl."

"How do you know things like that, O. Henry's daughter?"

"I just can't believe anybody's named Athol, that's all."

"No child of mine."

In January Klara goes to have coffee with Michael and Brad. She heads over to a shop with rotating fans on the ceiling and pretty young help behind the counter, coffee served in thirty European styles. Brad and Michael are nervous before they go. They bicker over what to wear. Brad's T-shirt, "I Can't Even *Think* Straight," is too much, says Michael. This pisses Brad off. "We're meeting a *dyke*, for God's sake." But Brad relents, takes off his leather jacket, pulls a sweater over the shirt. They don't talk as they head over to the café but things go well: On the way back Brad drapes an arm around stiff Michael and sings. "A *baby*, a *baby*, we're gonna have a *baby*!"

That's how I imagine it, but there are some specific things I know. Michael was the one who first visited Napoleon; he met the kid at Klara's place of work. He didn't want Brad to go. I picture it like this: Michael telling Brad that he's just certain Brad will fall in love too easily, that he, Michael, will be able to make a clear judgment. But Brad has suspicions—Brad reads Michael's mind: *Nobody wants to give a kid to a flighty little fag.* And when Michael shows up at the shelter, a Friday when he could have dressed casual, he's wearing an overcoat, a suit and tie, a show of his own substantiality. He crouches down on the floor. He leans his briefcase against the cinder-block walls. Napoleon hides behind Klara.

"He's beautiful," Michael says.

Klara laughs, embarrassed. For an instant she wants to say it's not Napoleon's beauty that has drawn her to him. She wants Michael to see the miracle that is this child. And Napoleon buries his face in Klara's breast.

"He's shy today," Klara says; she's nervous. "I've never seen him so shy."

She tries to pull little Napoleon over toward his new potential daddy—lifts him up in the air, swings him about, sets him sitting on her cross-legged lap, but when Michael gets too close Napoleon squirts over Klara's shoulder, plunges headfirst to the floor, and gathers himself behind her. It's real terror. Napoleon cowers from strange men. He's been raped before, Klara explains.

But even from over her shoulder—even with this chilling piece of news—Napoleon charms Michael. It's the kid's magic power—the one Klara told us about, the kid's power to make people love him. He squints and smiles and shows off, charming Michael. And it all works. Michael is imagining Brad playing with this kid—some seaside, some park.

When I was sixteen I was crushed, sullen, and angry. I lurked. Women loved me for it. It didn't matter where I was. Flat on my back in the town square on a sunny day in June, I was subterranean and furious. I got to Philadelphia at eighteen and people who were alienated or angry or otherwise split from the world liked to have me around. Massively depressed, but everyone took it for a James Dean cowboy cool. These days I'm worried and anxious and fatherly. I pace my comfortable house. I sit in the garden. Out of the shower, I shave. I comb what's left of my thinning hair. I put on a white shirt, a blue suit, a purple tie. My cheeks hang fat toward the collar. Heels clatter across the wooden floor downstairs. Julie calls, "Good-bye." I call, "I love you." I check beneath my chin for spots I didn't shave.

The adoption went through and soon began showing signs of strain.

"They don't know how to take care of a kid," said my

wife in bed, her body tense and nervous. "They take long quiet walks in Prospect Park. He throws rocks at ducks and squirrels."

It didn't take long before Michael wanted to give back the child. He'd call his mother on the Upper West Side for advice. His mother had no ideas.

"They can't handle the kid," Julie said. "It's too much for them. They lie in bed, putting him to sleep, and just before he falls asleep he starts screaming. *Stick it in me. Stick it! Fuck me up the ass!*"

"Jesus, can they do that?" I asked. "Give him back?"

"I don't know," said Julie, and she rushed her hands across her face. "I guess so. And I just can't imagine. . . ." Me, I can't help imagining.

Michael tells Brad that he has tried his best, that the adoption was something he needed to do, but that this boy is not for him, it's not possible. The kid makes the most fundamental parts of his life unlivable—he no longer sleeps, he no longer writes letters, they no longer make love; there is nothing in his life except Napoleon and work, and both of those are strained. Michael pushes his words forward hesitantly but forcefully. He says he's got to take care of himself. He doesn't always have to be his own first priority, but he has got to have a life in which he can function. There have got to be children, somewhere, who will let him relax in his couch as he listens to a three-minute song. There have got to be people, somewhere, who will devote themselves to this child as this child requires, that is to say patiently, twenty-four seven, for the rest of their lives.

I swear I could drive to Brooklyn and bounce Michael off walls. I could keep on bouncing him, fancy-pants Upper West Side fag, work his head like it's a basketball. The head snaps back. Blood stains the plaster—but this is not the story in which I do that. This is not the story in which I do anything. This is my life. My wife told me the ending. She took her hands off her ears. They were giving up the kid. It was over.

Julie dropped off to sleep. I headed down to the kitchen. I fixed myself a whiskey. I tried to think how Klara would handle this. Klara's tougher than I am. She's faced worse beasts than Michael—who is after all a kind and well-meaning soul. She doesn't have my tendency to hide or mope or run away or dream of violence. She would find him and talk.

So Klara invites him out to coffee again. It's late March and she has to trudge through a snowstorm—crazy New York weather, winter comes in bursts. She pulls off her scarf and her face is the color of a cooked beet. They smile and laugh about the snow. Michael gets coffee. Klara gets cocoa. She asks how Napoleon is doing. "Terrific," Michael says, and Klara turns stern. "This has got to be hard for him," she says.

"Oh, for all of us," Michael tells her. "It's terrible."

Carefully, Klara tries to invoke his obligations. She appeals to Michael on grounds of conscience. Michael, the lawyer, says his conscience is clear—depleted, he laughs, but clear. What about responsibilities? "I know," says Michael. "I know." Klara lets a word slip: *selfish*.

Michael has been waiting for this. He knows it's not true. He sees his adversary's weakness and presses his advantage. This is in that same nonsmoking coffee shop they met in before. It's crowded with people in sweaters, mothers with strollers, young women with novels, middle-aged men with laptops. Everyone looks like they attended the same private college. Ella Fitzgerald sings over the stereo. Michael takes a small sip of coffee, bends forward, and gives vent. He says: "I am being nothing more than honest in saying this adoption has failed."

Klara drops her hands to her sides. She's lost.

He says: "It's been only two months and I know I cannot do this. I am admitting my own failure—this isn't easy. Remember, you chose not to adopt Napoleon. You weren't willing to try. I was. I failed. I am not happy, I'm not proud, but I know that giving up now is far preferable to pressing ahead. I am incapable of being his father." He pauses. "Do you know what that means? That means I know I will grow to resent, to fear, maybe even to hate him." Michael bites his own lip. "This is a beautiful, wounded child, and I had wished and dreamed that I could tend to him. But I can't. I don't know how to do it. Understand? At night, he doesn't sleep, he doesn't let me sleep. At meals, if I eat, if I stop tending to him for a second, he panics. If I read, he begins shrieking. He needs a different person than me. Another parent. Someone else. I don't think I am capable of making his life better—and I know he is capable of making my life worse. I am selfish here, yes, but selfishness here is based in a reasonable estimation of my own abilities. I will fail as his father. I have failed. I continue to fail. And it is not generous to offer someone a failed father. It's hubris. It's idiocy. It's crap."

That dreamy look is in Klara's eyes again, as if they're scanning the horizon looking for land. She says, "I know you can do this."

"It's two months now," he says, "and in a year, if we keep him, it will only be worse to give him up. His attachments will be greater and so will ours and the whole thing will be so much more heartrending. To keep him on beyond, for the rest of my life—what would that accomplish? I know I can't do this. I've failed."

"But you said—" Klara's reduced to mourning. "You said you'd take care of him."

"And I was wrong, and I admit it. I can't." He cleans up some crumbs with a napkin.

At the day-care center which he still attends, Napoleon invents a game. He makes Klara pretend to be a train. He tells her to pull out of the station. As she begins chugging elbows, he starts to cry, "Don't leave me! Don't leave me!" They repeat this dozens of times a day.

Brad picks Napoleon up on April Fool's Day. He's wearing a springtime leather jacket and a pink T-shirt. The guy is an angel with clipped wings, looks like at any moment he's going to sob. He loves Napoleon. The kid's magic has totally worked on him. But Michael has given his ultimatum. And Brad can't imagine life alone.

"I am so," he says, "*so* the wife."

I'm furious, but that means nothing. Julie and I both know that we could take in Napoleon. She makes enough money. I could quit my job and stay with the kid. Nobody in the world would be better at it than I would. But like I said, my wife and I have plans. Two more months at the bank, and then we'll throw away the condoms. This time around, I feel cursed.

I see an article in the *New York Times* about people with gross facial deformities. I think, That will be my son. He will have extra holes in his nose. His face will be shaped like a radar dish. When I see an ugly or crippled toddler in Rittenhouse Square, a grade school kid in a wheelchair with an electronic breathing apparatus hitched up to the back—I think that will be my Jacob. Limbless, brainless, spineless, grotesque.

But Klara and Claire are tougher than I am. They're not easily shaken. Recently, Michael and Brad have approached them with a proposition: They want to co-adopt a child, the four of them together. They see each other walking in the park and they're friendly; they're on the same team.

I think of Napoleon, that poor tortured kid who on his own invented love, and all I can think is: He'll be lucky to live past fourteen. He'll be some miraculous, charming con man. He'll be a beggar or a jailhouse slut. I think of my father, peering into a room, seeing his dying child and his sullen teen. He knows that both of his sons have lost him.

A PENAL COLONY ALL HIS OWN, 11E

"It works as a," said Kevin, "a remarkable piece of apparatus." And he looked around the hallway that was familiar to
both him and me.

Kevin's skin was pale as a poached egg, his no longer red
hair cut short. He wore cuff links and a tie that matched his
breast-pocket handkerchief and he blinked slowly, lids shut-
tering, then revealing blue eyes. My old friend lurked somewhere in there, trapped behind layers of fat and years—the
leader of our most inspired games when we were kids, who
taught Zev Grubin and me to eat cat food wet from a can, to
hang by our fingers from his eleventh-story window, but
now there was a stiffness to his shoulders and to the muscles
under his cheeks.

"How you doing?" I asked.

"I assume you're here for the full tour."

In my memory, the apartment smelled of cat litter, but
now the aroma was synthetic orange. Below the plaque on
the front door that read 11E hung a brass sign, "The
MacMichaelman Museum of Kevin," and on the floor lay

the kind of humidity meter you find in museums and galleries, silently graphing dampness, also rows of cut flowers, bouquets of blown begonias, and, at the end of the hall where a coat rack had once stood, an elevated desk, a yellow sign above it welcoming me.

"Eight dollars is suggested admission, but, Davey, you can pay what you like." I rummaged in my pockets. Kevin spoke as he rang up charges. "I don't know if anyone—your parents, a news magazine I might have missed—has explained the museum to you."

"No."

What I had heard from my parents and old friends—Zev Grubin, better man than I, who lived in California but stopped by Kevin's every time he was in New York—was that Kevin had turned his parents' apartment into an exhibition hall of his own art.

I had kept my distance from Kevin since his first nervous breakdown, twelfth grade when the world had declared him mad. When I bumped into him after that at family events and parties, his stiffness and secret eyes creeped me—not something I'm proud of. When we were younger, our imaginary worlds had been linked. "Oh, but that's the way it is," Zev Grubin had consoled me over the telephone. "People lose track of each other, they grow apart." And when Kevin had first lost control of himself I had pretended it wasn't happening. "You were a kid then," Zev said. "It was a big shock for all of us. Past is past, Davey." So on this Christmas Day after I had dropped by my parents', I decided to take a trip to his place, make amends. It was the right thing to do and I felt good about myself, if a little uneasy. I tapped the buttons as I rode the elevator to eleven, rehearsed lines of conversation. I hadn't wanted to talk to Kevin about my life—not that I am successful enough to make anyone envious (I teach school, I write freelance), but I felt as though it would be unsympathetic to measure my independence and goals against his loneliness, his world that I imagined of confusion and grief. I decided I would talk to Kevin about Zev. I practiced comic anecdotes about Zev's film, how a video distribution company had managed to intersplice lesbian sex scenes into a story Zev claimed was inspired by Kafka. Also I would ask about Kevin's younger brother Ian—it seemed that could be neutral ground and I really was interested in Ian. I hadn't seen Ian for years and I would have been nervous talking to him. Ian, I figured, remembered all the ways in which I had abandoned the MacMichaelman family.

But, "This museum," Kevin said, easing himself off his stool, "was mine to put in practice, but understand: my father's in its conception and design. My father believed, you know, in decency, in bravery, in facing up to shames. I have tried to ingrain those values into every inch of this apartment, every floorboard, every doorknob. My father is gone now, but do not be troubled. It will be impossible for the next occupant, even if it is my brother Ian, no matter how he ventilates, sands, or rewires, to expunge completely from the apartment my monument to the revelation of—"

"How is Ian?"

Kevin cocked his head. "You asked about Ian?"

"I guess I did."

"Doing well, I suppose. Works as a pediatrician. Place of business is a small New England hospital. Is married to a woman once named Bonnie Sweet. Two children, very cute. Janey and Jimbo. But I am rambling on and here we are with the museum all around us. I think you'll find it a moving and judicious display. Herein I've recorded all those little slips of mine, those embarrassing acts and omissions, times I hurt someone unintentionally or made a fool of myself or revealed some peculiar awfulness in my heart—all of those shames of the past that once crept up on me while I waited for an elevator or dropped off to bed, times I said something stupid, told the wrong joke, wore the wrong clothes, behaved oddly. All those retroactive twinges of embarrassment that haunt me in the middle of the night, that pounce on me when I am idly perusing the cereal boxes in a grocery store. I have memorialized them here, so that, as the visitor travels through the museum, my feelings are indelibly imprinted upon my guests. Every artists seeks to create empathy—of course!—but here, I have managed to do so without fail. I have fashioned this apartment as a machine that transfers my repulsion toward my most picayune perversities on to you—mechanically, automatically. You see!"

A blue light flashed on, revealing a display case I had somehow failed to notice, the kind you might find in a secondhand jewelry store with a stained wood frame, green velvet backing, and a clean glass window. On the velvet rested memorabilia: Kevin's high school yearbook, opened to a picture of him with the knot of his tie too full and his hair cut in a puffy shag; Dungeons & Dragons game manuals, also graph paper, also pink and white and orange dice—ten-sided, four-sided, twenty-sided, in the days before desktop computers this is what we geeks played with, you needed lots of dice for D & D; pulp paperbacks with cover paintings of half-naked muscle-bound men with massively engorged swords; beside these, a single bedsheet folded to reveal nocturnal stains.

Above this case hung an egg tempera painting, a long horizontal in the mode of David's *Death of Socrates*, a figure much like Kevin's holding a single finger aloft, and above the colorful togas of onlookers faces of what seemed a fashionable party set, pretty women with bobbed hair and angular glasses, men with goatees and earrings, all of them reacting to the painting's central figure (Kevin) as though he'd let loose a stream of horse piss. *Wrong Joke,* read the identifying plaque.

"And somehow," I said, "these feelings of yours are impressed on me as I walk through—"

"Precisely. Feel. Beneath the floor runs a set of electrical currents—the point of these will become apparent soon enough—and within the vitrine lies a battery. The trembling comes through as a kind of warmth, almost undetectable, but the motions are precisely calibrated and correspond exactly to the code—"

"The—"

"You don't know the code?" Kevin adjusted his tie. "Forgive me. I have so many roles to perform here: curator, janitor, artist, CEO. Also I expected that your parents—they came up here, they visited, not into the museum, but—I expected they would at the very least explain the code. The whole thing is absolutely—in any case I am certainly the person to explain since I have here"—he patted the breast pocket of his houndstooth suit jacket—"my father's sketches."

"Your father's?"

"To be sure." He reached for the pink handkerchief that matched his tie and squeezed each of his fingers as though he were wiping the pistons of a powerful machine. Then he drew out a leather wallet. "The code is not too severe, I don't think, nor too uncommon. Perhaps you would like to see." He showed me a piece of paper creased at its folds and browned at its edges. It read:

•••• ——— —•••• —•—•—— ••••• —••••• —•••••••— •——•———•—••••—•—•—••
•••• ——— —•••• —•—•—— ••••• —••••• —•••••••— •——•———•—••••—•—•—••

```
••••  ——— —•••• — —•—— ••••• — •••••  —•••••••  — •——•———•—•• •• —•—• —•——
••••  ——— —•••• — —•—— ••••• — •••••  —•••••••  — •——•———•—•• •• —•—• —•——
```

"Morse." He ran an explanatory finger along the dits and dashes. "'Honesty is the best policy, honesty is the best policy, honesty is the best——'"

"And is every visitor told what the vibrations——"

"No."

"They don't get told that it isn't——" I put my hands on the display case. "I mean, it could be just, for instance, the rattle of a noisy dishwasher downstairs."

"No. I am explaining this to you, Davey, because you are an old friend. I feel you have a certain kinship with these devices. I am letting you in, as it were, the game behind the game. But no, I would not explain this to every visitor. There would be no point. They would feel it. Leaning a pants leg unsuspectingly against the display, the very essence of the message would tremble through their chinos and be absorbed into flesh. Look." Kevin passed his hand through a shaft of light. All I could see was strange shadow play on his palm, but once he flipped a switch and the rest of the room was thrown in darkness, what came clear were letters in Cyrillic script. "The same sentence," he said, "in Russian.

"It's in the wood grain, too. Seven years of work. And if I were to give you a magnifying glass and allow you to crawl across the floors, you would see it everywhere, in Finnish, Maltese, Maldavian, Slovak, Chuvash, Pashto, Tamil, Brahui, Dzongkha, Uighur, and Hiri Motu, as if the whole world were crying out my father's motto: 'Honesty is the best policy!'"

I swallowed, and a cold gray stone made its way down my throat.

Kevin's father, Clarence, had died just a few winters before; both Kevin's parents had been on a TWA flight that plunged mysteriously into the Long Island Sound. I had been on vacation in Ecuador that December and had missed the MacMichaelman funeral. My mom had put my name on some flowers she had ordered, and I had meant to write a condolence note to Kevin, had even bought the proper stationery, written the note to Ian, put that note in an envelope which stayed on my kitchen table to remind me to call my parents so that I could get his address, but then I had spilled coffee all over it. I had never expressed my condolences, not to anybody. "Well," Zev Grubin had once said, "you should have. You really should send something. It's never too late, you know." And staring at the foreign blue letters on Kevin's hand, I thought: This is my chance. Be a more decent person. I had visited, I could continue to visit Kevin, I could be his friend, and I could tell him how bad I felt—all I needed was the opportunity to apologize.

The lights flashed on. I looked at the thin boards of the polyeurethaned floor. Kevin asked me to take off my shoes. "So the soles of your feet can absorb the writing even as they rub it out."

"You expect me to read," I asked, even as I untied my Adidas, "Hiri Motu through my—"

He held up a hand in response and drew back the curtain that hung behind the display case, revealing the MacMichaelman living room. It was just as I remembered: the matching yellow furniture, the old rug, the grand piano with the pictures dust-free and carefully maintained. When we were younger, Kevin and I had imagined ourselves there to be crusading knights and wolves eating caribou. We had spread his toy soldiers across the floor and the couch and the coffee table and had staged crazy anachronistic battles: Roman centurions and Civil War grays against space men, Union cavalry and a ragtag band of oversized Indians. Now

Kevin had performed a weird miracle with the space. The living room seemed to be reproduced in full, yet ringed around it was a white-walled, bare-floored exhibit of memorabilia, all labeled and catalogued and displayed under glass. In a black bordered frame hung an undersized T-shirt from the Camp Oglagla all-star softball game. *Kevin Eleven*, it read, in print that mocked the twenty-four-hour store's. Behind a clear Plexiglas case stood an arcade-sized Asteroids game, maybe the same old one from Amil's Pizzeria, piles of quarters at its base. And in the frame above the couch where the MacMichaelmans had once hung a reproduction of Brueghel's *Tower of Babel*, Kevin had placed a sample of his own work, a self-portrait, his face painted over six feet high, brush strokes so fine the texture of the image was almost photographic. Kevin's chin, his left ear, and the top of his head were cropped by the frame, giving the impression that his enormous, innocent, pale, quiet, angry face was about to explode.

I crossed the rug to the grand piano, picked up a small picture: Clarence and Dorrie, taken just a few years before they died. They looked young in the photograph, she with her red hair in its Prince Valiant bob, he not so good-looking but with a thin face that was kindness itself in my memory.

"You'll have to put that down," Kevin said. "I'll have to ask you to step away from the exhibit."

I did as I was told, setting the frame on its angled stand; the velvet backing quiet against the wood, the faux-leather cool against my hand. Then, "Kevin," I began. "Oh—I don't know—don't you feel—don't you think you're being, being just a little bit hard on yourself here?"

"Pardon?"

"I mean, to feel ashamed, we all have things—what I mean is, we—I can't imagine your father—"

"Don't be a Philistine, Davey. What do you know about my dad? His desires, his secrets, his art. *Hard on myself.* That's Ian's line. How can you, of all people, say—but I guess it's nothing to be concerned with. No. I can see what you're doing here. I suppose you're simply exhibiting a normal partial response to the museum. Yes. The beginning of appropriate feelings. That's how your words should be understood, that's how I will understand them. It happens before the full effect of the museum is felt, this kind of resistance—"

"I—"

"Let me explain—"

"I guess I know about the museum. Now—"

"You know everything—except the most important part. You see. We are already on the move!"

And it was true. What had initially seemed an ordinary wood floor concealed cog wheels and a conveyor belt. We were being drawn toward the dining room. A diaphanous curtain fell behind us and the living room lights dimmed. The shapes of the furniture behind blurred before they were completely obscured and as I looked back I imagined Clarence and Dorrie MacMichaelman on the sofa, crouched as if they were mourning Kevin and not the other way around. Was that it, I wondered, the whole museum, an expression of grief for his lost parents? And then me, I thought, what had I denied myself in missing their funeral if not an opportunity to grieve? Tears welled up in my eyes. I thought about this trip through the so-called museum as a substitute ceremony, a time for expressing sadness about what, as I now saw it, had not only been Kevin's loss but also my own, because Clarence and Dorrie had fed me doughnuts and sandwiches when I was a kid, had loved me, and sure enough I had also loved—

With a bang, the floor jolted. A spring snapped and we two were thrown forward, Kevin and I sent stumbling into a rail that divided the dining room in two, the smaller section for viewing, the larger for museum display.

"It's fucking Ian's fucking fault!" Kevin roared, pointing at the busted conveyor belt. "Davey, I tell you, I have called him. I talk with Ian for hours, tell him how much money I need and for what. This place can't run on love alone, Davey! Somebody better give him a talking to, somebody better straighten him out, before—Oh, Davey. Look at my work and say it: Tell me I have not been a good son! Tell me I have not labored to achieve all my father could have dreamed!"

But I couldn't answer. There, on the other side of the rail, the MacMichaelman dining room was spread out in exquisite display. On the tablecloth lay the family's good china, on the sideboard a large silver platter. Once again, Kevin had achieved his trompe l'oeil magic: He'd preserved the old room exactly as it had been while somehow enlarging the dimensions around. The space was now big enough to accommodate wide display cases and a visitors' aisle. Mannequins posed in old clothing—torn jeans, a red beret, an army surplus book bag with the charms and amulets that in junior high school hung from Kevin's; a peace sign, a picture of Jim Morrison, a rabbit's foot, a bumper sticker that said *I Break for Hobbits and Unicorns.* I looked at it and remembered Kevin shaggy-haired and weird in his father's old overcoat but to me brilliantly attractive. There woud a single mattress in a glassed-in case and above it another original MacMichaelman canvass: artful brushwork, shades at once of El Greco and of Lucian Freud, a dorm room with a Bob Dylan poster on a cinder-block wall and a naked boy curled on a mattress, his knees drawn up, his ass to the viewer, his arms reaching toward his crotch.

"*No Sex My Entire Freshman Year*," Kevin read the title card. "Ian, of course, thinks that maybe I shouldn't make a point of this. He says my prolonged virginity is not something that will capture the public's imagination. You know, Davey, what really cheeses me off—and I'm speaking here of course as a friend, a private citizen, not the official voice of the museum—is that Ian combines these specific criticisms with his protestations of brotherly love, and then he doesn't give a fucking extra cent to the museum. Perhaps—and I'm only saying maybe—if he took a more active interest, perhaps then I would be more receptive to his commentary. I'm not talking about selling out—my integrity is *not* up for auction, okay? Still, my work is about intimacy, and a financial relationship is a relationship, is it not?"

"I really—"

"Of course. But why don't you look into this cabinet? Another one of those displays to which Ian is less than sympathetic. *Hard on myself.* Same words as yours. Coincidence, I'm sure. But look. See?" Kevin directed my attention to a darkened window in the wall. "The last letter my mother ever sent me."

"I couldn't—"

"Read." His eyes narrowed.

So I cupped my fingers to the glass and peeked. The last page of Dorrie's note went:

> is that we do spend a lot of time wondering what you're doing there, honey, and we would very much like to learn. I have called several times and though I know you need your freedom I still think it would be nice, especially for daddy, if you would drop us a line. Just write whatever you feel. No pressure. I love you.
>
> Love,
>
> Mom

Set around the letter, framing it as cherubs would the baby Jesus, were six stamped postcards, each with the MacMichaelmans' address in Dorrie's loopy hand.

I thought about her and Clarence, how frightening it must have been to send their brilliant, troubled son off to school. But they had done it, trusted him as they had to, and appreciated the possibilities he could offer, whereas I—

"Genuine," said Kevin. "The cards are. Same ones she sent me. The letter, I'm afraid, is a facsimile. Davey, why don't you take in the audio component of the display."

A pale green rotary phone hung on the wall—the same one that had once hung in the MacMichaelman kitchen, the number scratched out under the plastic dial, electric tape holding together the chord. I lifted the receiver. There was a dial tone, a ring, and then I heard a recording: Kevin, his voice slightly higher (maybe as he had sounded in college), and his father speaking through the tape hiss as if from beyond the grave.

Kevin: Hello?

Clarence: Hello!

Kevin: Dad? That you? Oh, man, I've got to—

Clarence: I'm just calling to say hello, Kev. Your mom has been—

Kevin: Dad, I'd love to talk but—

Clarence: Would it be okay if I called you back?

Kevin: Definitely, definitely, um—

Clarence: What's a good time? No pressure here.

Kevin: Well, I'll be out tonight.

Clarence: This weekend?

Kevin: Um, great.

Clarence: We fly to Paris Monday, so—

Kevin: Have fun. Okay. I gotta run.

Clarence: Do what you need to do.

"'Do what you need to do,'" said Kevin, when I had rested the handset in its place. "'Write what you feel.' Do you see how my parents' words have shaped my work? Can you understand? Ian of course thinks what I do here is inappropriate. He gives me platitudes—how I ought not dwell in the past, how I should strive for the future. Crap!"

"Your parents," I said, "were wonderful—"

"And you're impressed by the museum?"

"Speechless."

"Good." He grabbed my arm. "For now I would like to exchange a few words with you in confidence. You have arrived at a crucial juncture, Davey. The museum is three months behind on mortgage payments now, five on maintenance. The apartment will soon be lost. New Year's Day marks the end for me. Eviction. It's a shock—"

"I'm—"

"Listen. Have you ever, professionally, done any fundraising?"

"Not since—"

"Good enough. I have a plan. Tomorrow, up in New Hampshire, there will be a grand breakfast. I want you to go there as my representative. Six-hour drive, I'll supply the car. His family along with the families of several of my cousins will gather around his dining room table for one last holiday meal. He'll be serving waffles, just as my father did the morning after Christmas. That's the one thing Ian took from the apartment and it's the one way he keeps up the family tradition—waffles! So they will be stacked on steaming plates, banana waffles and blueberry waffles, sausages and pitchers of syrup. That's when you will strike. Just as soon as Ian mentions my name, you will burst in, his old friend, Davey Birnbaum, now teacher of advanced electives at the

School for the Humanist Culture, occasional book reviewer for *Time Out New York*, private, unpublished scribbler of his own stories—you will stride right up to the breakfast table, lay your hands where everyone can see them, and shout your unshakable convictions! Yet perhaps you won't shout. Perhaps you will simply take a seat at the table. You will just say a few words in a whisper, even, so that only Ian will hear. You don't have to mention anything specific; in fact, you need not worry about your speech at all, for the words will come out of you as if by inspiration—as we stand here now, the museum is working on you, inscribing those words onto your feet, into your ears and eyes, forcing even your little mitochondria to feel the precise and wrenching anger you ought! So if, in speaking to my brother, you sense that you have anything personal to add, don't. I'll take that upon myself, when I arrive a few minutes later. If my indictment doesn't drive Ian out of his kitchen and into the New England snow, force him to fall to his knees and cry out, 'Oh, Kevin, my wiser, older brother, how I humble myself before you!'—that's my plan!"

I didn't know what to say. I wanted to grab Kevin and cry for him. I wanted to smack him in the head. I wanted to fall to my knees and wail over his parents, plead for his forgiveness, but a strange deliberativeness came over me.

"No," I said. "This is all so. I can't explain. Kevin, this museum of—it's. We all have things we regret. Things we did or didn't do in the past—"

"You?"

"Of course—"

"You, Davey? You feel those things, too? Anxiety? Regret? Shame?"

"Kevin—"

"Oh, yes! Come on! There's just one more thing I have to show you, just one more!"

He pulled on my arm. We walked through the old French doors into the corridor that ran between Kevin's bedroom and his parents'. In that narrow hallway, when we were younger, Kevin and Ian and Zev and I had played at being hockey players and basketball stars. We had argued about Dr. J's height: Was he six, seven, eight feet tall? Now the hall was carpeted and the walls hung with elaborate picture frames. *To thine own self be true*, read one oil-painted sampler, and around the letters rabbits leapt and unicorns strutted. Beside it a silver gelatin print, black and white, recalled at once the work of Cindy Sherman and the famous still from *Public Enemy*, Cagney shoving a grapefruit in Mae Clarke's face; *Thirds*, it was called, and in it sat the same people I'd seen before in egg tempera—goatees, glasses, sharp bobbed hair, now dressed in Armani, and bulky Kevin lunging across their table for one last slice of prosciutto. We stood before his bedroom.

The doorway had been transformed into a small viewing area with gray carpeting and a low Plexiglas partition. The room itself was a mess, scattered objects all around, but each was labeled with a small blue numbered sticker and next to me was a map, an annotated guide to the spread: Lego, pornographic magazines, model glue, a ham radio, and the taxidermied corpses of the MacMichaelman family pets. Kevin's bed had been moved to the center of the room—I recognized the Eskimo sheets he had had when we were little kids—and on the wall across from us hung an exquisitely rendered painting. It was over ten feet high and at least that wide, heavy with darkness, the chiaroscuro sensual but also creepily cartoonish. In the blurry center of the black emerged forms, which as I stared revealed increasingly baffling detail: the arches and apses of a cathedral, stained-glass windows in sunlit blues and reds, the frames showing Kevin sulky and alone, his parents pleading, an airplane exploding, waves washing against a Long Island shore. Standing at the entryway to his bedroom, I felt myself drawn across the floor as though into the texture of the oils themselves, where I discovered clever renderings of wood carvings: ancient oak sculptures of vacations, MacMichaelman family dinners, the four of them playing bridge. This cathedral was a Chartres built to commemorate Kevin's grief. The hideous gargoyles outside, I knew, were all Kevin's face, shouting, screaming, fanged, and lurid, and the pews for his parents' funeral were packed except for one seat that was lit and empty, and that belonged to me. The force of the thing hit me: terror, grief, remorse. I felt myself not responsible but representative of everyone who had abandoned Kevin.

"It's really my favorite," he said.

"I'm so," I told him, "so sorry." But Kevin seemed not to hear me.

"Ian's big on my more strictly representative work, the self-portrait, things like that. 'You have real talent, Kev,' that's what he says. 'I think art school might be a great idea.' Like, as if that's supposed to be encouraging. But to tell you the truth, when I look at most of my paintings I just see pigment, you know, the brush strokes, the goop of the paint sitting there on stretched canvas. This one, though, works with the machinery of the whole museum. There's so little in it, but it's almost pixilated, almost alive——"

"I wish," I said, "I wish I could have been there for you——"

"You don't think it's too heavy-handed, right? I mean, that's what it's about, in a way. Impressing its point on you. It's coded——I've actually, with a tiny little needle scratched in the traces of the words you need to hear, 'Honesty is the best policy,' and when you look at the painting really hard, like you're doing now, I think of those little needles scratching back on your cornea, maybe even hurting you a bit. Of course, the whole layout of the room is designed to reflect that sentence. It all spells it out, all that junk. See how the bed and the painting make up the *i* and its dot? You get a better sense if you look back and forth between the room and the floor plan over here——"

"It was wrong of me, so wrong——"

"Davey?" Kevin turned my way. "What are you talking about?"

"I wish, I wish I had been——had gone to your parents' funeral. I feel——"

"You feel?" he seemed disoriented. "You weren't there? I'm honestly not sure what you're getting at here. Remember, the museum, this museum is not about you. Anyway——"

"I should have, I should have at least sent a note——"

"A note?" Kevin, nonplussed. "That's what you take from this? All this tells you is that you should have sent a note? Like, a condolence card?"

"Just to say how sorry. I just feel I was inappropriate, you see——"

"Oh, right!" Kevin struck his head. "That was what I needed! A little note, nice blue paper, *Love, Davey*. Like I didn't get enough of those. And like yours, after all the years, after everything, would have some special kind of——"

"I could have been a better friend is all I'm saying——"

"Davey!" Kevin bit his finger. "Shit!" He kicked the wall. "That's all this is to you? You come here, you see the whole fucking museum, I lay out my case——Your paranoid, orphaned, manic-depressive, solitary, delusional, grieving, schizophrenic friend reveals to you his sorrows large and small, casts all his hopes upon you, and you're sorry you didn't send a note?"

"I'm just feeling kind of inadequate."

Kevin's arms flailed. His fist smashed the nearby photograph. His whole body trembled in a spasm of frustration and grief. It was then we heard the knock on the front door, the quiet, "Hey?," the friendly, "Kev? Bro?" Ian called as he walked through the exhibition halls, "I brought you Christmas dinner, Kev. Kev?"

Who moaned miserably on the floor, deaf to everything.

"Kev?" Ian turned the corner. He was thinner than I remembered and balding, carried a Styrofoam cooler heavy with food. "Christ," he said when he saw us. "What's going on here?"

Kevin was a crying heap. I apologized.

Ian said, "I'm not sure I know what——"

"Doesn't matter," I interrupted. "I'm sure you don't want me here."

And as I backed out of the apartment, I heard the two talking, Ian consoling Kevin. "Hope it's still warm," he said, opening his cooler. "Long way from New Hampshire. I brought a video of the kids, too. And some frozen waffles. Nice of Davey to come by. Did you guys have an okay time?"

I tied my sneakers in the front hallway, thought of the putative Dzongkha, Pashto, and Hiri Motu sentences on the floor. Ian, I noticed, had kept on his loafers, walked right over the madness said to be imprinted there. He had tried to meet Kevin as a brother should, as a friend ought to have, without concession to the other's delusions or lies.

And I tell you, since that day I visited Kevin's, I've felt terrible. I can be standing alone in a shower, riding a crowded subway train, and suddenly it hits me: the shame that stops my breathing short. It's not the big things that bother me— that I avoided Kevin for years, that I failed him in his times of illness and grief—Kevin's in a hospital now and I do my best to visit—it's the little ones. Why did I put my hands on that glass case in his front hallway, trying to argue with him about Morse? Why did it take so many years to chase me up to his apartment? And why haven't I told Kevin, even now, that I found his paintings beautiful?

THE SPEEDBOAT

When people ask how I met Tom, I tell them we're neighbors. I leave it at that. The truth, as is often the case, would embarrass everyone. I was getting off the train. I'd been in the city late watching videos of myself conducting focus groups, was one of not too many stragglers emerging from the subway. Dark of night, pleasant spring—you come out of that station, right next to the park, the cool of Brooklyn evening after the heat of Manhattan day and the uncivilized jostlings of a subway train, and there is a hint of release. Must have been ten o'clock, a Wednesday. I came home as I often do, wanting a drink. I like a glass at the end of the day. It helps me sleep, but I'm a lightweight. Two and I get up slow in the morning.

That night I climbed out from the subway stairs and I heard a small shout and a clattering to my left, from across the street, beside a park bench where drunks often sit. I knew something bad had happened. When finally I turned, I saw a woman collapsed. I'm nearsighted and so couldn't

175

make out the scene. What seemed to me a Walkman lay on the ground. What seemed a bearish drunkard, indeterminate race, crouched above. I'd turned and paused after the yelp and the crashing sound. No one else had bothered to look. There's social pressure at work even in the face of calamity, and in New York social pressure is to walk straight past. I don't want to give the impression of myself as a Good Samaritan—Lord knows I'm hardly that—but the sight was ambiguous and frightening. I went for a closer look.

I'll admit I kept my distance. The bulky man kept his head bent, tending to the fallen woman. I took in just his exaggerated bulk and the darkness of his clothes. I assumed he was somehow sinister. From across a bank of parked cars, I asked whether there was anything I could do. What had happened? Should I call an ambulance? The man disregarded me and murmured importunities to the woman. I thought the whole thing a put-on, this man somehow bullying this woman, pretending to care for her, pretending to be her intimate. On the park bench from which I assumed he'd risen sat an empty bottle of seltzer water, nothing sinister in that. A street lamp burned yellow above. There were no cars moving in the street.

The details at this point begin to lose their order. I know that a woman rushed up from behind me, older, with a head of thick dyed-black curls and friable plastic glasses. Her beaklike nose twitched and twittered and she asked if the fallen girl had suffered a seizure. I think this woman and I composed the same story: This girl on the ground (we'll call her a girl for now, to differentiate her from the older woman) had left the subway train, had collapsed, and this park-bench drunkard had risen to tend to her. He was thick around the waist. He wore navy blue sweatpants and a navy sweatshirt. The fallen girl wore sandals and a vest and had dropped a

Walkman and a woven shoulder bag. Early springtime, she wore socks beneath the bands of her sandals. The big man persisted in calling her 'Honey.'

"Was it a seizure? What happened? Did you see?" The beaky woman took charge. This was fine by me. I could smell liquor, but it didn't seem to be coming from him, rather to infect the general vicinity. At some point the bearish guy looked up, his delicate, spectacled, hairless face, and half whispered the word "Alcohol." This was Tom. He wasn't such a big man, taller than I, but softer, and with a high-pitched, nervous voice. It was nervousness that gave him that hint of dishonesty.

The woman wanted to feel the girl's pulse. She stretched for the girl's thin, uninhabited arm. Tom whispered initials. They weren't DTs, but something like that, some term common in the rhetoric of alcoholism.

"She should see a doctor." The woman didn't understand Tom's hinting.

He said "Alcohol" again, this time loud, so she would hear.

The woman blinked behind her glasses, the news weighing in on her. "*There's* the bottle." And like a prop in a dream it appeared, behind the crouching couple and to the left, its screw top peeking from a paper bag, Johnnie Walker. That bottle and not the Walkman had fallen with the clatter I'd first heard.

Tom was massaging the blond girl's neck and her legs and shoulders, as if to keep blood pumping around. I stepped away to get a better view of her face. This was Alison, though I didn't learn her name that night. She was pretty enough, but drawn and idiotic and haggard. I could see in her face what she ought to have been, athletic and a private-college girl, streaky hair and a mannish nose and very nice skin with freckles: a former member of a high school field hockey team. Her eyes—I can't match words to their color-less, slovenly ease.

The beaky woman insisted on an ambulance. This was alcohol poisoning, she said. People died. A passing dog walker pointed to a police car parked not too far away; they might help. The girl on the ground—Alison—began insist-ing, drunkenly, sloppily, but definitively, that that wasn't at all what she wanted. "Thank you," she murmured. "Thank you kind people."

I was inclined to agree with her, but something kept me at the scene. I don't know what, a desire to get the story straight and see it to its tentative end, a desire to see if the woman with the glasses would manage to hold sway, or something simpler: lurid curiosity. The woman began talking about doc-tors. Tom volunteered that he was a doctor. The woman demanded what sort of doctor Tom was.

"Mathematician," he had to say. "But my brother's a psy-chiatrist." And Alison, too, began flashing her faltering class credentials. "I'm an ESL teacher," she said, from the ground. "An ESL teacher."

The beaky woman wanted to check out Alison's pupils. Tom is the sort of guy who carries with him a small black penlight, probably also a Swiss army knife, probably also his digital watch doubles as a calculator. He pulled that light from the Velcro pouch at his hip, let the woman go ahead with her inspection. Maybe she worked in public health, an adminis-trator at a local hospital. She shone the light on Alison's nose and cheekbones. I'd had just about enough. I said my piece, that maybe she needed professional help, that the case looked bad to me. I'd call an ambulance, I offered. I'd hail a cab.

"I'm an ESL teacher," Alison said again. "Thank you kind people." Minus the sepulchral cast, it would have been a modern-day Dean Martin drunkard routine.

"We live right around the corner," said Tom. I didn't mention that I did, too. I wished the two of them luck.

That night, I got home and there were messages on my machine from my mother and I called her and I fixed myself a whiskey. For a moment the stuff looked nauseous and toxic, honey-gold in its bottle; but I thought what the hell, and by the time I had my first sip it was reassurance itself. After the news and sports scores, I headed to bed. The next morning I flew to Ohio, to continue my research on direct mailings. I flew from Columbus to Washington State, then down to Yorba Linda, California, and out to Austin, Texas, and then back home. I stayed in hotel rooms, saw airport lounges, read magazines, trod the vacuumed carpets of American life. I had a calibrated drink every night, to help me sleep, never two, never in a bar or hotel lounge. I'm not a social drinker.

My father drank until he was laid splat out on the floor of our Upper West Side apartment. At the cusp of adolescence that was nightly routine on 89th Street. I helped my father to bed, helped him off the ground. He was always in a stupor, not quite blacked out. I put my twelve-year-old arm around his warm bulk. He told me he didn't need any help while he wobbled beside me to bed. My memories of those nights are confused. I have no idea where in the apartment my mother was. I don't remember my sister present. I remember my father's manly smell, and his weight, and the difficulty of getting him off the narrow, shiny floorboards, pleading with him as he lay, waking him. There was something tender about the way he emerged from his miasmatic wallow. You'd think these would be memories of disgust or horror, me schlepping my dad through the foyer, but in fact these were the times in my adolescence when he was most manageable and close. He was infantile, and so my father and I were boys together.

As I say, the details are a haze. I wonder if it was assigned to me as a task: Get your father off the floor, like set out dishes, or clean up your room. I wonder if it was something to which I was driven by filial loyalty, to cup the scraps of his dignity in my palms. It was terribly important to me that my father didn't sleep on the floor. Some nights he got drunk in bed, lay on the covers in just his underwear, emptied half a bottle of vodka into his breathtaking belly, traffic from West End Avenue sending lights around the room. He never suffered hangovers, woke me up bright and early, holding a glass of orange juice, got me ready for school. Twelve years old and I was altogether a mess but not in any conventional way. I screwed up deep into myself, couldn't keep my teeth brushed, couldn't wear my clothes right, didn't like to have my hair trimmed, didn't smoke marijuana or do my homework, was terrified of girls, abstained from cigarettes and drinking, only broke things in my own room—kicked a hole in a wall, punched out panes of glass in windows four stories above the sidewalk, took a baseball bat to my own bed. I masturbated, nightly, staining my bedsheets, and in my fantasies I was tortured horribly by the sorts of women who model bathing suits for *Sports Illustrated*.

There was a terrifying moment in adolescence when the dean of my middle school called me into his office and asked if everything was all right at home. He told me all my teachers had gathered to talk about me. Miss Scheinholdt, Ms. Tucker, Dr. Krowl. I imagined them in a room, one after another, saying I had promise, but . . .

"The haggard masturbator," that's from *Lolita*. Family mythology has it that this dissolution of mine was essentially causeless. My older brother died; my father fell into his alcoholic wallow, and there I was, a mess. That rage, that destructive urge to smash things—at thirty-four I'm too old, I've lost it.

Tom introduced himself to me in a fruit store on Seventh Avenue—Seventh Avenue in Brooklyn, that is: clean, short, turn-of-the-century buildings, white people shopping with strollers and Labrador retrievers. I was buying lemons. He had no obligation to say hello, but Tom came straight up to me with an extended pink palm, no flinching. His lettuce-laden shopping basket swung behind him.

"I wanted to thank you," he said. "I wanted to apologize. For that night."

His face was soft as a plush pink eraser. He was bald and handsome and hearty. I'd heard on *Seinfeld* that one step in an alcoholic's recovery is to apologize to all those he's hurt, and I guessed it was my duty to shake hands and tell him there was nothing for which he had to be sorry.

"Yes," he insisted, his soft face grave, his voice carrying on in an authoritative stream. "You were very decent. I know you live right next door to us, and I wanted to introduce myself so that you wouldn't see me on the street and think, That louse, that terrible drunken clown. I've seen you around." Tom's voice had brass it had been missing that awful night by the subway station. He wore a loud Hawaiian shirt, a mathematician in summertime. "This is the first time I've gotten up the nerve to introduce myself. Tom Elsworth. We live in the building next door and I thought you thought I might be avoiding you. I see you, you know, when I go Rollerblading. I see you when I walk my dog."

Baffled, my hands weighing lemons, I said nothing but my own name. He kept his eyes on me and smiled, and on Tom's part this was work. He was building himself, right there, so as to erase any lingering image of the Tom Elsworth in the dark sweats with the beaky woman and the bottle on the pavement and the girl sprawled and semiconscious. He was renovating, so that none of that would exist, and I had a funny sense I could see the scaffolding and saws, all the work that went into sprucing up his image. "We're having a party tonight," he said, "you should come."

I dropped my fruit. The lemons bounced across the pink and white linoleum tiles, the sawdust on the grocery floor.

"Ten o'clock," he said. "Party time."

"H-how's your wife?"

"Alison." That was the first time I'd heard her name. "She's not my wife."

And though I was interested, I skipped the party. I heard sounds of it, across the air shaft but up a flight. When I went out, ten P.M., to buy myself a bottle of whiskey, I saw a pack I placed for incoming guests. Skinny men and long-haired women, shorts, skirts, dungarees, not quite hippies, not quite intellectuals, anything but stockbrokers, the sort of young people you associate with vaguely good works.

I was born a cripple and, relatively late in life, learned to walk. My brother was run over by a speedboat in the summertime. We were up in the Finger Lakes. I was at the Reisses' cottage next door. Mrs. Reiss saw the accident. I heard her scream as a dog's pained howl.

Recently, I did some work for an alliance of airline companies following a rash of crashes in the fall, and the CEOs and spokesmen, before Congress and news cameras, did what they could to assuage fears. I flew from Columbia, South Carolina, to Baton Rouge; Madison, Wisconsin, to Cheyenne. My luggage ran through X rays, across conveyor belts. I strode on moving sidewalks, past plate-glass windows, watched aircraft lurch and launch over asphalt fields. In lounges computers measured ambient din and set television volume accordingly. In rooms with lifetime-guaranteed carpeting and wood-veneered furniture, we served coffee and glazed doughnuts, sat hairstylists and bank tellers in front of consoles and monitors, showed them executives stammering into microphones, had them turn dials left and right. Our sample was a geographically spread group of consumers, indexed to age, race, gender, income, politics, leisure habits, education, likely resources for news, frequency of flying, size of family, travel budget, career. The team produced a forty-seven-page report with a nineteen-page index, as well as a one-hundred-and-fifty-four-minute video, the same twenty-two minutes of testimony replayed seven times, each video testimony sequence keyed to an overlaying graph, the graph displaying respondent reaction to each spokesperson's words and gestures.

If anyone ever gives you an argument that this sort of research is crap, believe every word. Companies adore the stuff, particularly their spokespeople—something about the massive artillery of technology and staff assuring them that the world cares a whit what they're saying. Ask me: The longing to fly is tied hopelessly to the longing to crash. Figure each word that's spoken over the intercom—flight attendants' warnings, captain's happy chatter—has been tested and approved. Formalized codes have been instilled in training seminars, the same regimen in courtesy parceled out to executives at Disney and security guards at the Met. The entire apparatus rests under one umbrella heading: Quality Control. There's constant effort toward inoffensive neutrality, and yet the resultant rhetoric and mold-injected plastic interiors lead to brutal fantasies of fucking and death. Stewardesses are the objects of sex fantasies. The mile-high club makes it in the john. Do you strongly disagree, disagree, agree, agree strongly?

These days I favor sweater vests and khaki pants, loafers and argyle socks. Recently, I've hired a woman to water my plants and vacuum my apartment. I'm only there a few weekends a month, but I like it neat. Work is difficult and I sometimes get testy. I prefer to travel alone. Ticket, driver's license, credit card, corporate ID. From hotel rooms I call my answering machine and find rambling messages from my dad. He is a mass of energy and rage, a sixty-nine-year-old retiree, a quiet drinker, less spectacular than in my youth. Pitching drunks have left gaps in his intelligence, and my father's rambles stall and bolt, an old train climbing a hill. He sends me letters filled with irrelevancies, back issues of magazines whose purpose I cannot decipher. I never mentioned those nights when I helped him to bed. I don't want a scene out of psychodramatic theater, the final confrontation between father and son. My suspicion is he has no memory, no idea.

I'd every intention of going to Tom's and Alison's until about nine that evening. Then I began imagining what might pass at such goings-on. Confident Tom in a bathroom helping Alison vomit, holding her back as her muscles spasmed. Those soft, pink, bearish hands. His mathematician's forearms beating a wall. Children of account executives performing scenes from Bukowski, domestically, for their friends. My life in my twenties wasn't so different than theirs. I failed out of three different colleges. There was a fair amount of marijuana—let's not get into it—other drugs, never heroin, nothing that bad. Lurching affairs with terrified women—Effie Paul, whose father had blown his brains out with a gun. You think your own tragedies are astounding. We're trained, I think, to make them monumental, the tales of our own making. I was lying in bed with Effie, the first night after we'd fucked, and I began in my stoned way to pontificate: Most folks, I ventured, hadn't seen the horrors of the world as I had. When I finished my ramble, Effie paused, and then haltingly made her own. The whimpering family dog, the blood on the carpet, her father in his study—alone, Effie found the corpse, brain dripping from the top, like a bottle of purple horseradish whose neck has shattered. The cruelty, for her, lies not so much in the suicide, but in those who made the tragedy her mother's, those who refused see the tragedy as her own.

This wide and universal theatre
Presents more woeful pageants than the scene
Wherein we play in.

That's Shakespeare.

Tom and Alison threw parties most weekends. This became clear sometime after he introduced himself in the grocery. I hadn't previously noticed the regular partying, or that it always came from the same spot across the air shaft. After meeting Tom in the fruit store, I gauged the shifts in their weekend moods by shifts in music, in volume, in ambient din. Low-key Miles Davis: I pictured one or two other couples, hashish, stir fries, ice cream for dessert. Before the last guest left, Alison would burst into tears. I imagined her standing in a corner of a room, bawling, flailing tense arms, forbidding Tom to touch her. He with pink palms open, demonstrating that he wasn't her monster. Other nights, I could hear peppy music, a couple of years out of date, serviceable party tunes, danger lurking beneath middle-class fun. Would she end up making a pass at a colleague or a friend, slurping a drunken tongue across Tom's cousin's beard? Self-immolation, mutual humiliation, they'd invite all their friends.

The third time I met Tom was on the train. We rode in from Manhattan together. Friday evening and he sat smack next to me, which is not polite among slight acquaintances in New York. At West Fourth Street, I was sitting alone, staring at a newspaper. The place beside me was empty. He took it.

"Tom," he said. "And you missed our party." They were having another one, that night.

He had a funny habit of tracing his tongue across his upper lip and he bobbed about, jolly-like, in his seat. He was working these days in the computer lab at NYU; his co-workers were great, a fun crew. His folks—he said "folks"—had a place on Deer Isle, Maine, and he and Alison were heading up there for Labor Day. His pits sweated in his pink, collared shirt. Sweat beaded across his forehead. Spectacles traced white lines in his flesh. His head didn't look to me like a plush pink eraser this time, or if it did, I was most conscious of the hard bone underneath. Most people would avoid a stranger like me, someone who happened to live nearby and had witnessed what had to be a moment of keen embarrassment, but not Tom Elsworth. That massive round cranium, he was beating me to death with it—motorboats and seals and good times up in the Maine ocean so cold only a lunatic would swim. I wanted to read my paper—the president, blow jobs, his wife—Tom wanted me to leer at his own sad, sick drama.

After Grand Street and Chinatown, the train buckled and burst up out of the ground, the Manhattan Bridge, long girders fashioning Xs, Ms, Ws, and Ns, the massive city at night. All the towers in midtown with their windows lit, work going on through dinnertime. We had chugged over Chinatown, and midriver you could see it all: the Brooklyn docks and tanks, power plants and refineries all busy with electric light.

"These parties," Tom said, as the subway pitched and the fluorescent lights flickered. "It's mostly Alison's idea and by now it's really taking on a life of its own. Every other weekend, and by now people know—it's great, really, great, I don't mind the setup, though cleanup can be a drag. We had to throw out a couch not too long ago, but hey. And the thing that's really great is more and more, I don't know most of the folks who come. I don't even have to do the inviting. Sometimes people show up on the wrong day, but, you know . . ." He was a chipper cipher, the beady eyes in the pink, padded face. "Alison, well, the drinking is a little bit heavy but—"

I raised a hand to quiet him. But no.

"She's just . . . unhappy, I guess." He was pushing his poor busted life at me like it was some badly baked pie. Tom was saying it to me, not in so many words, but clearly, *My life is out of control.* Maybe because I had witnessed it, seen him bottom out, and there was nothing he could lose with me— at least that's how I understood it then—he was saying it to me, right there on the train, *I am such a mess. . . .*

The train trundled underground and into darkness, and after DeKalb Avenue I caught my reflection in the black window—dashing tunnel light bulbs breaking up my view—but the jacket, the tie, the mustache. I was his elder. He was massive and pink and gesticulating beside me, but I looked like somebody's dad. We climbed out of the subway station, walked up Seventh Avenue, past the fruit store, and turned right. In front of his building I said the obvious.

"You live here?"

Tom snorted. "If you can call it living."

For a second I thought—hard to tell in the streetlight—

that behind his glasses his eyes were welling up, but then he smiled and darted up the steps. "I'll see you tonight?"

"Absolutely."

Crazy idea, but I wanted to see it: Tom and Alison's party from hell.

At home, I felt sick. There were four messages on my machine, my mother, twice, seeing if I was all right. My father, rallying me for a war with Iraq—caught up in some vision of heroic Jews, strapped like movie stars into jet planes, ready to bomb the hell out of the most dangerous villain the planet could offer. The other was my housekeeper, who said she was moving to Detroit. The plants were dry. I'd left dishes in the sink and there were mouse droppings in the kitchen.

Effie Paul had been through years and years of analysis. I hope that I can say, without bitterness, that if anybody needed it, she did—not because she was entirely crazy, but for what she had been through. Effie liked to rag me for my incommunicativeness, couldn't believe I was a Jew. So out of touch with my feelings, she said. Said I was posing as some midwestern invention of American manliness. Said that in the mirror, she and I looked like two immigrants right off the boat. Wide-faced like my grandmother, tough as hell. Smart. I'll admit straight out, I couldn't take the pressure: her constant desire to know me. Tell me a secret, she'd say, the two of us alone in bed. Every night, that's what she wanted, more than lovemaking, another secret. I was to confess who I am.

Effie had one room on East Sixth Street, one flight above an Indian restaurant, six locks on the door, bathtub catty-corner to the stove. Her bedclothes perfumed with curry, whiffs of coriander and tumeric in her morning hair. We slept in a biriani of odors, luscious basmati rice. I'd find cockroaches in my shoes before I left. Nothing to be done, life above a big-city restaurant, they'd crawl across the pillows of her bed. Effie's place was decorated in beads and unframed photographs. She'd painted the floor a hideous shade of green. A long, tasseled curtain sectioned the bed from the rest of the room. The futon lay on the floor, covered with pillows of all shapes. With magic chalk she'd bought in Chinatown, Effie drew lines around the mattress. This was to keep us safe from vermin.

"Tell me a secret." She believed in Tarot cards and astrology and that drug companies were importing flus from Asia in order to keep their sales high. She'd graduated from Yale, treasured her Djuna Barnes, her Céline, her H.D. She wrote poetry, worked as a waitress (paperbacks in every corner of the little room, typewriter on her kitchen table)—what the hell were we doing with our lives?

"A secret," I'd say.

She was insatiable, wanted particular masturbatory fantasies, adolescent desires. She would let loose a prize of her own—her heart an ocean trawler, dragging nets through childhood, dredging for glimpses of her father. He called her Gin, from the back end of Ephiginea, stroked her small hand when she suffered the flu, said, "Oh, oh, darling Gin," told her how awful to him was her pain. The man swung from rage to contrition. When Effie told me she feared for her own tendencies toward suicide, I would shut my eyes to it. "Please," I told her, with a hand up. "Please."

"Men should be as they seem," that's Iago, and who won't agree with him? Effie's married now, to a blond poet who tends to destitute schizophrenics. She was short-legged but cute, had a funny walk, almost a waddle. When I see anything like it—doesn't matter where the hell I am, Massapequa, Charlotte, Boulder, Taos—there's a surge in my gut and I hope it's her.

Before the party, I did something I do infrequently. I had a drink to steady my nerves, two fingers of whiskey in a juice glass. I chewed a stick of gum and rinsed my mouth with Scope. Killing time, jittering about my apartment, trying to make things right: I watered the plants, I washed the dishes, I wiped up the mouse shit from around the stove. Phone calls to return, I dialed the two-one-two of my parents' number, but hung up quickly. From next door, I could hear sounds of the party. What was Tom doing in there? A watchful eye on his girlfriend? Could he open the door to the bathroom and find her sucking a colleague off? Soft pink Tom, staggering from the bathroom toward the bar, fixing himself a drink. He'd stay up with her, late at night, to make sure she didn't choke on vomit.

Before I left, I swallowed a second whiskey. I didn't leave until after eleven o'clock, and if I was worn from traveling and drink, I didn't know it.

Tom and Alison's, top of the stairs: Two heavyset guys pushed at each other like young bulls. In the little rooms, knots of people joined in heated, laughing discussion. No one I knew, no one I'd ever seen, all of them younger than I. At a table in the living room sat a comprehensive display of liquor bottles, sliced citrus, and a bowl of ice. A lanky girl was hilarious, had commandeered the bar as her station. "Angelee specials," she cried. She was long-faced, strangely middle-aged just past twenty. "I'm servin' Angelee specials." I asked for a ginger ale. Disappointed, she splashed vodka over the ice in my cup. "What are you, anyway?" She said it like we were at a costume party.

Don't get the wrong impression: I wasn't going there just

to see them ruined. Tom was an ass but there was a sweetness about him. And it was interesting: this crashing failure, this crazy display. I wanted to see how he spoke of it. More than that, I wanted, I hoped that if I could—not *tell* Tom, but somehow *imply* my own—I don't know; I wanted some bond, not just to watch him, I wanted intimacy. But I got piss-ass drunk that night.

I looked around for Tom, but found Alison, deep in conversation in the apartment's quietest room, vastly more beautiful than I'd remembered her. I suppose that shouldn't come as a shock. To see her in a dress, with her hair washed and pinned, she looked a lot better than she had drunk and sprawled across a sidewalk, and even then she'd looked all right. She was taller than I'd imagined, and joined by two almost equally beautiful women. They unfurled skinny arms, shifted weight from hip to hip. "*Totally* on the make—*that* guy—know what I mean?" The room bulged with sweat, perfume, and sound.

"Tom invited me," I interrupted them. "I'm the neighbor."

Alison had no idea. She was sloppy drunk, a drink in one hand, her gray eyes bleary but joyful, and she said that her boyfriend was up on the roof. She offered, as a puckish afterthought, a martini. I declined, but she insisted. Janica—whoever that was—had made martinis, she said. They were fab. Her friends all laughed. I laughed with them. Alison raised a hand in the air. She wouldn't take no. She pressed her plastic cup to my lips, spilled her drink across my chin, dribbled it down my neck.

"Oh—I'm so—I'm so, I apologize." But it was expressed with hilarity, with confidence in her own charms. She touched my shoulder, bracelets gliding on her arm. "I am sorry, I am—"

"Oh, it's fine." I disapproved of her.

"Did you—did you like the martini?" Her eyes widened, petulant and puppyish.

"My tie," I said. "Enjoyed it quite a bit." But, conciliatory, I took a deep swallow, finished off her drink. One of the girls applauded.

There were two options then: to head out into the night, home alone and to bed—I'd already had too much to drink, it would ruin me for Sunday—or to climb up a ladder and out onto the roof and see Tom. I hesitated in the front hall-way. I was going to leave: This was just kids having fun, nothing like what I'd wanted to see. But then Alison came up behind me, not following me but looking for someone else. She pointed the direction to the ladder to the roof. I didn't want to play the idiot further and so climbed. The alcoholic blur had set in—two and a half whiskeys at home, the vodka and soda downstairs, the half martini on top. I had trouble with the little ladder, my feet slipped on the black metal rungs. The scene under the stars appeared easier, more spa-cious than the one downstairs. A portable machine blared Mexican music. Tom held court in a corner, surrounded by three young men, laughing and hearty. I jammed my hands in my pockets. This wasn't at all what I'd come for. Despair, lurking offstage, seemed temporarily written out of the drama.

Tom saw me, clasped me heartily by the shoulder, glasses glowing disks in the night, and he gestured, beyond his mathematical friends, to a garbage can of ice and green-bottled beer. I had one, figured what the hell. I came back to the circle of Tom's friends and laughed with them. Someone told a story about ice fishing, falling through the ice. I sup-pose I drank quickly, just out of nervousness, sucking my beer. One of Tom's pals, I believe his name was Andy, headed off toward the garbage pail, saying, "Who needs more?" Tom told everyone that I did.

"Won't you even give me time to swallow my own spit?" That's what Job asks, his most reasonable, outraged demand. I know you're not supposed to mix liquors, but the mixing isn't what makes you lose control. They say infidelity never broke up a marriage, alcohol never drove a man to despair; it's the demons that precede the drinking or stray fucking, and those things lie deep. The affair on the roof had been mostly masculine, the one downstairs ruled by the girls. But about halfway through my third beer, the women began climbing the stairway, their dresses caressed by breezes.

What I remember, what I don't—one thing is for sure, there's more of the latter than the former. I felt large and spectacular, absolutely aglow, but as I fumble back, I know I was shouting. I can remember the force of my breath, my tongue beating against the insides of my teeth, the way my throat got sore. I went on about conferences, fucking in hotel rooms, fucking in bathrooms, fucking in elevators. I hope I said nothing about Effie Paul, but I fear that I did. "Once I went out with this girl and she said she'd kill herself if I dumped her." Was this boy talk, or did this talk go on with women? I can't remember. There was conversation about fashion—what do I know about fashion?—something about my jacket and tie. I remember taking my tie off and tossing it over the side of the building. This seemed to grant me good audience, and I remember taking off my jacket, too, whipping it as a stripper would above my head, and then hurling it out onto Berkeley Street. I remember Alison, clutching herself with laughter and wide-eyed schoolgirl glee. "Oh, my God! Oh, *my* God!" I remember crouching on my hands and knees in a corner of the roof and puking.

I remember, vaguely, Tom taking me home, gathering my clothes from the street. My keys were miraculously still in my jacket pocket. Tom walked me up the steps to my apartment, walked me into my place. He wiped off my face, let me puke again in the bathroom, put me on my bed, unbuttoned my shirt, took off my pants, slipped off my briefs. He scrubbed my face, held a washcloth and a basin of warm water. Though I remember this clearly, in retrospect it's a bad dream. I was like a baby in bed, and Tom ran his hand over my limp, drunken dick, like a falconer ruffling the feathers of his bird, up and down, just once, ineffectually. Then—and I'm sure of it—he slipped a pink digit up my ass. God knows what possessed him. There I was, vulnerable stranger. I don't think I protested, just lay there on my bed. I see myself squint-eyed and swollen-faced and barely able to talk. He was so sweet, so caring, the secret pink sadist. His little gambit at molestation was almost an afterthought.

The next day, around noon, Tom called. "You alive?" he asked, chipper. "Quite a time there last night, Buddy-O. Wouldn't have pegged you for it. Alison says you come to every party, from now on."

I groaned.

"Come over, if you can make it. We'll take care of you. Feel responsible for your condition, pal."

I dropped the receiver, disconnected the call. Then I lurched out of the bed, guts swimming. I tried to wrangle my throbbing mind around the events of the night. Tom wasn't half so busted-up as I'd previously thought. I made a guess: He had bought the bottle that night Alison drank herself to the verge of death. Maybe he hadn't emptied it down her throat, but he was the one conscious and clearheaded at the end of the night, and he'd been with her the whole time.

Before I'd played stripper, had Tom egged me on? Gotten me drinks? Drawn a crowd around me? I think I remember that he had.

"Buddy?" he said, the second time he called. "You okay?" For a second time, I hung up on him. Was it because I'd seen her smashed on the sidewalk? Because I'd been interested? Was that why he went after me? On the edge of tub, I rubbed my sore temples. I tried to puke, but nothing came up. I drew myself a bath. I had been so focused on pink Tom—Tom as the man in misery—but now I saw Alison. No matter what passed in their parties, Tom kept control, masterfully. She obliterated large portions of her brain.

My phone rang again, when I was dizzy and toweling off and drinking coffee. It was Tom, still full of the heartiness of the day. He wanted me to come over. There was nothing I could say. I knew that if I began talking about abuse, he'd just start laughing. "Sure, guy. Sure." The night behind us seemed a dark, strange dream.

I hung up on him a third time, but fifteen minutes later, he appeared at my door—worried, maybe, or just faking it. Alison was with him and she worked as a kind of social armor. What could I say in front of her? Tom played up an almost fatherly concern. "You can't take care of yourself, buddy, not in this state. Come over."

"Please?" Charming Alison smiled, her head tilted to one side.

And I did. She scrambled up some eggs. We had mild Bloody Marys, hair of the dog. I chewed slowly, was able to hold the food down. It was a long, loose morning spent with the *Times*. Tom sat on the floor beside me, his funny pink head by my knees. Alison sat some yards away, on a cane chair at a wood table, their shaggy black mutt, Arthur, curled at her feet. Tom kissed Alison, long and passionately, each time he got up for a new glass of water. Late afternoon, I helped them sponge and mop their place. Alison did the bathroom, which stank. I wasn't the only guest who had vomited. She had, too. Tom laughed almost approvingly. He vacuumed. With a spray bottle of oil soap, I cleaned tabletops and bookshelves. Monday came, and I took a plane to Tulsa.

I've been back several times now, whenever I'm in town and they're having a party. I show up and don't meet too many people. Sometimes I have a beer, but mostly I watch. Tom looks at me with a knowing smile; he thinks he's got my number. No one there seems to have anything substantial to say. That's what a party is, I guess. Dionysus, god of wine, is also the god of theater. I'm not a good social mingler, but they have the sorts of affairs where you don't have to do much in order to feel part of the show. Sometimes people ask me how I know Tom and Alison. I tell them that I live next door. This isn't, I'll admit, the best answer—not the answer people really want to hear. Friends of theirs from work, from high school, from college, from graduate school, even people who've met them at other parties shy away from me. In their eyes, I suppose, I'm the lonely older guy who has nothing better to do with his weekend nights than hang around at his neighbors' apartment, sipping water, and looking in on younger people's fun. I've seen Tom, from a corner, point at me and whisper. At these parties, he blooms. Alison, with her pretty, flighty desperation, makes me uneasy. I'll pass her at the drink table and she'll wave a hand in the air, a little hint of striptease.

I called my father recently, the anniversary of my brother's death. He was up in Cape Cod; since my brother's death, we avoid the Finger Lakes. We talked about Philip Roth's latest novel, the strange warmth of this past winter. I'm working with a fast-food chain, right now, test-marketing pies. In focus groups, we sit respondents around a white, ovoid table. On one wall is a mirrored window. Video cameras film the scene. We discuss the crispness of crust, attractive shades of golden brown, the firmness of fruit, sweetness, tartness, warmth. Behind the mirrored window sit executives and note-takers. People lend us their yearnings and these we exploit, the better to serve them in the future.

Summertime, the speedboat humps the waves. Ripples off its wake buff the shore. My brother's is an easy, confident backstroke, something that as a ten-year-old I envy. He's got plugs in his ears. He's susceptible to infection. I'm playing with checkers indoors, me and Joe Reiss. We're pretending the plastic disks are space ships; they can fly. The boat drivers are Pakistani teens, drinking their second Sunday beers. The motor grinds. Mrs. Reiss howls. I mistake her cry for the panic of a dog.

THE DEAD FIDDLER, 5E

1.

What happened was this: Dr. Lenzner suffered a crisis of faith. He stopped believing in talking cures, dismissed outright the work of Freud. The crisis arrived in waves of night waking, three A.M. anxieties.

"They are praying to me," the psychiatrist told his wife as he stared at the dark ceiling. "They expect some kind of sorcery——"

"Nonsense, Seymour," said Ms. Feibish-Lenzner, sleepy-eyed. "You give them what they want, what they need, no less. And the rates are reasonable. So rest."

But her practical thinking did little to assuage Dr. Lenzner's worries. He worked his practice hollowly, nodded at each analysand, and said, "I see," or, "What comes to mind?" And hating himself at the end of each day, he sought solace. Where? Kundalini yoga. Rolfing. Vegan cuisine. Even, in the end, the local synagogue, a fact which worried Ms. Feibish-Lenzner terribly. A nervous woman, she feared for her husband's business—imagined that he would betray his beliefs, dispense halakic commentary in the secular arena of his practice. The gentiles might stand for this, she reasoned, but the Jews?

Dr. Lenzner saw his patients in a small room beside the kitchen in apartment 5E. Where in decades past a dumb-waiter had risen, there was now a hollow between the office and the dishwasher, and it was possible through this cavity to eavesdrop on the dreams and worries of those who lay on the doctor's couch. The first time Ms. Feibish-Lenzner crept to the kitchen expressly to listen in on Dr. Lenzner's business, she did so in order to assure herself that he said nothing mad, that he scared away no patients, and what she heard was a sense of unease, as if all of them knew the doctor's mind was elsewhere. So when in his midnight hysteria her husband next tossed in bed and woke her, she offered up a simple plan: She would work with him, attend secretly to his patients, and then on discreet index cards outline suggestions for what he might say to each. In this way she would ease her husband's burden and leave him to attend to his spiritual needs. So it came to pass that Anna Feibish-Lenzner, Phi Beta Kappa, Radcliffe '59, ABD in sociology at Yale, some-time volunteer for left-wing causes (West Way no, Ruth Messenger yes), VP of the co-op board, maintainer of the family finances (otherwise unemployed), sat daily in a pants suit, sipping blended herbal tea and writing in the margins of the *Nation* and *New York* magazine thoughts that ought to have been her husband's.

Mornings before work and evenings after, Dr. Lenzner jogged up to the Jewish Theological Seminary on 123rd Street and pored over the Gemara, the Annotations and Commentaries, the Midrash and the Zohar. He worked with rabbis and graduate students. This went on from February to April, and Ms. Feibish-Lenzner was mortified late that spring when he started to close his office early on Fridays, when he refused on Sabbath to answer phones, ride the ele-vator, fry an egg, or tear toilet paper from a roll. She forbade him from wearing a yarmulke while working—it would scare patients away—but the doctor grew his beard. He donned his prayer shawl and phylacteries daily and though he bobbed and prayed beside a big-screen Hitachi TV, he looked like one of the ancients. He had a high forehead, and under shaggy brows eyes that combined the sharp glance of the scholar with the humility of a God-fearing man. Ms. Feibish-Lenzner, red-haired, a head taller than her husband, and still good-looking, trembled, but her husband's silent religiosity endowed him with an aura of wisdom palpable to his patients, and as his faith in his own abilities dwindled, his practice grew. Leading editors and intellectuals, musicians, sculptors, and actresses came to 5E to unburden themselves. Their stories of raging fathers, of peculiar sexual obsessions, of nagging phobias, these wafted through the space where the dumbwaiter once rode, and in the kitchen, Anna Feibish-Lenzner scrawled in the margins of her magazines, "Valium for this one," or, "Just keep him talking, nothing wrong here." She knew it was not her advice that attracted their devotion, but the doctor's world-weary person, the comic sadness of his face. Confident and strong in the confines of 5E, Anna Feibish-Lenzner grew increasingly guarded socially. No more dinner parties, no invitations accepted. She never went out with Seymour. And when before summer he asked permission not to accompany her and their lovely daughter Jessica out to their place in Sag Harbor (he wanted to head to the Catskills, a small community equipped with cheder and shul), Ms. Feibish-Lenzner granted his leave happily. August, she lay on a striped blanket, sipping bottled water under the cerulean sky, the crash of waves around her, the cries of children, cracked open a Coppertoned eyelid, and admired the sand-caked arch of her daughter's foot. Maybe, she thought, this will all turn out for the best. If she could just hang on until both kids got through college, then the practice, the apartment, the marriage could all go.

But September came. Young Jonathan Lenzner, a prince who suffered terrible allergies, back from a summer playing tennis abroad, packed his trunk, shipped off a box of books, and headed to Princeton for his junior year, happy to flee his ever more nutty family. That same morning, without his wife's knowledge, Dr. Lenzner donned a skullcap for work. He had been wearing one all summer up in Spetonak, and such was the implicit orthodoxy of his carriage, the religious devotion inscribed in the lines of his face, that Ms. Feibish-Lenzner, going over the morning patients with him, didn't notice. In fact, it took three weeks for anyone to remark on his yarmulke, and when a patient finally did, it was because she thought confusedly that Dr. Lenzner with his skullcap was somehow hatless. This was a joke at which the analyst and analysand chortled together, one of the few times that Dr. Lenzner was able to reveal his true self while posing in his professional capacity, but as soon as he laughed he thought with a shudder of his terribly perceptive wife across the way: What would Anna make of his laughter? What if she laughed in turn? He touched his skullcap, ran his hand across his beard.

By strange coincidence, the day that Dr. Lenzner's kippah was discovered was the day that Ozzie Beller, his daughter's boyfriend, caught the cold and infection that killed him. An itch in Ozzie's throat became a raging fever. His temperature rose from 103° to 107° and when finally he got to St. Luke's, it was too late. At his funeral teenage girls embraced, rubbing tight-fitting dresses. The boys, usually so full of zits and sexual energy, seemed subdued and infantile with their dark suits and pale, stunned faces. All the kids were demonstrative in their mourning except for lovely Jessica. Stripped translucent with grief, she did not stir or speak. Nor did she cry as the coffin was lowered into the ground. And when she came home from the burial and her parents helped her to her room, her face seemed a mask behind which there was nothing—not the girl who this year was to edit the school literary magazine, nor the one who in her first try had scored fifteen-seventy on the SATs. And in Ozzie Beller's death, Dr. Lenzner did not see random calamity. He recognized the hand of the Lord. He would have said, just one year earlier in his clean-shaven days when he saw himself as a man of science, that it was preposterous to assume in a universe of billions of human lives that the Lord would focus on him— Seymour Albert Lenzner, M.D., Ph.D.—and would in response to his smallest action take the life of a young man. Lenzner would have located such belief in a childish egotism whose religiosity was simply a continuation of the infantile narrative, with God playing the part of the stern parent. But now bearded mystical Lenzner, after saying his midnight prayers, shook.

October came. The leaves turned in Riverside Park, and tumbled down along the playgrounds by the drive. Schoolchildren frolicked and homeless, psychopathic veterans stared, their eyes bleary with gin and crack cocaine. Soon would come the season for standardized testing and lovely Jessica was going to miss the opportunity to apply to colleges early. Horace Mann was understanding, thought perhaps the girl should take a semester off. But her mother was less so, and felt that Yale might not want the kind of student who after the death of a boyfriend fell to pieces. Now it was she who woke after midnight, eyes wide with visions of her daughter's failure. Robe tied tight and face shining with moisturizer, she went to the back of the apartment and there saw lovely Jessica, cross-legged in the middle of her room, singing softly and rereading the storybooks of her childhood, *Stuart Little, Charlotte's Web.*

Clothes disappeared from the corners of Ms. Feibish-Lenzner's closets, and when in despair, she dashed from her husband's practice to peer at the now-melancholy view of 89th Street, she saw her daughter walking toward the park wearing flowing paisley outfits with bell-bottoms and frills. Lovely Jessica was regressing. At seventeen, when she should have been bursting with aspirations, infatuations, and lusts, she was dawdling back to a second childhood—was in her mourning full of whims and fancies. She did not allow herring or radishes to be mentioned in her presence and averted her eyes from the neatly packed chicken in the refrigerator. Once, she found a fly in her breakfast cereal and then would not eat for the rest of the day. Ms. Feibish-Lenzner phoned her daughter's oldest friends, hoping to draw them close to the girl in her time of grief, but lovely Jessica had grown altogether too strange. On the day, for instance, that Abigail Pererra was to visit, she abstained from eating all morning, afraid she would puke at the sight of Abbie's face. In sadness and bewilderment, Ms. Feibish-Lenzner longed to turn to her husband, but what had once been her Seymour was now a shell of a man. With his long gray beard, his skullcap sitting high on his distinguished head, he was, from the outside, a picture of pompous rectitude. But Ms. Feibish-Lenzner knew it, even his Judaism had become skewed. Up in the seminary on 123rd Street, he sobbed, he confessed horrible crimes, and in his office, when meeting patients, he would read off the cards his wife had given him, but would silently mouth the Yom Kippur prayers. Every day for Dr. Lenzner was the Day of Atonement. He ate a single meal, exactly at sundown.

Halloween approached. Ms. Feibish-Lenzner woke at night to see her husband silhouetted against the bedroom window wrapped in his punishing all-night Judaism and from the back room heard her daughter sobbing in the dark, crying out not for her dead boyfriend or for her fearsome mother, but for water. It was as though a fire were raging within Jessica, consuming everything. She drank water by the gallon and Ms. Feibish-Lenzner had to replenish her supply every day, toting cartfuls back from Red Apple. Sweating from the trip home, unpacking the big plastic jugs, she found her husband pacing nervously, examining notes for the day. The weight of her burdens nearly broke the woman. She suffered terrible visions: Her daughter might run outside and stand in the way of a truck, she might traipse into the very room in which Dr. Lenzner saw patients—Ms. Feibish-Lenzner had the super affix a padlock to the hallway in the back of the apartment and stowed her daughter safely away. A temporary measure, she assured herself, just until things calmed down, but it came to pass that while she sat in the kitchen, trying to listen to stories of other people's worries, her daughter screamed and pounded on the locked door. Anna Feibish-Lenzner was overwhelmed. Tears obscured her notes. The *Times'* magazine tumbled to the floor, and she found herself unable to retrieve it. Mornings, after he returned from synagogue, the doctor looked to her for his index cards, and she handed them to him blank. Either he did not notice their blankness or there was nothing to say. Lenzner sat silently through the sessions with his patients, nodding, keeping time to his private prayers.

The practice flourished still. Dr. Lenzner's sleeplessness etched fierce lines in his face. Under the weight of constant atonement, his beard grew gray, his hair turned white. Film moguls flew cross-country to visit. Their limousines dropped them at the unprepossessing building on West 89th Street; they gave their names to our doorman, rode the little push-button elevator to the fifth floor; Ms. Feibish-Lenzner, unable now to comb her hair or dress herself stylishly, let them in and led them to the doctor, and there, in a tiny room by an Upper West Side kitchen, they came face-to-face with a sage.

"Yes! Yes!" one screamed. "It was not that my mother did not sufficiently love me, but that I never loved my mother!"

An article appeared in "The Talk of the Town," describing but not naming the Upper West Side shrink in whom the media elite invested the power of miracle. Ms. Feibish-Lenzner knew what we, her neighbors, understood: that the Lenzner apartment, which heads of Hollywood studios and even (clandestinely) some European ministers of state had seen as their Mecca of mental health, was in fact Bedlam. Kevin MacMichaelman, Zev Grubin, and I, stealing into Central Park on Thanksgiving night, saw lovely Jessica wandering Sheep's Meadow, collecting fallen leaves. We called to her—red-haired, sparrow-breasted, the most beautiful girl we knew—and then assumed she was deaf. Rumors spread: She was dabbling in magic. Among the senior class at Horace Mann her name became a synonym for unlucky. Her princely, adenoidal brother Jonathan, out in college in New Jersey, had a conversation in which the words Jessica Lenzner were used in just that way, but after he bridled, he quickly calmed, and assumed that he must have misheard.

2.

December came. The pipes in our building were declared suspect. Plumbers cut holes in walls. The elevator floor was covered with a dropcloth and all day workmen rode up and down carrying drills and saws and sections of filth-encrusted drain. The super assembled the aluminum Christmas tree, also set out a plastic menorah, also hung a sign that read *Happy Holidays*, gold-trimmed red letters strung together above the lobby mirror. Tree salesmen brought in pines from New England, and the needles perfumed Upper Broadway. Ms. Feibish-Lenzner was not surprised when, December twenty-second, after his evening prayers, her husband announced his resolution—he was going to give up his practice and deliver himself into a life of religious devotion. What surprised her was the care he had taken for his family.

Dr. Lenzner explained that he had agreed to sell his apartment—together with his office and the recommendation that his patients continue their therapy with the buyer—to a Dr. Henry Morgenbesser of West 103rd Street, a tenured professor at Columbia, and the best-selling author of *How to Reclaim Yourself from Your Past*. Lenzner, speaking fluently but emphatically, almost as if performing a stage speech or a sermon, proposed to give his wife the entirety of the proceeds from the sale, a small fortune, really, all that money together with the house in Sag Harbor, so long as she would agree to one condition of their divorce. The condition concerned their daughter, the lovely Jessica. Dr. Lenzner demanded that she never return to Horace Mann, that she give up her plans for college and all her former ambitions. He proposed that she move to Brooklyn with him, that she see a psychiatrist for her grieving and a rabbi's daughter for her religious training. Furthermore, he surprised his wife by announcing, he had brought a photograph of his daughter with him in his journeys out to Williamsburg, and had arranged a marriage for her. The prospective bridegroom was one Shmelke Motl, a scholar. Dr. Lenzner would not, of course, marry off his daughter without his wife's consent, he told her, but if she refused to consent, he would not sell to Morgenbesser; there would be no money at hand.

If she refused to give her consent, Dr. Lenzner said—and here his strange detached voice did not take on any fury, but rather became more detached, almost as if it were not his voice at all and had no relation to his features—if she refused to give her consent, they would continue with things exactly as they were. Heads of corporations and of motion picture studios would visit Dr. Lenzner, he would sit in his office reciting silent prayers of atonement, she would be in the kitchen, no longer keeping notes, but sobbing. And their daughter would remain locked in the back of the house, drinking endless gallons of water.

It was just past the winter solstice, a Sunday, five o'clock and gloomy. Ms. Feibish-Lenzner sat on their unmade bed. She looked at the bookshelves in the bedroom—her husband's Freud, Buber, Nabokov, and Kafka. Seymour Lenzner had once been of her culture, but now (there was no use pretending) he was gone. She looked at her husband, a bearded eccentric all dressed in unkempt black, and there was no sign of the vigorous, Cornell-trained intellectual she had married. His offer lay before her and in it she saw what she could only call the handiwork of the devil. She imagined herself in Sag Harbor, a wealthy divorcée, ready to start life all over again. In the mirror behind her husband she saw her reflection—beneath her sorrow and exhaustion, she was still vigorous. It wouldn't be a bad life. All she would have to do was disown her only daughter.

"And Jonathan's Princeton tuition?" she asked.

"I would do my best to cover that," her husband intoned—or was it a voice from behind him, somehow speaking through him?

Just then the lovely Jessica began beating on the locked

door to the back of the apartment, screaming for water, screaming for mercy. Dr. Lenzner withdrew to fetch her drink. Ms. Feibish-Lenzner fell back on the bed, sobbing.

She thought over her husband's proposal and realized she had nothing with which to bargain. Unemployed, penniless, powerless, she was all those things her feminist friends had told her a woman could be, and worse, a failed mother— without an idea of how to save her daughter beyond the vague notion of committing the girl to psychiatric care, a notion already comprehended in her husband's plans. Unable to think on her own, she would have called a friend, perhaps my mother, Mimi Birnbaum, whom she had so assiduously been avoiding, and tried to talk over her position, but she could not imagine where such a conversation would begin. There was too much madness to confess. Ms. Feibish-Lenzner cried to the ceiling as her husband had done on so many anxious nights, and realized that all this time when she had thought her husband and daughter mad, she had been as crazy as either of them. Tears brimmed over and fell on the bedspread. She sobbed at the thought of her lovely Jessica as the shaven-headed wife of one—what did her husband call him?—Shmelke Motl. And yet who was she, she who had mishandled her husband's breakdown so spectacularly, who had for her own daughter indulged in techniques for the treatment of mental illness borrowed straight from *Jane Eyre*, who was she to say that Dr. Seymour Albert Lenzner, therapist to Nobel Laureate novelists and leaders of the world's powers, who was she to say to him that he didn't know what was best? Her husband's solution to the affair was at least graceful, and left everyone attended to and comfortable. Again, she saw herself alone in the beach house in Sag Harbor, freed from the entanglements of the past months— a new Anna Feibish-Lenzner, maybe just Anna Feibish again. But the very tempting quality of this vision compelled her to argue against it.

If she were to give in to her husband's plans, she would simply be sacrificing her daughter's happiness for her own. Yet, hadn't she been doing that all along, simply without acknowledgment? And could she be certain that her grief-wracked daughter, having suffered both a mental breakdown and her own parents' cruel response—could she be certain that the lovely Jessica would ever recover? Head on to Yale? Become the cardiothoracic surgeon she had once hoped to be? Ms. Feibish-Lenzner could not imagine any such thing. But she could with the help of a dark, selfish voice in the back of her head envision the lovely Jessica becoming enraptured by the rituals of religious life. Perhaps a set of rigid laws and duties was exactly what the girl required. And in the Williamsburg life that Dr. Lenzner proposed, she would be tended to by not simply a psychotherapist but also a rabbi, a husband, a father. Was it simply her own anti-Semitism that rejected this picture? Each week, she could take the Jitney in from Sag Harbor to visit, help Jessica tend house and raise Shmelke Motl's several children.

But to play her daughter like that would be a betrayal of everything in her life and education and history. For what had her parents come to this country? So their granddaughter could live the ghetto life of her great-grandparents? In the same costumes, with Crown Heights project toughs to take the place of marauding Polish peasants? When her husband came back to the bedroom, his forearms and face covered with his daughter's fierce scratches, Ms. Feibish-Lenzner was curled in a ball at the head of the bed, shuddering.

"Well?" he asked, head hanging low.

"I agree to everything, God help me. Everything." She

shut her eyes and opened them, blinking away tears. "Just let me visit her, Seymour. Let me see her every once in a while."

"Of course."

"And what's more," she started, "I would like to have a week with her. A week with my daughter in the apartment, before this marriage to your Hasidic friend. Is that too much to ask?"

"Not at all," said the doctor.

The bedroom around them, their books, their posters, the wardrobe that had been built for them, it all seemed then a set of ruins, monuments to their wrecked marriage. Dr. Lenzner pulled out a prayer book, a prayer shawl, and his phylacteries. Then he brought his daughter to the living room and, with Ms. Feibish-Lenzner lurking behind him, described for the lovely Jessica her prospective husband. Shmelke Motl was small and dark. He did not look like much, but had the head of a genius. Because he was an orphan, the householders provided his meals; he ate at a different home every day of the week. The lovely Jessica listened without a word.

When Dr. Lenzner left for the Jewish Theological Seminary, where he now was an unwelcome guest, Ms. Feibish-Lenzner ran out to Zabar's and came home with her daughter's favorite childhood meal: kasha varnishkes and pot roast with gravy. The lovely Jessica rocked over the plate as if it were a prayer book. Soon afterward, she retired to her room. Ms. Feibish-Lenzner, exhausted from the day, crawled off to bed. Dr. Lenzner, as soon as he returned from his last trip to the conservative Harlem synagogue, slipped in beside her.

At midnight, he was sleeping while Ms. Feibish-Lenzner, trapped in misgivings, listened to the sounds of night—the sirens and car radios. She watched the beams of headlights pass across her room from east to west, in the opposite direction of traffic. She heard the mewing of cats in the alleyway, the wandering shouts of degenerates. She hoped to hear her daughter slip from her prison, to hear her flee down the fire escape, hoped that, if on this night her daughter should escape her room, she would leave and never return.

Half in dream, she imagined the lovely Jessica, beautiful and mad, running down through the three tiers of Riverside Park, across the West Side Highway to the wide Hudson, and then following the river upward through Westchester and Putnam Counties, Dutchess, Columbia, Rensselaer, and then from Albany to Buffalo, all the way across the state, past the Finger Lakes, out to the Great Lakes, Erie, Huron, Superior. Bundled like a pioneer trapper against the Minnesota winter, her daughter would press on fiercely through North Dakota—if she could score fifteen-seventy on the SAT, if she could handle academic pressure at Horace Mann, and still set records, *sophomore* year, for the cross-country team, she could do this—her beautiful, brilliant daughter could follow the Marias River in Montana, up to Glacier National Park, right to the border of Canada, far as far could be from her crazy parents.

But that was not to be. Shmelke Motl awaited.

The clock's glowing green digits shifted from 1:59 to 2:00. The betrothal contract was already drawn up, ready to be signed. She had bargained for the extra days so that her son could come home. She had harbored hopes that Jonathan would act as their deliverer, that he could see where they had all gone wrong and release them from their folly and save her lovely daughter. But now when she thought of Jonathan out in Princeton she thought of him living a life far distant from hers. Princeton, just across the river, a little more than an hour's drive away, seemed now miles removed from her grasp. At a quarter past two, she decided that she would never burden Jonathan, that she would call him and tell him not to come home. "Stay away! It's all madness here!" At two-thirty, her mind twisted by doubts and fears and anguish, it seemed imperative that she call him. She had no expectations. She planned to scream at him: "Your father is a danger to you! I am a danger to you! Stay away! Stay away!" But when a voice came from the other end of the line, Ms. Feibish-Lenzner realized that she was telephoning another universe. She heard a girl's laughter in the background. The voice—Jonathan's?—was drunk and smoke-burned.

"Yo?"

And Ms. Feibish-Lenzner slammed down the phone. The single syllable, "Yo?," could have been just about any stoned and boozy nineteen-year-old in the country—black, Jewish, Puerto Rican, whatever—the vocal cords slathered up by sex and drugs and sleepiness, yet she was sure the voice was her baby's. Also, she recognized the erotic quality of the background laughter. Her son was fucking some chippie, right then.

Ms. Feibish-Lenzner imagined Jonathan and his nude friend under a poster for some rock and roll band, the room full of incense and marijuana smoke, a bottle of Jack Daniel's and (she hoped) a box of condoms by the bed. And she believed suddenly that her phone call had played into some kinky game. This girl was up above her Jonathan, maybe he was handcuffed to the bed, and this thin, blond poopsie, her breasts young and high and firm, had held the phone to him while they fucked, and at the click of the broken line, Jonathan had kept talking, playing.

"Hi, Mom," he'd say.

And the girl's mouth would drop into an outraged O.

"Oh, yeah, nothing much"—Jonathan smirking to this girl and speaking to no one—"just screwing Kelly Traynor. Oh, she's great. Supple and giggling."

Kelly, wagging a naughty finger, would catch on. "Let me talk to her." She'd ride Jonathan up and down, she'd bring the phone to her overlipsticked mouth. "Hello, Ms. Feibish-Lenzner"—with a big smile—"I just wanted to leave a message for you—" And then she'd burst with it, orgasm, and let her cries and groans out into the dead line of the phone, Jonathan's laughter interrupted meanwhile by his own explosive shouts—

Ms. Feibish-Lenzner caught herself.

This night, when her world was falling apart, to fall into sexual fantasy featuring her son and, in the role of Kelly Traynor, some pug-nosed bimbo she'd seen perhaps in a television movie of the week? It was madness. Calling him was madness. She was further gone than she had feared—but this thought gave her electric mind reassurance.

In divorce court, she knew, this agreement she had just made with Seymour would not, could not stand. And now she was imagining herself on trial, listing all the crazy things she had done, naming them, and lecturing the judge, "*Non compos mentis*, that's the phrase, Your Honor. You see, Judge, this agreement I made was just part of it. Just another crazy thing I did when in the grip of madness, and now all such agreements should be rendered moot, null, and void." Her husband, she knew, would have a harder time reneging on the sale of his practice. Morgenbesser wouldn't easily relinquish what he had paid for so dearly. But her daughter—once she got her wits back and even if she didn't get her wits back—would have no problem annulling her marriage to Shmelke Motl. Being forced into an arranged marriage when she was out of her skull—if that didn't make a contract worthless, she couldn't imagine what would.

So, as two-thirty in the morning crept toward three, Ms. Feibish-Lenzner found reassurance. In a year's time, and with the right psychoactive drugs, the lovely Jessica would be back at Horace Mann and ready to apply to colleges. Jonathan would be happily heading toward graduation from Princeton, concealing from his friends the complex meshugaas of the Lenzner family. She'd sell the place in Sag Harbor, maybe she'd rent a small apartment in Riverdale in which she and her daughter could spend their weeks. Lenzner himself would be remarried, and good riddance. Perhaps in two years his passion for Judaism would fade and he would fly out to the Himalayas, shave *his* head, don saffron robes, and become a follower of the Dalai Lama. Whatever. It was good-bye, Seymour.

She turned to look at him, the grand, rabbinic head that lay on the pillow beside her. It was never quite dark in their apartment. The lights of 89th Street shone in. Ms. Feibish-Lenzner didn't like curtains—they reminded her of her parents' house in Queens—and she had never managed to buy adequate shades. So in the dead of night she could see him clearly, her Seymour, yarmulke pinned to his head, strong nose pointing at the ceiling, mouth agape, considerable beard spilling across the bedspread. What strange things we humans are, she thought, liable to change so utterly over time, and yet—she touched her husband with a nostalgia verging on affection. She kept away from the beard, caressed his cheeks and nose and forehead, careful not to wake him. She moved close, to take in his smell. She ran a hand across his chest and thigh. She felt his penis, erect under his flannel pajamas.

Oh, my God, she told herself, you really are insane.

She pulled back the sheets and bedspreads, pulled down

his pants even as he snored, hiked up her own nightgown, and felt her vagina. This was the craziest thing she had done yet. And it made perfect sense to her, to fuck him good-bye, to have him one last time before their marriage dissolved. He slept, he didn't stir. She lowered herself on him, eased them both through it. Like a boy, he orgasmed, whimpering in his sleep. She, too, felt a rush and blossoming, then crept off him carefully, wiped him with a Kleenex, pulled up his pajama pants, and tucked him in. She was disturbed by her own behavior, yet strangely tranquil. He was crazy, but he was no longer hers.

She shut her eyes, rearranged herself on her pillow. For the first time in months, the Lenzners rested peacefully side by side.

3.

Wind came off the Hudson, lofting plastic bags into trees. Old snow rose in helixes around flying newspapers. Ghosts blew through town, Ozzie Beller's crying like a pigeon in heat. The walls in the Lenzner bedroom were hollowed, pipes had been pulled from within, and the cum-cries of the middle aged lovers (one still asleep) wafted between rooms and into their daughter's. There, the lovely Jessica moaned in a language not her own.

It happened that night was the first Sunday of winter break and that we three were one floor above, Kevin MacMichaelman and I in sleeping bags, Zev Grubin in his bed, all of us beneath posters for *Star Wars* and the Dallas Cowboys Cheerleaders. On the floor lay Dungeons & Dragons game books and notebooks and paraphernalia—descriptions of monsters and spells, odds charts for magic working and thievery failing, complex rules of combat, four-sided, six-sided, eight-sided, twenty-sided dice—and in one corner a hole Zev had drilled through the floor, hoping someday he would glimpse lovely Jessica's boobs. Her wakeful mumblings came through that hole, and in my dreams, I imagined her invaded by a spirit from the past, a dybbuk—a fiddler claiming to be a hundred and fifty years old, buried in a shtetl in Poland and returned to speak Yiddish out of Jessica's closed and pretty mouth. We stood in the elevator traveling up, she and I and some others, and though it seemed Jessica was haughty and beautiful as ever, the babe of the building and I barely pubescent with corduroy patches sewn by my mother onto the knees of my jeans, this fiddler communicated with me despite her and from within her, listing my desires and perversities in my grandparents' rhythms, words lost on me but the meaning clear, everything I wanted to do to lovely Jessica's nude body—fetishes, spankings, parts I wanted to suck, the fiddler from Pinchev knew Yiddish for it all.

At 6:01, Jonathan Lenzner stood at a train station, waiting for northbound New Jersey Transit. He had missed his mother's phone call—wrong number, it was Frankie Marchand down the hall who had said "Yo." Jonathan was a fair-skinned boy with a tennis player's build and a posture on the verge of maturity. Out in Princeton, despite his runny nose, he seemed a natural leader of men, though in the presence of his parents he was forever nervous and annoyed. Jonathan wore a bright blue parka, carried an oversized gym bag, and his dark hair was cut short. Torn by contrary impulses, he was heading home early without warning the Lenzners and almost against his will. His sister's plight had him worried. His family seemed distant and secret and weird. Jonathan practiced imaginary backhands in the cold. And in Brooklyn, Shmelke Motl hustled through frozen Williamsburg. He was short and lean, his black hat tipped forward to reveal under street lamps the dark crescent of his yarmulke against his pale shaved scalp. His little legs strode toward his rabbi's house, where he would have perhaps a roll and a cup of coffee and then the two would take the train to Manhattan, the IRT uptown, the reb to pay a call on Shmelke's prospective bride, while Motl in his hand-me-down shoes and long cotton coat would wait below in Riverside Park.

And in her bed, Ms. Feibish-Lenzner dreamed contentedly. All she needed on her side was time—the game played out, she would win. Maybe some legal battles, she would survive, then, divorces secured and remedies in hand—lovely Jessica would not suffer forever, the loss of one lover (even Ozzie Beller) could not be so severe—her husband would become a weird ghost of her past (and maybe that was all Seymour aspired to be) and the future would stand before her promising as sunrise.

At 8:36 A.M., Jonathan and the rabbi arrived simultaneously. Young Lenzner, nose bright pink and the rest of his face pale, was surprised to see the cleric standing in the lobby in his broad black hat and velvet waistcoat, but not nearly so shocked as when the man got off the elevator with him and rang the bell of 5E. Rabbi Pinchas Gershon, a heavyset man in his middle thirties with a sparse blond beard and a benign smile, extended a pink hand to Jonathan, the rabbi seemingly friendly and reasonable until he explained that he was there as a representative of Jessica's future groom.

"Her future—" Jonathan sneezed.

The door opened and he saw his father, gray-bearded and dressed black. Jonathan had not been home to witness his family's changes over the fall semester, and if Dr. Lenzner's costume-party appearance explained at least part of the rabbi's mystery, it hinted at deeper and more unlikely goings-on.

"Holy crap," Jonathan gasped.

"Seymour," said Gershon, with a flourish of his friendly palm.

The psychiatrist did not look up to meet his son's eyes.

And in the Lenzner living room was no ordinary scene. On the coffee table—an antique wooden door set upon legs fashioned by a Cape Cod blacksmith—were bagels from H & H, as well as cured olives and sliced onions and a tray with three kinds of cheese. Beneath the spare modern canvas on the wall—a trace of pink against an off-white background—Ms. Feibish-Lenzner was setting down a fruit bowl heavy with bananas and grapes. The lovely Jessica, in a floral patterned dress which covered her from her wrists to her ankles, sat stiffly in a rocking chair.

"What the—" Jonathan began.

Ms. Feibish-Lenzner startled at the sight of her son (she knew she should have spoken to him, should have warned him away), but the lovely Jessica did nothing but weep. Her red hair was combed behind her delicate ears. Her complexion was like dried plaster. Tears ran from her eyes, the only movement on her face. Jonathan dropped his ski jacket on the floor, just as he had every winter since he was three.

"Jess?" Her bone-white hands gripped the rocker. "Pop? Ma?"

Ms. Feibish-Lenzner, advancing to greet her son, shot him private theatrical gestures he failed to comprehend.

"Who is—" He pointed at the rabbi. "No—" He withdrew from his mother's embrace. "I—"

Dr. Lenzner raised a hand in the air. "All will be explained."

"Like, *that's* supposed to . . . ?" Jonathan turned to his sister. "Jess? Pop, you cannot expect . . . Jess?" He hoped for at least a smile, but the poor girl was blasted.

"It's understandable," said Rabbi Gershon, "that under

the circumstances she should be somewhat nervous, somewhat shy——"

"A befitting modesty," Dr. Lenzner suggested.

"Fuck," Jonathan squeaked. "Dad, how can you . . . ? Who
is this? Ma——"

"Jonathan," Lenzner said. "The rabbi is a respected man
in his community and an honored guest in our home. I
would have you treat him with civility. And Rabbi Gershon,
forgive my son. He is an unexpected visitor this morning and
the circumstances of your arrival have not been fully
explained."

"Oh, please." The rabbi blushed. "No apologies on my
account."

"Come to the kitchen, honey," said Ms. Feibish-Lenzner.
"I need some help with the cream cheese."

"The fucking——" Jonathan began. Were they mad, or
playacting? Was this the beginning of some strange surprise—relatives to leap out from behind couches and reenact
highlights of his bar mitzvah? He was so dizzy and baffled
that when his mother pulled him by the hand to the kitchen,
he followed. Ms. Feibish-Lenzner—wearing an apron over
her black Charivari blouse and skirt—took her six-foot-tall
son through the swinging door. Behind him Jonathan heard
the rabbi say, "Oh, nothing, Doctor. Please. I assure you. In
my business, we see much worse."

The Lenzner kitchen had not been remodeled in years. It
was the same stove in which his mother had baked his childhood cakes, the same cabinets that held on high shelves
china for Thanksgiving and Seder, the same Formica-
topped table on which he had eaten hot dog lunches with
his grandmother when he was two and on which more
recently Ms. Feibish-Lenzner had kept notes on her husband's patients, also the same dumbwaiter cavity which,

when he was a kid, made Jonathan think of spirits rising from the deep.

She looked terrible. Ms. Feibish-Lenzner was doing her best, wore lipstick and blue earrings and around her throat chunky black beads, but she had aged since he had been at Princeton. Her eyes were red-rimmed and sleepy. The skin hung loose from the corners of her mouth. Her tongue tip touched her lips, but she seemed unable to say what she wanted.

And her son was a stranger in front of her. If he felt like a child, Jonathan looked to her a young man, handsome, strong, more innocent than she, but (she suspected) wiser. Ms. Feibish-Lenzner stammered, feeling sure he would pass judgment on her, as if he were representative of more powerful forces—as if behind Jonathan, or maybe through the hole in the wall where the dumbwaiter had once run, there were others listening. Quicker than words could come from her, she imagined her sentences flying up the dumbwaiter shaft and into neighbors' kitchens. Nell Grubin would hear in apartment 6E, Nell née Herrington, heir to two generations of scholarship at Harvard, and if she, Ms. Feibish-Lenzner, could look over Nell's shoulder and read the notes that would soon be scrawled in the top margin of Nell's *New York Review of Books* (right there, above a David Levine caricature of Susan Sontag), she would be devastated, because Nell, upon hearing the words rising from the dumbwaiter shaft, would scribble down the truth, that the lie Anna was living was not the lie she understood, but something much more fundamental.

"Don't you dare do a thing." Her two hands grabbed Jonathan's one. "I have it all worked out and the way we get what we want is to let them do their worst—"

"What we—" Jonathan felt himself recoiling.

"We're on the same team. You must trust me, you must believe me, right? I know what you're thinking—she's crazy! But that doesn't mean I'm wrong—"

"Ma—"

"Your father is out of his mind." She was speaking fast, hoping she could get the words out before squirming Jonathan could register the totality of his disbelief. "But the way out of this—and it's a bigger problem than you understand and I've been thinking about it, I haven't been thinking about anything else—is just to let him go. Let him sell everything to Morgenbesser—"

"Morgen—"

She waved a hand. "Then divorce me and get Jessica married to Motl—"

He was pulling away, standing up straighter, and looking ever more confidently opposed to her.

And what was strange, really, was that Ms. Feibish-Lenzner, as she continued to speak— "but I'll stand in front of the judge and swear on my mother's grave"—felt all of her sympathy on Jonathan's side. She kept on whispering— "let Seymour go through with his cockamamie plans, then we'll pull out the rug"—but she was feeling something else—confusion, repulsion, distrust of herself—feelings registered on Jonathan's face, and inside her, her best, most loving motherly heart was privately urging him on to action.

She was distant from the scene. Another, happier Anna Feibish-Lenzner hovered before her not in space but in time, just a few seconds in the future, and this Anna Feibish-Lenzner had a moment of clear vision: that Jonathan would never let his sister marry Shmelke Motl. He would ruin all his mother's and all his father's plans. And this, Ms. Feibish-Lenzner knew, was just as it should be.

So she smiled inwardly as aloud she laid out the final

touches of her disastrous plans—"sell the place in Sag Harbor, move to California, let Jessica start anew"—and felt her own pretensions flying from her. She was not, as she had hoped to appear to Rabbi Gershon, the good Jewish wife intent on marrying her daughter off, nor was she the scheming, deluded mother she offered up to her son, neither was she what she most feared that Jonathan saw, a selfish woman who for convenience's sake would hide from the worst crises in her own home. She was good (she hoped so). She was loving (she felt it). Jonathan pulled his mother to him and as if in agreement kissed her head. Then he walked into the living room and smashed her world to bits.

Not long after that December 22, the Lenzners got their divorce. They sold 5E on the cheap, were never heard from again. Rumor has it that Ms. Feibish-Lenzner is a high school drama teacher now, lives in San Diego. The same whisperers say that the doctor suffers from strange ailments, that he has given up Judaism, seeks everywhere for cures. Drinks tincture of tarantula. Wears hats in the shape of pyramids. These rumors I cannot vouch for, but Jonathan and Jessica, I see them sometimes.

He is a real estate lawyer, married, and owns a brownstone on a quiet Brooklyn street. Jessica is his tenant upstairs. Still beautiful. I see her some mornings, a ghostly girl, an absolute knockout. Mostly, I feel I know too much about her past. I don't want to embarrass her, make her think of times best forgotten. So I never say hello, though Jessica and I wait side by side sometimes for the 7:10 train. Once or twice, she's tried to catch my eye.

Yesterday, for instance, book bag on my back, cardboard coffee cup in hand (I teach English at the School for the Humanist Culture), I was reading I. B. Singer, preparing hurriedly for class—a senior elective, Jewish Ethics and Aesthetics, something I feel unqualified to teach, but proposed because I knew the chair would go for it. The train was late. I looked up three times from my book and each time found Jessica staring at me.

She didn't smile. She didn't say hello. The train came finally and rumbled by us and in its hot wind and shrieking breaks I saw her examining me and suddenly saw myself as though through her eyes—or perhaps the eyes of that Polish dybbuk of my twelve-year-old nightmare.

She knew that I knew her, she knew that I was ashamed to say hi. Moreover, she knew that I didn't understand the book I was reading, and that I was unqualified to lecture a bunch of bright eighteen-year-olds about it. Furthermore, she knew (the dead fiddler informing her) where I had been the morning of that December 22, right upstairs surrounded by dice and books for role-playing games, that I had spent that night pretending to be a wizard named Pipik, that I had had those quasi-erotic dreams about her riding the elevator and a spirit speaking through her in lascivious Yiddish. She knew that I was writing this story, the one in your hands, that I was making up slanders (her mother's sex fantasies?), and that I was recounting her family's misfortunes in some quasi-Old-World voice, a folk-tale voice, as if my own were inadequate.

Lovely Jessica looked at me and she knew all this and I looked at her and I knew she knew, and so I shut my book of stories and dashed to a different subway car.

Oh, fiddler from Pinchev! Oh, role-playing games! Throw the dice, see what comes out of me next.